CHIMERARED

INDIGO

CHIMERARED
INDIGO

WRITTEN BY **PHOENIX RED**

EDITED BY **KATHARINE VAIL**

TBG PUBLISHING

Phoenix Red
ChimeraRED: Indigo
P.   cm
Summary: Moving to a new underground city on her home planet, ChimeraRED works to
find her father amidst a new threat while also finding her true purpose in the process.
ISBN <978-0-578-19219-2>

TBG Publishing
Printed in the U.S.A
Second American Edition 2017

www.chimerared.com

To Chimera, D, Mar, Nat, K, Deija and the Universe

CONTENTS

Contents

CHIMERARED
INDIGO

Introduction

My name, ChimeraRED. I've been here on Tychon 1 for seven and a half lunar cycles. This region is more beautiful than the others. In fact, I think it's the most beautiful on the planet. I would know . . . I've traveled across the regions from the sleek white structures of Tychon 2, the grime and soot of Tychon 3, all the way to Tychon 4 with its political corruption.

I'm an Automally . . . at least that's what they call us. We call ourselves Reds. You're probably wondering who they are. They . . . are those who are not like us. You see, a small group of us have a gift . . . the gift of elevated consciousness. A consciousness of the beauty, inspiration and connection between one's self and the creation of something . . . something beautiful because it was made to be, not because of its quantum properties.

The Greys, with their large round heads and slanted eyes, are a reflection of their color, lacking vibrancy, liveliness and emotion . . . most of them at least. Their only concerns are math, science and the physics of the universe. We call ourselves Reds, referring to the bright, free, creative personalities. The Greys are against us. They created a committee to find and slaughter us. Somehow, they believe our free thinking is a virus. A virus that if spread would bring destruction to Tychon. That's why the Tychon Broadcasting Group was created. To spread our message throughout the galaxy, to find an outlet for our creativity and to get help in our battle against the Grey society. But overtime, I came to realize, not everything is what it seems. This is our story. This is my legacy.

This first part of the journey starts several lunar cycles after I arrived at AzurNu, an underground city for Reds. Migrating here changed everything.

A New World

It is a cold Tychonian night as two hoverbikes streak across the arid underground terrain of Tychon 1. The glow of the hoverbikes' propulsion lights up the bikes and the ground underneath, reflecting the shadow of the bikes against the shifting terrain. The robes of the two figures atop the hoverbikes float like sails as the figures crouch behind their speed shields. As they approach a large singular rock formation, the hoverbikes slow.

The lead bike comes to a stop and powers off as the figure upon it sits up. Sliding off the hoverbike, the figure removes the cloak, revealing a female with dark hair and red eyes. She raises her wrist unveiling a mounted gauntlet-like device.

"ChimeraRed," the figure declares.

"Accepted. Welcome, Chimera," a voice on the device responds.

Pressing a button on the device, various clothing outfits are projected as holograms. Chimera taps one of the outfits and the device suddenly emits a bright light and begins to Chimera. Her cloak slowly morphs into a new outfit. After the scan is complete, Chimera dons a silver and red breastplate, black tights and a neck protector with spikes.

A second figure pulls up and slides off the hoverbike. Slowly removing a helmet, the figure shakes her hair free. A female donning a braided blonde Mohawk dismounts the second hoverbike. Her green eyes glow in the dimly lit underground as she too produces a wrist mounted device.

"StarChildRed," the second figure announces.

After a brief scan from her wrist device, her cloak transforms into a triangular-shaped skirt and inverted diamond-shaped top.

"Looks like you're faster on your digi-changer than your hoverbike," Chimera remarks sarcastically.

"I didn't know it was a race," StarChild responds, grinning. "When are you gonna get rid of that ancient wristcom?"

"Iona handed it down to me," Chimera replies. "She says it's been in the family for generations."

"Which is exactly why you need a new one," StarChild answers back.

"Very funny," Chimera declares. "Anyway, where is it, straight ahead?"

"Watch and learn," StarChild responds, walking up to a large rock formation. She waves her hand over the rock and a large platform becomes visible in front of her.

"Why is it so far from AzurNu?" Chimera inquires.

"I don't know why they don't have one in the city. Just relax, you're gonna like this." StarChild smirks as the platforms extends out toward Chimera and StarChild. The hum of gears fills the quiet night as they slowly begin to descend into darkness. Once the platform comes to a stop, Chimera and StarChild step forward.

"Are you sure this is a good idea?" Chimera questions, glancing at StarChild and then back at the platform ahead.

"Trust me, you need this. You never get out. Now come on, let's elevate," StarChild instructs, as she slides her hoverbike onto the platform and motions for Chimera to step forward.

Chimera steps forward and a magnet slides Chimera and StarChild's hoverbikes to the right of the platform, storing them with a group of other hoverbikes. Chimera and StarChild continue on, deeper underground until they arrive at a massive cave.

"Do you come here a lot?" Chimera asks StarChild.

"I've only been here twice before," StarChild responds. "It's your birth cycle, so we had to come."

StarChild leads the way as she and Chimera approach a faint

glowing pink and blue translucent wall. Glowing graffiti phrases like LIVE RED and DOWN WITH GREY sprawl across the rocks. Muffled bass can be heard from the other side of the rock. As Chimera and StarChild enter a narrow dark tunnel, the bass becomes more audible.

"The way in is right over here," StarChild explains, as she points.

StarChild presses her hand against a small device attached to a protruding rock and a holographic puzzle appears. After putting the puzzle into sequence, she taps the completed puzzle and grabs Chimera's hand. An orange circle of light appears on the ground as Chimera and StarChild step into the middle. Within seconds Chimera and StarChild are de-particularized, fading away like small specks of shiny dust. They both re-particularize on the other side of the rock, inside a RED Energy Station.

"Welcome to *Elevated Existence*," StarChild announces.

Chimera glances around in awe as she stands in a crowded subterranean room filled with shifting lights, pulsating sounds and eclectic Reds.

"You should see your face," StarChild comments.

Chimera continues to study the room.

"So there are two main areas!" StarChild shouts to Chimera, trying to make herself audible over the influx of sounds. "This is the main floor."

As Chimera and StarChild move through the energy station pushing past other Reds, a brightly lit spiral of red lights in the center of the room houses a projection of an artist performing.

"Who is that?" Chimera asks, referring to the hologram.

"That's ElectraRed," StarChild answers. "This is her song Indigo. You've never heard of her?"

"No, I haven't really listened to a lot of music," Chimera answers.

"Yea, forgot you're from the surface," StarChild retorts.

Chimera elbows StarChild as StarChild laughs leading the way toward another area. Blue and pinkish purple lights flash periodically, lighting intervals of darkness with colors to fuel the celebratory mood. As StarChild stops, a small floating bot approaches, scanning Chimera and StarChild. The bot projects a digital image of a drink.

"You want something?" StarChild asks Chimera.

"No, I'm good," Chimera responds.

StarChild pulls up her wristcom and types something in. She pulls out a hologram of a specific drink from the wristcom and inserts it into the bot. Within a few seconds, a small door opens from the midsection of the bot and two triangular-shaped bottles are dispensed. StarChild grabs the bottles with her left hand as the bot scans the wristcom on her other arm.

"Six credits processed," the bot announces as it completes the scan and floats away.

StarChild hands one of the bottles to Chimera and proceeds to open her bottle.

"I didn't need one!" Chimera exclaims, as she begins to smirk.

"Today marks the beginning of a new chapter, Chimera. You don't have a choice," StarChild states.

Chimera shakes her head. "What is it?" she asks.

"Just taste it. I promise you'll like it," StarChild instructs.

Chimera opens the blue, triangular bottle and smells its contents.

"Um you can drink it for the both of us," Chimera declines.

"Oh no," StarChild begins. "You're not getting out of this one."

Chimera and StarChild glare at each other for several moments before StarChild cracks a smile. After a brief exchange of stares, Chimera's smirk turns into a smile.

"You see, you can never keep a straight face," Chimera declares.

"Fine, give it here," StarChild instructs as she snatches Chimera's bottle. StarChild takes a sip of the fluorescent liquid in her bottle. "Yum, always so good!" StarChild brags, continuing to consume the beverage.

"That's totally not gonna work," Chimera states, as she glances around.

Music fills the air as Reds move to and fro across the room. While Chimera is busy glancing around, StarChild positions the bottle in front of Chimera and when Chimera turns, StarChild stuffs it to Chimeras lips and begins pouring the fluorescent liquid into Chimera's mouth.

"Star!" Chimera explains, stepping back after consuming a mouthful.

"Sorry, you had that coming!" StarChild exclaims, snickering.

Chimera hesitates for a bit, takes a deep breath, and sips her beverage.

"You know what?" Chimera declares.

StarChild raises her hands, motioning for Chimera to finish her statement.

"That wasn't half bad!" Chimera admits, continuing to drink.

"I told you!" StarChild quips. "You just never trust me."

The two settle in, connecting to the music, and sipping their drinks. Chimera and StarChild get comfortable, enjoying the atmosphere for half a degree when something catches StarChild's attention.

"Isn't that . . . AriesRED?" StarChild exclaims.

"Who?" Chimera questions.

"It's a friend of mine," StarChild responds hopping up. "Hold on, I'll be right back."

"What?" Chimera asks, as StarChild slides off to catch up with Aries.

"Did she just leave me here by myself?" Chimera mutters rhetorically, standing up to see StarChild fade off in the distance.

Chimera plops back down into her seat and settles back in. After several moments, Chimera notices a Red across from her who is also alone. Leaning on a lit handrail, the Red watches the holographic performances projected in the center of the room. As if he feels someone watching, the Red Chimera was glancing at turns and locks eyes with Chimera. She quickly looks away and continues listening to the music. As she watches Reds move and gyrate to the music being pumped into the room, Chimera periodically looks back at the mystery Red against the rail. Without warning, the Red pushes off the rail and begins toward Chimera.

"Err, is he walking over to me?" Chimera whispers to herself.

As the Red is about to reach Chimera, another Red jumps in front of Chimera.

"Hey, you look familiar!" declares a long-haired brunette Red.

"Do I know you?" he asks.

Chimera glances at the Red for a moment.

"Sorry, I . . . think you have the wrong Red," Chimera responds.

"I'm Solar," the Red says, raising his palm for the Tychonian greeting. "You seem different. Where are you from?"

Chimera leans back a bit. "I'm . . . from far away," she answers.

"Oh, an outlander," Solar proclaims. "I figured you weren't from here. I'm from AzurNu, born and raised."

Chimera nods, catching a glimpse of the Red from the rail step back and slowly disappear into the crowd.

"What are you doing here alone?" Solar asks.

"I'm actually here with someone," Chimera answers. "She stepped away for the moment. I should probably go check on her." Chimera peers past Solar searching for StarChild.

"You seem like you're not elevated, do you want to boost?" Solar asks.

Before Chimera can respond, a hand grabs her.

"Hey, sorry to interrupt!" StarChild exclaims hollering above the music again. "Come on I want to show you something."

StarChild leads Chimera away as Solar is left standing alone.

Chimera and StarChild move across the room toward a tunnel.

CHAPTER ONE

"I didn't get your com coordinates!" Solar exclaims to Chimera as his voice is washed away by the pulse of throbbing sound frequencies and Reds chatting.

"I got us a pass into *Immersion*!" StarChild exclaims.

"*Immersion*?" Chimera remarks, crossing through the transparent tunnel that reveal jagged rock formations outside the passageway.

"Only the coolest place on Tychon!" StarChild proclaims, continuing to lead Chimera by the hand.

Chimera and StarChild reach the crossing into *Immersion* and stop at a moat like waterway of light blue glowing water that separates *Elevated Existence* from *Immersion*. StarChild stops in front of the bridge entryway and retrieves a contact-like device from her wristcom. She places the single contact into her right eye.

"What's that thing you put in your eye?" Chimera inquires, approaching StarChild to look at the contact.

"It's a virtual overlay," StarChild answers. "It's the only way to see the digital door code." StarChild inputs a sequence into what looks like thin air to Chimera. Nothing occurs, so StarChild reenters the code.

"Oops, I think I know what I did wrong," StarChild declares. She tries again correcting her mistake and suddenly a small square drone descends and scans StarChild and Chimera.

"This is a lot to go through. What's *Immersion* about?" Chimera questions, glancing at the drone strangely as it scans her.

"It's existence . . . on another level," StarChild responds.

The drone completes its scan and the entry door opens. A platform floats across the divide to Chimera and StarChild. The two enter the platform and float across to *Immersion.*

Once the platform reaches the other side of the divide, Chimera and StarChild step off. A giant door opens and they descend down into *Immersion.* Entering in, Chimera is greeted by a giant room on a circular platform filled with more Reds.

"This is awesome!" Chimera exclaims.

"You haven't seen anything yet," StarChild replies.

As Chimera and StarChild walk down a lucite staircase, tube-like devices the size of large pillars sprawl across the room. Neon and bright colors within the tubes swirl slowly, like lava flowing down a pipe.

"What are those?" Chimera asks, pointing at one of the tubes.

"And I'm the one that lived under a rock?" StarChild jokes.

Chimera glares at StarChild.

"They're sound tubes!" StarChild exclaims. "They sync to you when you pass by and track your movement. They play music only you can hear from the level of your brain's frequency."

"Seriously?" Chimera asks.

"I know, crazy right?" StarChild states. "It's like your own personal sound system."

Chimera and StarChild continue through *Immersion,* as sweeping lights of multiple colors fill the room. Some Reds move to the sound of the music while others move slowly, as if in a trance.

"Why are they moving like that?" Chimera whispers to StarChild watching the Reds.

"They're immersed," StarChild replies. "They're connected to the music. Just relax, and let the music take you too."

Chimera relaxes and takes a deep breath. As she closes her eyes, she begins to feel the music. The sound tubes sync with Chimera and begin to send her brain new signals. StarChild relaxes as well, letting the sounds connect to her thoughts. Chimera and StarChild both become one with the music, spending the night entangled in the dimension of sound.

On the region of Tychon 4.5, Lord PrychonGrey, supreme ruler and leader of the Grey autocracy known as the Tychon Federated Union, arrives. His royal transport lands at one of the Hue-man breeding facilities in the capital province for Grey dominion, called Prychon

City. Lord Prychon is accompanied by his advisor AlvisoGrey, his royal messenger NintiusGrey and his imperial entourage.

Upon landing, Lord Prychon and his entourage exit the transport and make their way to the entrance. As Prychon enters, a glaucous light flashes throughout the facility and the lights dim. Two Greys in metallic armor greet the entourage at the entryway and lead them down the corridor. As the entire group heads through the main corridor of the facility, the floors project green pentagons. These pentagons track each member of the entourage and display their identity via holograms that float above each member's head. The walls of the facility project streams of various information and statistics that relate to the breeding facility.

After Lord Prychon passes through the lab corridor, other Greys stop to perform the royal Grey greeting, placing their left arm across their chest, extending three fingers out and nodding his head.

Lord Prychon's entourage continues to the end of the corridor and reaches the planosphere, an elevator-like contraption that alternates small dimensional panels which lead to the various floors of the facility. One of the Greys steps forward and slides his hands across a panel. The door opens and a collection of cerulean colored panels are visible. One of the panels slides into place and the entourage steps through the portal.

Descending several levels, Lord Prychon reaches the main breeding lab for Neophyte production. The entourage exits the portal and moves across the lab toward a large control center on the right side of the room. The breeding lab is a large, sprawling hangar-like room that is dark grey with accents of green. Curved arm-like devices balance small incubators that are suspended in midair. Inside the incubators, lay Hue-man Neophyte specimens.

Three Grey scientists are active inside the control room. Nintius approaches one of the three Greys.

"Lord Prychon requests a status report, Kamio," Nintius projects to the Grey telepathically. "What progress do you report today?"

As Lord Prychon enters, Kamio and the other two scientists turn to him and perform the Tychonian greeting.

"Specimens are at low supply, my Lord. We need more test subjects," Kamio projects telepathically to Prychon.

Prychon steps forward and checks one of the display screens in the control area. He turns to the second Grey in the lab.

"What is your suggestion, Rhea?" Prychon questions. "Increase efforts to abduct more Hue-mans from earth or clone the Hue-mans we contain here on Tychon?"

"As the abduction specialist," Rhea projects telepathically, "I wholly understand the benefits and hindrances of a domestically engineered workforce. That aside, my suggestion . . . clone the neophytes we contain here on Tychon. To travel to earth and abduct more Hue-mans for breeding is far less feasible."

"Perhaps she is correct, sire," Alviso begins. "We face war with the Corrillians in the outer galaxy, a shortage of resources here on Tychon and the threat of political instability with the weakening economy, sire," Alviso explains telepathically.

"The Corrillians are no threat!" Lord Prychon declares aloud in Tychonian. "Once Racheon and the Grey Army are fully prepared, we will wipe all of them from this solar system! A stronger Hue-man workforce will yield more resources! More resources means a stronger economy. A stronger economy means a stronger army."

"Very true, my Lord, yet if we concentrate our capabilities on domestic affairs, we will have a greater effect," Alviso advises.

"What say you, Starchus?" Prychon asks the third Grey scientist.

"Subjects from earth present a more potent DNA foundation," Starchus states. To duplicate Hue-mans that we contain here at the farm would present diluted test subjects. That dilution is the root issue with many of our Neophyte underlings now."

Prychon turns and steps away from the control center toward the breeding floor where a sea of incubators extends as far as the eye can see.

Lord Prychon mediates on his decision. After contemplating, he addresses Kamio, Rhea, Starchus and his entourage, "Very well, prepare a new campaign for earth abductions."

"My Lord, I must advise that this will further strain our capabilities," Alviso warns.

Lord Prychon turns to Alviso, "We will amass all test subjects needed for a new, stronger generation of Hue-mans. We will create a super race that will harness victory."

All other Greys nod in approval except Alviso, as Prychon projects his mandate.

"That is all," Prychon acknowledges. He turns to Nintius and projects another thought privately.

Nintius nods, then turns to address the group. "Lord Prychon would like a word with Kamio privately."

Nintius, Alviso, Rhea, Starchus and the remainder of the entourage begin toward the exit of the lab as Kamio remains.

The next rotation, Kumeno, the first sun on Tychon, rises around the 7th degree. The sun heats up the early morning terrain like an oven. Chimera awakes, sliding off her sleeping pod.

"Ugh, why do I feel so dizzy?" Chimera says to herself as she steps onto the cold floor of her dorm. "What is there to eat today?" she mutters, touching the screen on her food storage unit. Scrolling down the inventory list, she sighs.

"I gotta go get something to eat," Chimera proclaims.

Retrieving her digi-changer, Chimera dresses herself and leaves her dorm. On her way through the dorm corridor, Chimera hears a voice call her from behind. She turns to see OmegaRED, leader of the Reds on AzurNu.

"Where are you headed in such a rush?" Omega asks.

"*GRUB*, to get something to eat," Chimera responds to Omega. "I could eat a whole Mountain Gnarl right now."

Omega begins laughing.

"Have you started studies yet?" Omega questions.

"Not yet but I'm looking forward to it!" Chimera exclaims. "Just waiting on approval from the Foreign Affairs Bureau."

"How do you like it here on AzurNu so far?" Omega inquires, placing his hand on Chimera's shoulder.

"It's . . . different," Chimera admits. "I feel like . . . a whole new world has been revealed to me. And I don't know why she would leave this place."

"She did what she did to keep you safe," Omega replies. "After your half-brother Ignis was killed, she left. Left to start over."

"I guess," Chimera mentions. "I kind of rather not talk about it," she adds shaking her head. "Seems like running away. Running away never solved anything."

"I agree," Omega begins, "but you must learn to pick your battles. I'm on my way to a meeting with the council. Why don't you come by my chateau sometime and we can talk more."

"That sounds good. I'll talk to you soon," Chimera says, continuing on her way.

Leaving the living quarters zone, Chimera heads down the main corridor toward Tiberius Station, the main hub for AzurNu's hover-rail known as the *RedLine*. The hover-rail is a suspended train that carries Reds to the various zones of AzurNu.

Reaching the station, Chimera climbs the platform and boards the hover-rail. She rides the *RedLine* to Viand Station, the stop for cafes and diners on AzurNu. After deboarding the hover-rail, Chimera makes her way to *GRUB*, a food establishment.

The area outside the Viand platform is busy with the hustle and bustle of daily AzurNu life, as hundreds of REDS walk to and from, searching for a bite to eat. Chimera enters and orders an insta-meal from one of the food conveyor lines. After retrieving her food, she scans around for a place to sit. Eyeing an empty seat at a table with several other Reds, she heads over with her food tray.

"Sorry, this seat is taken, Automally," a Red at the table retorts.

"I'm not an Automally," Chimera snaps. "I'm a Hybrid."

"So you say, Automally. Go sit at a table with your own kind," the Red orders.

A few other Reds at the table snicker, as several others are quiet.

Chimera clenches her first, but gains control of her temper and turns away. She heads to another table that is empty. It's near the 10th degree, and *GRUB* is packed with Reds looking for a quick meal to begin their day. While eating her insta-meal, Chimera overhears two Reds at a table across from her conversing about something that catches her attention.

"Yea, I'm really not supposed to know about it, but I overheard my brother talking about it," the first Red whispers. "He's part of a conspiracy group that tries to get info on Enforcement. He thinks they really exist, so they started a network of Reds that hunt for proof."

"I really . . . can't say too much," the Red on the left declares.

"I don't want to be kidnapped at moon's rise," he whispers.

"You're not gonna get kidnapped," the second Red remarks. "That's a load of rubbish. Just tell me what you heard."

"Shhh," the first Red snaps, glancing around nervously. "We shouldn't even be talking about this here."

"Sorry," the second Red whispers back.

Both Reds glance around, as if they feel someone watching. Chimera, who was leaning in to hear their conversation better, quickly turns around and pretends to type on her wristcom.

"I think there's going to be an attack on Trytech," the first Red whispers.

"Trytech?" the second Red questions in a low voice, seeming confused.

"Yea, the Grey Weapon Lab," the first Red begins. "They make advance weapons for the Grey Army."

"I think you're too into this conspiracy stuff," the second Red proclaims. "Besides, it would be suicide and probably start a war."

"Don't underestimate the Enforcers," the first Red warns. "The revolution is imminent."

"Reds would never attack Greys," the second Red assures sarcastically. "Plus, there's no such thing as the Enforcers."

"The Enforcers exist!" the first Red snaps. "And they're going to tip the scales . . . change things so we won't have to live here underground anymore."

"How could the Enforcers exist, yet nobody seems to know about them?" the second Red questions. "Besides, even, if they did exist, how could they carry out this attack tonight? Curfew is at the 30th degree.

That means no flights leaving from the docks."

Chimera is so engrossed in the conversation, she doesn't notice she pushes her tin juice box toward the edge of the table.

"It goes down in the DM," the first Red answers. "From what I heard, somewhere around Bay 17. They . . ."

Suddenly, there is a sudden crash as Chimera leans too far in and knocks her juice box off the table.

The two Reds conversing are startled by the sound and turn. Chimera accidentally locks eyes with one of the Reds and then quickly leans down to pick up her juice box.

"We should go," the first Red suggests, standing up from the table.

"Dammit," Chimera mutters to herself, realizing she may have spooked the two Reds.

Quickly finishing up, she messages StarChild with her wristcom to meet her at the Zen Lounge. Chimera leaves *GRUB* and heads toward the lounge which is on the east end of *Create*, the creative zone of AzurNu with entertainment and recreation for Reds.

Arriving at the Zen Lounge, Chimera spots StarChild and waves her over.

"There's going to be an attack tonight!" Chimera exclaims.

"Hi!" StarChild proclaims. "Forgot your manners?" she jokes, putting her palm up.

"Sorry, hi . . . there's going to be an attack tonight!" Chimera reiterates. "I thought this place was all about 'we come in peace?'"

"Ok, calm down," StarChild demands, laughing a bit. "Tell me, what are you talking about?"

"So . . . I was at *GRUB* grabbing something to eat when I overheard two Reds talking about an attack. They were saying something about a group called like the Enforcers? Supposedly they're gonna raid a weapons factory tonight."

"Enforcers!" StarChild exclaims, before adjusting her tone. "Enforcers?" she repeats again, now whispering. "C'mon, let's head back to our quarters."

"Why?" Chimera questions.

"Because, we can't talk out here!" StarChild whispers aggressively.

StarChild grabs Chimera and leads her out of *Create* back toward Viand Station. Hopping aboard the hover-rail, StarChild motions for Chimera to stay silent as they hover back toward the living quarters zone. Once they reach the room, StarChild places her palm on the door scanner and the door slides open. She peeks around to make sure no one has followed them, and then darts inside the room with Chimera. She waits for the door to close.

"I know you're new here, but there are like three things you should never do here!" StarChild explains. "Number two on that list is to talk about the Enforcers. You don't want anything to do with them, or the weird stuff that supposedly goes on."

"Wait, you can't just start at number two. What's number one on that list?" Chimera inquires.

"My digi-changer! Never touch my digi-changer!" StarChild exclaims. "And the third is to stay away from all Greys!"

Chimera smirks. "So the Enforcers are real?" she asks.

"I'm not saying that. I'm just saying stay away from anything related to that," StarChild snaps.

"Now who needs to relax?" Chimera replies.

"Chi, this is serious," StarChild warns.

"Just tell me if they exist or not," Chimera urges.

"Like I said, I don't know," StarChild answers. "And to be honest, I don't want to know!"

"We'll they're planning an attack tonight so there may be a kernel of truth to it," Chimera states.

"Like I said, I don't want to know!" StarChild repeats, covering her ears with her hands.

CHAPTER ONE

"They're leaving AzurNu after sundown tonight," Chimera mentions loudly, so that StarChild can hear her.

StarChild removes her hands from her ears. "Why are you telling me this?"

"Because I'm gonna check it out tonight," Chimera answers.

"Are you insane?" StarChild exclaims.

"I need action, some adventure," Chimera declares. "Plus, I'm tired of sitting back and feeling like a caged animal. There are a lot of rules here."

"Yea, those rules are to keep you safe," StarChild remarks. "Besides, I took you to *Elevated Existence* yesterday."

"I know, and I'm grateful for that," Chimera answers back, "but I feel like there's something missing. Don't you feel a little cooped up here? Don't you want to get out and see what else is out there?"

"You've only been here for a short amount of time!" StarChild exclaims.

"Look, I'm going with or without you," Chimera declares, folding her arms.

"Definitely without!" StarChild responds. "Breaking curfew to look for some secret group that probably doesn't exist . . . you're going to get yourself exiled from AzurNu."

"At least I would have some excitement in the process," Chimera mutters, heading to the other side of the room.

"Can't say I didn't try and warn you," StarChild says, shaking her head. "I'm going to studies," StarChild adds, grabbing a small, triangular device off a table by the door before exiting.

SEEDS OF REBELLION

That evening around the 25th degree of rotation, Chimera wakes up and slides out of bed.

She is about to change when she receives a call on her wristcom. "Hello?" Chimera answers, still not fully awake.

"Chimera, it's Athos from Tychonian Science studies," the voice announces.

"Hey!" Chimera responds.

"Greetings, what are you doing?" Athos questions.

"Just getting ready to care of some stuff, why?" Chimera responds suspiciously.

"Oh, did you want to study for the Levels of Existence exam that's coming up?" Athos asks.

"I . . . I would but I can't," Chimera explains.

"Oh, how come?" Athos inquires.

"I can't really say," Chimera replies.

Suddenly, StarChild interjects, "You're still going through with this?"

"I told you I was," Chimera replies.

"Well you have one major problem," StarChild whispers.

"What?" Chimera inquires, turning her attention from her conversation with Athos.

"You said everything's going down at one of the bays in the DM," StarChild begins. "Access to that area is locked down after curfew so you'll have no way of getting there."

"Hold on, Athos, I'll have to comm you back," Chimera remarks, turning her attention back to her wristcom.

"Wait, you guys are headed to the DM tonight?" Athos questions.

"I . . . think you misheard," Chimera responds to Athos.

"You guys are planning something aren't you?" Athos declares. "Tell me, what's going on?"

There is a pause. Chimera looks at StarChild who shakes her head vigorously and motions for Chimera to keep quiet about the night's activities.

"No . . . we're not getting into anything tonight," Chimera reiterates.

"Well that's too bad because I know how to get into the DM after curfew," Athos replies. "But go ahead, you can comm me later."

"Wait!" Chimera exclaims.

"Chimera!" StarChild snaps in a loud whisper. "You can't tell anybody!" she warns.

"I trust him," Chimera replies back to StarChild. Returning to her wristcom conversation.

"Trust me about what?" Athos questions.

Chimera turns back to glance at StarChild who shakes her head again in disapproval.

"There's something going down tonight," Chimera reveals. "I'll loop you in, but you can't tell anyone one!"

"You have my word," Athos promises.

"Ok," Chimera continues. "From what we heard, there might be a raid led by the Enforcers."

"The Enforcers?" Athos questions.

"Yea, if you get us into the DM then you're in! We could use an extra pair of eyes plus you're a walking encyclopedia," Chimera jokes.

Athos chuckles. "A raid . . . sounds risky. You know what?"

Chimera awaits his response.

"I haven't been on a covert mission in a while. I'm in," he confirms.

"Elevated!" Chimera exclaims. "If you can get to the Civilian Exit docks without being seen, we'll meet there and head to the DM together. If anything happens, we'll meet back at my dorm."

"Copy that, what unit is your quarter?" Athos asks.

"717," Chimera responds.

"I'll see you soon," Athos replies as he and Chimera end the call.

Chimera uses her digi-changer to change into a dark, one piece jumpsuit. After dressing, she grabs her magnetic backpack known as a magpack, and quietly slides out the room. As she turns to head down the corridor toward the docking bays, a hand grabs her by the shoulder.

Startled, Chimera jumps and turns to see StarChild.

"What are you doing?" Chimera whispers to StarChild. "I thought you were curfew patrol!"

"I am," StarChild states sarcastically.

"Not funny," Chimera snarls. "What are you doing out?"

"Are you kidding me, I couldn't let you go alone. You wouldn't last a minute without me."

"Yea yea, you just needed some action too," Chimera whispers with a slight grin.

"Well I doubt we'll find any action, but look what I did find roaming the halls," StarChild says, revealing Athos from behind a wall.

"Hey," Chimera greets Athos with her palm as he approaches.

"Good to see you," Athos acknowledges.

"C'mon, let's get out of here before we get caught," StarChild urges as the three begin down the corridor.

Chimera, StarChild and Athos head up toward the *Docking Major* bays of Tychon, just east of the Council wing.

"This way," Athos instructs. "I know an alternate way into the docks."

CHAPTER TWO

The three of them are almost to the main corridor of the dock's diamond-shaped passageways with vented floors and exhausts pipes, resembling the interior of a spacecraft. Steam seeps through the pipes, creating a layer of fog in some areas of the corridor.

Making their way through the corridor, Chimera suddenly stops. "I hear something," Chimera warns.

"What?" StarChild questions.

"Quiet!" Chimera demands. "Sounds like footsteps."

Several moments later, footsteps become audible from an intersecting hallway behind them.

"Let's hurry up," Chimera urges. "I think there's a guard coming."

Chimera, StarChild and Athos pick up the pace and begin to jog. Reaching the split where the council and dock corridor cross. The three of them are about to cross the last hallway before reaching the corridor when a shadow appears ahead of them.

"Hold it!" Chimera exclaims, realizing they may be trapped.

Chimera, StarChild and Athos jump back against the wall of the corridor as Chimera looks around searching for an escape route. The shadow grows larger as the figure approaches and the footsteps behind them continue to grow louder.

"What are we going to do?" StarChild asks frantically. "I knew this was a bad idea."

Chimera strikes the wall behind her in frustration.

"We'll get out of this, don't worry," Athos reassures StarChild.

Chimera turns and hits the wall with her fist again.

"What are you doing?" StarChild asks. "That's not helping. We're going to get caught!"

"It's hollow. I think it's a utility room or something," Chimera states, surveying the wall behind them.

"This is not the time to explore," StarChild warns.

The shadow rounds the corner and begins to shrink as something approaches. The footsteps from behind grow closer as well and a voice rings out.

"Is someone there?" an unknown voice calls out.

As the figure behind approaches, Chimera finds a latch and slides the door behind her open.

"Hurry, in here!" Chimera commands, pulling StarChild into the room. Athos quickly follows as the three of them stumble into the room. Chimera closes the door as quietly as possible and a few moments later, the figure stops in front of the room.

"We're caught!" StarChild whispers.

"Shhh," Chimera instructs as she places her hand over StarChild's mouth.

Through several slits at the top of the door, Chimera and Athos peer outside.

"I think it's a curfew guard," Athos whispers.

The guard looks around before turning to his right, looking

directly at the utility room. Chimera quickly grabs the handle to jam the door as the guard reaches out and begins to try and open the door. StarChild covers her face, believing it is only a matter of moments before the three are caught.

All of a sudden a voice rings out, "Hey Fleek, what are you doing?"

The guard turns and lets go of the door.

"Cypher, how goes it?" he greets. "I heard something around here and was checking it out."

"Hmm, was probably Ekko," Cypher explains. "This idiot's been a pain in the ass all night. Has some song stuck in his head that he keeps singing."

Suddenly, a third voice rings out. "Indigo, Indigo, I'm holding on to letting go," the voice sings, off-key.

"Ow, I think my ears are bleeding," StarChild remarks sarcastically. "Just take us to detainment already."

"Infinity have mercy," Fleek, the guard outside the closet door, declares.

"We thought we heard someone else," Cypher admits. "Me and Ekko just finished up a sweep of the Council wing. C'mon let's grab a corvee."

"Sounds good, you buying?" Fleek asks.

Cypher chuckles as the two walk off.

"Where did you get that song from, Ekko? You sound terrible,"

Fleek inquires.

"My youngest, she's been playing it nonstop. Now it's stuck in my head," Ekko responds as the three guards turn a corner and disappear.

After waiting for some time, Chimera edges the door open slowly and pokes her head out.

"Ok, it's clear," she whispers to StarChild and Athos, emerging from the room slowly.

"That was too close," StarChild whispers, glancing around to make sure the coast is clear.

"Told you we'd be ok," Athos reassures.

Chimera, StarChild and Athos sneak down the corridor, headed toward the docks. They are nearly to their destination when a security drone appears in the distance approaching from a passageway on their left.

"Not again," StarChild says, seeing the drone.

"Don't worry, I'll handle this," Chimera confirms, raising her wristcom. She programs something on her wristcom and a blue laser appears. She points the laser in the direction the drone came from. A red light on the drone lights up and it rotates back in the direction of the laser. The drone then flies back down the hall from which it came.

"That was genius!" Athos proclaims, grinning at Chimera.

Chimera smirks, as they continue on, finally reaching the end of the corridor.

"C'mon, this way is the best way to the DM," Athos instructs, leading Chimera and StarChild down a small hallway.

"How did you find this way?" Chimera asks.

"I know everything, remember," Athos replies.

Chimera, StarChild and Athos arrive to the *Docks Major* and are greeted by a massive entrance with multiple doors. Three hallways lead to the dock and entrance. Chimera and StarChild lay crouched in the shadows of the far left hallway. Chimera peeks around the corner to survey the entrance.

"Ok, so the good news is there are only two guards," Chimera whispers back to StarChild and Athos.

"That's good news?" StarChild inquires.

Chimera glares at her.

"Kidding," StarChild begins. "I hope you know you're not the only one with tricks up your wristcom. Watch this." StarChild pulls up her wristcom and proceeds to type something. After a few moments, a small floating sphere emerges from StarChild's wristcom.

"I see there's some warrior in you after all," Chimera jokes, glancing at the small sphere and then back at StarChild. "What is that thing?" Chimera asks.

"My secret weapon," StarChild announces.

Chimera shakes her head as StarChild glances back down at her wristcom. She presses a button and the small sphere rises and darts off past the main entrance of the docks to the far right corridor that leads away from the docks. After a pause, StarChild presses another button on her wristcom and whispers, "Load Dug simulation 3."

Suddenly, the sound of a muffled voice can be heard, emanating from the corridor that the small sphere entered.

"What's that sound?" Athos inquires, looking at StarChild and Chimera.

"It's my conversation simulator," StarChild explains. "I use it when I'm in the middle of something and I don't want my beau to know!"

"You let Dug have fake conversations with an artificial intelligent ball when you're busy?" Chimera declares, shaking her head.

"It's the virtual chat add on, don't judge me," StarChild responds.

"Let's see if it works," Athos whispers.

"Wait for it," StarChild says with one hand up, as if counting down for something.

"What are we waiting for?" Chimera asks sarcastically.

"Wait for it," StarChild repeats, peaking around the corner.

As if on cue, the two guards are suddenly alerted to the sounds of the voice deriving from the third corridor on the right.

"What's that noise?" the first guard asks.

"I'm not sure, sounds like someone in corridor three," the second guard responds.

"Night patrol's already swept that section, no one should be in there," the first guard confirms. "Let's check it out."

"Shouldn't one of us stay and keep sentry on the door?" the second guard suggests.

"No, go check it out," Chimera whispers, as if her thoughts could influence the guards.

"C'mon, don't make a fuss," the first guard responds, as the two of them move toward the corridor where the sound is originating.

"Here's our chance, let's go!" Chimera exclaims, as she, StarChild and Athos sprint for the door.

Reaching the door, StarChild tries to open it.

"It's not opening, must be locked," StarChild announces.

"Let me take a look," Chimera proclaims, as StarChild slides out of the way.

"Hurry, they're coming back," StarChild warns. StarChild presses another button on her wristcom and the sound of the muffled voice suddenly stops.

Chimera looks at the door and notices a small round panel with five indentations. She places her hand on the panel and twists it to the right. The panel slides back and the door opens.

"Nice!" Athos remarks.

"Let's go before they see us," Chimera exclaims.

Chimera, StarChild and Athos slip through the open door and

disappear into the darkness of the loading docks. Just before Chimera closes the door behind them, the little sphere darts through the door as well and back into the tiny entry on StarChild's wristcom.

Inside, the massive docks are relatively dark with the exception of a few spotlights.

"It's freezing in here, isn't it?" StarChild asks.

"Yea, feels like we're outside," Chimera remarks.

"I don't think the heating ducts extend to the docks," Athos explains.

"So tell me guys, what are we actually looking for?" StarChild questions.

"I'm not sure," Chimera responds. "Anything out of the ordinary."

The docks are a large open indoor area filled with spacecraft, desert speeders and other transportation vessels. Stacks of supply crates create silhouettes that appear as mini skyscrapers in the dark of night. Chimera and StarChild continue in, peering around the dimly lit area. Athos heads in a slightly different direction.

After passing a large transport ship, Chimera sees the control tower for the docks.

"C'mon, let's see if we can get up there and get a better view," Chimera suggests.

Chimera and StarChild sneak across the cement vented floor,

stepping carefully.

"Everything looks the same, especially when it's dark," StarChild whispers as the three circle past a group of small fan generators twice.

Chimera and StarChild reach an L-shaped structure adjacent to the control tower.

"We can get a better view from those stairs," Chimera suggests.

They climb a pair of metal stairs to reach the top of the building. At the top, Chimera moves to the other edge of the building to climb a second pair of stairs.

"This should give us a view of the whole dock," Chimera explains.

"I really think we should go now. There's nothing here," StarChild warns. "Besides, I think we've already broken every law here."

"We've come too far to go back now," Chimera replies.

"I agree," Athos adds climbing the structure and joining Chimera and StarChild.

"Besides . . ." Chimera begins, stopping mid-sentence. Her eye catches something just beyond what looks like a hanger, next to a large inverted elevator lift.

"Hold on, I hear something," Chimera whispers, crouching down and moving closer to the edge of the rooftop. Athos crouches down as well and edges closer to get better look. StarChild remains in place, arms crossed.

"Get down!" Chimera exclaims, motioning for StarChild to crouch down as well. StarChild quickly ducks down.

In the distance, a group of figures all in black cloaks stand huddled in a circle around another figure.

"What are they doing?" StarChild questions, moving in to join Chimera and Athos.

"I have no idea," Chimera answers.

"Looks like some sort of ritual," Athos responds.

"I have an idea," Chimera exclaims. "That ball of yours, it's like a two-way radio right? Does it have a listening feature?"

"Yea, it does," StarChild replies.

"Ok, great," Chimera declares. "Can you send it over there where those figures are so we can hear what's going on?"

"I'll try," StarChild answers.

StarChild once again dispatches her voice sphere, and sends it toward the huddled figures. The sphere floats quietly to the group and begins to relay the conversation from the cloaked figures.

"When we arrive at the LZ, we hit it hard and fast. No mistakes, just the way we simulated. This is what we've been training for, Enforcers. We're retrieving the weapon crates and plasma ray schematics," a voice explains.

"Sounds like that might be the leader," Chimera whispers.

"You might be right," Athos adds.

"So they really exist?" StarChild replies. "And . . . that attack you were talking about before, that's what they're preparing for?"

"I think so," Chimera replies. "Can you turn up the volume on your wristcom a little?"

"Sure," StarChild replies, adjusting the volume on her device to hear the cloaked figures clearer. Chimera, StarChild and Athos continue listening in.

"We come back with the weapon crates and schematics or we don't come back at all. If we fail or if any one of us is caught, the repercussions could be disastrous. We meet back at the LZ at the 2nd degree to rendezvous with transport and return back to base. Any questions?"

There is a brief silence.

"Are we expecting heavy resistance?" another voice in the huddle asks.

"Our objective is to remain unseen, but make no mistake, you are authorized to terminate all Grey resistance on site," the leader instructs. "Any other queries?"

There is another pause

"Alright, let's head out then," the leader instructs.

The figures all move toward the elevator lift in unison, behind the lead figure. The elevator gate opens, revealing a medium-sized airship. They all load onto the elevator.

"We gotta find a way to get to follow that elevator and get up top," Chimera explains.

As all the figures step onto the elevator, the ship door slides up and they begin to enter.

"Are you saying what I think you're saying?" StarChild asks.

"Yea, we're going to the surface," Chimera responds.

"In the history of bad ideas, this is the worst I've ever heard, and I've only known you for a lunar cycle," StarChild remarks.

"It's now or never! Something big is about to happen and we need to know what it is," Chimera declares, as she walks back to the stairs still crouching. When she reaches the stairs, she looks back and asks, "Are you guys coming?"

"We've come this far, why stop now?" Athos replies.

"How did I let you drag me into this," StarChild remarks. "You owe me big time."

The hum of the elevator can be heard as it begins to rise up toward the surface above ground.

"Don't worry, it'll be worth it," Chimera remarks.

"If I do this, you're on quarter cleaning duty for four rotations, and I get half a planetary rotation worth of your hot water credits," StarChild negotiates.

"If we can get to the surface before they're gone, you've got a deal," Chimera states.

"How do you plan on doing that?" Athos asks. "If we follow them we'll be seen."

"Give me a moment to think," Chimera exclaims, as she sprints down the stairs, reaching the ground level.

"We could go back to our quarters, hatch a plan and be suicidal rebels another rotation," StarChild replies sarcastically.

"Hatch, that's it!" Chimera proclaims. "StarChild, you're a genius!"

"I am?" StarChild asks.

"Yea, you guys look for an access hatch," Chimera instructs. "Whoever maintains the ventilation systems here needs some sort of way to get to the surface."

"How are we going to find that?" StarChild inquires.

"fan exhaust duct, somewhere where the fumes get released," Athos chimes in.

Chimera, StarChild and Athos dart across the dimly lit docks toward the area where the figures entered the elevator.

"Keep an eye out for any vents," Chimera suggests. "Somewhere where you see smoke rising."

Chimera, StarChild and Athos continue looking for hints of a ventilation system.

"I see something!" StarChild exclaims, pointing to a large bladeless fan above them, with a billow of smoke rising toward it.

"That's it!" Chimera exclaims. "We need to find the hatch that leads to the tunnel."

Chimera checks near the fan and notices a platform to the right of a giant generator box.

"We have to get up to that platform," Chimera states.

"The stairs, right over there," Athos states, pointing to an elevated stairway near the platform.

The staircase is connected to the platform and extends down but does not reach the ground, leaving a gap of about twelve meters.

"How do we get up there?" StarChild questions. "We need a ladder or something."

Chimera looks around for something to provide a boost to the stairs. She clenches her fist and begins to pace back and forth. The hum of the elevator fades away as the figures reach the surface.

"We're running out of time. They're almost to the surface," Athos warns.

"I have an idea!" Chimera exclaims suddenly. "Bring a few of those crates, quickly."

Athos and StarChild head to a stack of crates and each take a side. They begin to lift the top crate over and down to the ground.

"These things are heavier than they look," StarChild professes, as she and Athos struggle a bit with the crate. Chimera joins to help hoist the crate and the three of them set the crate a short distance in front of the stairs.

"We need two more," Chimera instructs.

Chimera, Athos and StarChild retrieve two more crates, sliding them from the pile and onto the first crate they set in front of the stairs.

"Ok, now what?" StarChild inquires, leaning over out of breath.

"Now is the hard part," Chimera says.

"So that was the easy part?" StarChild retorts to Chimera, as her communicator sphere picks up a few faint sounds from the elevator reaching the surface.

"Alright, it's time," Chimera announces. She takes several steps back, aligning herself with the crates and the stairs.

"What are you doing?" StarChild asks.

"Stepping outside the box," Chimera replies.

"Literally," Athos adds.

There is a silence as Chimera gets into position, and then begins to run full speed toward the stairs. As she approaches, she springs off the crates she placed on the ground and soars through the air. Chimera nearly reaches the staircase with the tip of her right hand but falls short and lands on her feet with a thud.

"You almost reached it!" Athos exclaims.

"That's like a fifteen-meter gap or something," StarChild declares. "I've never seen a Hybrid jump that high."

Chimera is silent, focused on the stairs in front of her. She returns to her original position a good distance away from the staircase. She hunches over, takes a deep breath and closes her eyes. After getting focused, she sprints off again toward the stairs. Once again, Chimera steps atop the crates using them as a springboard. On this second attempt, time seems to slow down as Chimera sails through the air as if a jetpack were propelling her. Nearing the staircase, she extends her right hand again and catches hold of the bottom rung on the staircase. Holding on with her right hand, she grabs hold of the stairs with her left hand as well and pulls herself up.

"Wow that was some jump!" Athos exclaims.

"Who are you?" StarChild adds.

"I ask myself that question every day," Chimera declares, as she pulls herself up and climbs the staircase. "C'mon, let's get you guys up here now."

Chimera presses a button on the stairs which extends the staircase down. StarChild grabs hold and begins to climb up the stairs. Athos follows.

"Let's go, we gotta hurry if we want to catch them!" Chimera proclaims.

Finding the escape hatch, Chimera begins to twist the access wheel on the door clockwise.

"What's behind there?" StarChild asks.

"The service tunnel, I think," Chimera replies. "It should connect to the ventilation system. Help me with this." Chimera grunts as she tries to open the hatch.

Athos and StarChild join, turning the wheel slowly as it becomes less resistant. Eventually it stops as the vault-like door creaks open. A rush of cold Tychonian air blasts through the open hatch.

"Almost there," Chimera states as she steps into the tunnel and begins to climb a ladder on the wall of the tunnel. A blinking blue light provides sporadic bursts of the light as Chimera, StarChild and Athos scale the relatively dark tunnel.

"Smells like Dyloid," StarChild remarks.

"Yea, watch your step," Chimera advises.

Water drips down from above as the walls sweat from the moisture of the night. The three continue up the ladder to the top of the tunnel where they reach a second access hatch.

"Hold my legs while I unlock this second hatch," Chimera instructs.

StarChild reaches up and grabs hold of Chimera, supporting her by her thighs. Athos holds StarChild in place with one hand as well, holding onto the tunnel ladder with his other. Chimera works to open the second door. The creak of an old, heavy door rings out as Chimera finally opens the second hatch. A burst of twilight rushes through the opening and Chimera is greeted by a rush of cool air from the night winds. Chimera climbs out of the tunnel onto the cool subsurface of AzurNu. She turns and reaches down to help StarChild and Athos up.

"Here, take my hand," Chimera offers as StarChild grabs hold and is hoisted up out of the tunnel.

"You ok?" Chimera asks StarChild.

"Yea," StarChild answers.

Athos emerges shortly after, peering around as he rises out of the muggy tunnel.

"Look, there's the ship right there," StarChild announces, pointing to a rock covered enclosing, covering the elevator lift.

"Let's catch them before they lift off," Chimera urges.

"How are we going get on?" StarChild inquires.

"It looks like a Tiberian cruiser," Athos exclaims. "Most of them have a storage bay at the bottom of the ship."

Chimera, StarChild and Athos rush to the ship, still crouched to avoid being detected. There are no traces of the figures outside of the craft and the buzz of its preflight boosters is audible. The ship suddenly throttles up, preparing for takeoff.

"Hurry!" Chimera exclaims.

They reach the maintenance bay underneath the main hull of the ship.

"How do we get in?" Chimera inquires.

"I don't know. Ask the encyclopedia," StarChild responds glancing to Athos.

Athos places his palm on a panel on the side of the bay and a knob slowly protrudes. Athos turns the knob and then presses a button, causing the bay door to slide open. Chimera and StarChild dash inside the bay. Athos peers around to make sure they were not seen, before entering the bay and shutting the door. The ship throttles to full power and then rises and begins to glide forward. Once clear of the rock enclosing, the ship ascends quickly and tilts to the left. It speeds off heading west.

First Strike

The ship quietly sails through the Tychonian night flying toward Tychon 3, the industrial region for Grey Production. Stars in the sky twinkle like flashing beacons, filling the night with the story of the galaxy. Chimera and Athos peer out the translucent bay walls, watching the terrain below them rise and fall as StarChild clutches the wall. Soaring over the outskirts of Tychon 1 for half a degree, the ship enters the outer borders of Tychon 3.

"Wow, is that Tychon 3?" StarChild asks unlatching herself from the wall to see ahead.

"I think so," Athos replies looking down as well.

"You know, I can count on what hand the number of times I've been above surface," StarChild mentions, watching the shifting scenery.

As the ship approaches Tychon 3, sprawling grey structures cover the entire region like a network of bunkers and towers. The industrial landscape replaces vegetation and plant life, giving the region a dark grungy feel. Factories and oddly shaped structures connected by tunnels and hubways stretch across the land, as far as the eye can see. In the distance, what looks like Reds appear, moving about through the hubways. Smoke and ash pumped out over many lunar cycles blacken the sky, adding to the region's gloominess.

"What is this place?" StarChild questions.

"It's where the Greys bring the Marooners to work," Athos replies.

"Marooners?" Chimera asks.

"Yea, Marooners . . . or Inbetweeners as you probably call them," Athos answers. "Gene modified Hue-mans."

Chimera stares in disgust at the sea of factories populated with drudge-like Hue-mans moving about.

The ship slows and begins to descend in an open area just outside the outskirts of the region. Touching down, the ship shakes a bit before coming to rest on the dry surface. Not far away sits a Grey transport ship. After several moments, a blast of air is heard as the main hull door opens above them.

"Do you think they'll come down here?" StarChild asks.

"I hope not," Athos replies.

The figures from the ship appear, gliding down the open hull door. They don black masks that make their faces impossible to see. Chimera, StarChild and Athos hide behind a large rotating octagonal machine in the center of the bay, unsure if the figures will enter.

"Reds?" StarChild whispers.

Chimera doesn't answer, as she watches the figures exit the ship.

The figures board a hover platform and glide off toward the transport ship. Once they arrive, the figures step off the hover platform and enter the transport ship. After waiting a bit, Chimera and Athos check to see if any other figures are around. Seeing there aren't any, Chimera, StarChild and Athos exit the bay of the ship. After stepping outside, they search their surroundings and sneak to up a nearby hill for a better vantage point.

"I think that's it right over there," Athos remarks, pointing toward something.

"What's over there?" StarChild inquires.

Athos directs Chimera and StarChild's attention to a massive pyramid structure to the north of their location.

"Trytech," he states. "You said they were coming to hit a weapons factory right? They make weapons the Greys use . . . phasers, blasters, sentries, drones."

"And what about that weird structure over there?" StarChild asks, pointing to an array of open pits with tube-like structures around them.

"I think those are mines," Athos answers, still whispering. "For transium."

"The translucent stuff?" Chimera asks.

"Yea," Athos responds. "Transium is what makes aircrafts

transparent, like when they disappear."

Chimera, StarChild and Athos continue to peer out, studying the landscape.

"So many structures," Chimera mentions.

"Are there Greys here?" StarChild inquires.

"Yes," Athos replies. "They keep watch over the inbetweeners . . . making sure everything operates in a manner they deem fit."

"How long have they been here?" Chimera inquires.

"We don't know for sure, but from what I've learned in Advance Studies it's been like this since before we were here," Athos remarks.

"I need to come to your Advance Studies with you some time," Chimera mentions.

"You should," Athos replies. "We are studying Advance Tychonian Science. I'm-" Athos stops mid-sentence, as he notices something. "Look, they're nearing the outer border," Athos points out, spotting the transport ship.

Chimera pulls out a tiny magnifying device and repositions herself to get a better look.

Chimera watches as the transport ship passes a patrol tower.

"I can't believe that worked!" Chimera exclaims.

After entering the outer perimeter, the transport disappears into the distance. Chimera kneels back down.

"What do we do now?" StarChild asks.

"Now, we wait," Chimera responds. "Keep watch, they'll be

back."

"Yes, your majesty," StarChild retorts sarcastically.

Chimera, StarChild and Athos lie quietly, as the brisk Tychonian air gusts, kicking particles of dirt and sand around. Chimera falls asleep as StarChild does shortly after. The two are asleep for nearly two degreess when Chimera is suddenly awaken by Athos.

"Chimera, wake up. I see them!" Athos exclaims.

Chimera turns over and catches a glimpse of a ship approaching.

"Wake up!" Chimera exclaims to StarChild.

"I'm awake," StarChild says in a half sleep voice.

Crossing the perimeter to the outer zone, the ship continues back picking up speed.

"C'mon, we need to get back to the ship," Chimera instructs.

"Look!" StarChild exclaims. "There's another ship coming."

Chimera retrieves her magnifier once again and takes a closer look.

"It looks like a Grey security patrol," Chimera acknowledges.

"Another one of ours?" Athos inquires.

"I don't think so," Chimera answers back.

"That can't be good," Athos remarks.

"Not at all," Chimera replies, watching the second ship approach.

Suddenly, the patrol ship slows down and begins to turn around.

"I think the patrol spotted them," Athos declares.

"Yea . . . I think you're right," Chimera adds, watching the patrol ship pick up speed.

"What should we do?" Athos questions.

"We have to help," Chimera exclaims. "You guys stay with the ship. I'm gonna create a diversion."

"Are you sure?" Athos asks.

"Yea, trust me," Chimera remarks. Seeing StarChild still asleep, Chimera kneels down to wake her. "StarChild, wake up, you have to get back to the ship!"

"I'm coming, Dug, hold on," StarChild replies half asleep. Coming to her senses, she realizes where she is. "Sorry about that guys."

"I'll stay and help you create the diversion, Chimera," Athos insists. "StarChild, you can head back to the ship."

"What's going on?" StarChild questions.

"Get back to the ship, StarChild!" Chimera proclaims as she begins searching the ground for something.

"Ok ok, no need to get snappy," StarChild acknowledges, as she hurries back toward the ship.

The Enforcers and their commandeered transport continue back toward the ship.

"Do you think they can see that patrol ship coming?" Athos asks.

"I don't think so," Chimera answers.

"What's the plan then?" Athos questions.

"Find a container, or something like it, that I can put stuff in," Chimera instructs.

Athos searches his magpack as Chimera begins collecting sand from the floor.

"Here," Athos says producing a medium-size thermos. "Would this work?"

"That's perfect," Chimera remarks, continuing to collect sand in her hands. "Pour whatever's in the thermos out, quickly."

After emptying out the thermos, Athos exclaims, "I'm done."

"Ok, bring it here," Chimera says, pouring the sand she collected into the thermos.

"Now, do you have an antimatter canister with you?" Chimera questions.

"Yea."

"Perfect, detach it and hand it to me so we can attach it to the thermos," Chimera instructs.

"What are you making?" Athos asks.

"It's a distraction . . . an explosive one!" Chimera proclaims.

Athos detaches one of the canisters from his magpack and hands it to Chimera.

"Now hold this while I tie it up," Chimera orders. She produces a strap from her magpack and ties the thermos and canister together. The patrol ship nears, hovering several hundred meters away.

"It's now or never," Chimera announces. She grabs the thermos rig and heads to a nearby group of abandoned support pylons.

"Go, now!" Chimera shouts to Athos.

Athos sprints back to the ship and links with StarChild. Once Athos is clear of the blast zone, Chimera points her wristcom at the thermos rig and fires a laser. She then takes cover. Suddenly, there is a flash and an explosion which shakes the entire area and disintegrates the pylons. A fireball shoots up into the sky and the Grey patrol ship slows down turning toward the blast.

The Enforcers aboard the hover platform glare at the explosion. One of the Enforcers seems to notices the patrol ship in the distance, pointing at it. The figures quickly reboard the ship carrying several crates onboard. Chimera presses a button on her magpack and she quickly hovers back toward the ship.

After arriving, she opens the bay door and steps inside.

"How did you know how to do that?" Athos asks.

"I don't know. It kind of just came to me," Chimera answers.

"Did they see you?" StarChild questions, startling Chimera as she enters the bay underneath the ship.

Powering up the engines, the craft rocks as it lifts off the surface and climbs back into the sky. Chimera, StarChild, Athos and the unknown figures soar back toward AzurNu.

"I still can't believe I let you talk me into this!" StarChild exclaims.

Arriving back at AzurNu, Chimera, StarChild and Athos wait for the Enforcers to exit the ship and clear the docks, before sneaking out and returning back to their living quarters.

The next rotation, Chimera wakes early after a night of restlessness. StarChild is fast asleep in her sleep pod.

"I need to re-center," Chimera announces to herself.

Briefly changing, Chimera leaves her quarters and heads to *Infinity: Place of Peace* to meditate, located inside the *Create* zone of the city. Chimera arrives and meditates for a degree. After meditation, Chimera checks her wristcom and notices a message from Athos.

Come to lecture room X3 to sit it on my Advance Tychonian Science class, the message reads.

Chimera considers whether to accept the invitation, still exhausted from the previous night's exploits.

Chimera decides to go and begins toward zone 4, the Education wing of AzurNu. Reaching the lecture room hall, Chimera finds room X3 and pokes her head inside. The class is full of Red students. The previous professor has already rotated out of the room and the class is awaiting their next instructor. Chimera slowly enters the room as some of the other students seem to glance at her strangely.

"Chimera, over here," Athos calls, waving Chimera over.

Chimera walks across the room past the lecture platform into the seating arena. She walks up the ramp toward Athos, who is sitting in the mid-section of the seventh row. Chimera slides past the other students and takes a seat next to StarChild. Just then the lecture platform begins to rotate and the lecture agent slides in.

"The lecture Agent is IndusRED. He's really good," Athos whispers to Chimera.

"Last rotation, we discussed the levels of existence," Indus begins. "There are ten levels or dimensions of existence. Nothing else exists outside of these levels." He begins writing on a large holographic screen behind the lecture stage:

Lecture Agent: *IndusRED*
Subject: *10 Levels of Existence*

Level 1 =

Level 2 =

Level 3 =

Level 4 =

Level 5 =

Level 6 =

Level 7 =

Level 8 =

Level 9 =

Level 10 =

Once he's done writing, he continues. "Who can tell me what the first level is?" Indus asks.

One of the students presses the screen in front of them, which activates a floating sphere in the front of the room near Indus. Looking up, Chimera recognizes the Red.

"It's the Red from the club," Chimera whispers to Athos.

"Huh?" Athos questions.

"Nothing," Chimera whispers back.

"Existence is the foundation of all ten dimensions, encompassing everything in the universe," Solar responds.

"Correct, and . . ." Before Indus can finish his sentence, he is interrupted by Nexus.

"That includes all matter, space and consciousness," he adds.

Indus pauses for a moment, and then responds, "Correct, thank you. And who can tell me what the second level of existence is?"

Solar buzzes in again, turning to briefly glance and wink at Chimera. Indus pauses again, looking around the room before acknowledging Nexus.

"Yes, Nexus," Indus says.

"Matter is the foundation of all living thing in existence. All objects, beings elements, liquids, gases and mixtures are a summation of matter, comprised in various sequences," Solar responds astutely.

"Thank you," Indus replies.

A hologram of an atom slowly rotating appears on the holographic screen.

"The third level, who can tell me about it?" Indus asks the class.

Before Solar can buzz in again, Athos buzzes with an answer.

"Yes, Athos," Indus acknowledges.

Athos writes something on his screen and then transfers the note over to Indus's Master Sphere that displays Athos's answer on the holo-screen.

Indus reads Athos's answer aloud, his voice resonating through the sound amplifier inside the Sphere, "The third level of existence is Formation. All matter and beings composed of matter are created by formation. Formation is the arrangement of matter in any particular sequence to form a complex organic nuon."

The atom on the screen replicates, forming hundreds of more atoms. The atoms fuse together and take the shape of a Hue-man.

"Very good, Athos," Indus states.

"Nuon meaning being, object, compound gas, element or any other biological structure," Solar adds loudly.

"Thank you, Nexus, but please dial in your answer next time," Indus declares as the entire room begins to murmur, annoyed by Nexus's overachieving demeanor.

"What is the fourth level of existence?" Indus inquires.

Another student taps their screen.

"All matter follows the basic principles, rules and laws of physics," the student begins. "Matter is limited to these laws and must obey them in all dimensions lower than the eighth existence. Laws like the law of motion and the law of gravity, which govern time, space, the universe and all that's within it."

The Hue-man on the main screen retrieves a ball and throws it up in the air. The ball falls back to the ground shortly after.

"Great," Indus remarks. "Very well put."

"The fifth level of existence . . . who can tell us what it is?" Indus questions.

A student on the lower center row buzzes in and answers, "Consciousness!"

The screen in front of the class zooms into the Hue-man's head, revealing a brain.

"Right," Indus says. "And what is consciousness?"

"Consciousness is thought; self-awareness," the student proclaims.

"Exactly, consciousness is the knowledge of one's own existence," Indus announces. "Consciousness doesn't relate to objects or matter, but it's elevated to the state of a dimension. Who can tell me why?"

Another student dials in to answer, "Because it exists within it's own plane."

"Correct," Indus acknowledges, writing on the screen at the center of the room. "Consciousness lies in the dimension above Rules because there are no rules or limitations to consciousness. One can think of or imagine anything that he or she allows himself to. And what is the sixth dimension?" Indus asks, glancing around the room.

Solar buzzes in, looking around the room and stealing another glance at Chimera.

"I'd like to hear from someone new this time," Indus states.

Another Red buzzes in.

"The sixth dimension of existence is Time. Time is movement relative to speed, and doesn't really exist."

"Close," Indus remarks. "Time is movement relative to matter."

On the screen, the view zooms all the way out to display a planet slowly rotating around a sun.

"Since time is movement relative to matter, if no matter existed, the passage of time would not be quantifiable. Time is movement, you were correct about that. And because time is movement relative to matter existing in the seventh dimension, traveling forward or backward through time is only possible for beings that have mastered the next dimension on our ladder. The seventh dimension is very important, who can tell us what it is?" Indus inquires.

Athos buzzes in.

"Athos, tell us," Indus commands.

"The seventh dimension is Space," Athos states. "All matter within the universe exists within the realm of space. All matter is comprised of atoms, protons and neutrons with space between these parts. Space holds anything and everything."

"Yes, exactly," Indus answers.

A diagram of the Zeta Reticuli solar system appears on the screen.

"Space holds everything: planets, stars, light, sound, thoughts, rules, matter and even time," Indus explains. "Without space there would be nothing! Now, the last dimension on the limited quantum ladder is what?" Indus asks. He selects a student to answer.

"No Rules," the student answers. "In the eighth dimension and above, traditional laws and rules of physics don't apply."

"Right," Indus responds. "This is definitely a class of high thinkers. Now, an example of no rules would be like a black hole." The main screen zooms in to a black hole that pulls debris into its center. "A black hole has the capacity to swallow a planet and shrink its size to a tiny rock while retaining the planet's mass. Black holes break all rules of traditional physics. Wormholes are another example."

"I really dig this stuff," Chimera whispers to Athos.

"Yea, me too," Athos agrees.

"The ninth dimension of existence is Sub-infinity," Indus continues. "The unique aspect of the ninth existence is that anything is possible in the realm of sub-infinity, except for the creation of new matter from a zero-state. Sub-infinity is the separation between all other dimensions and the tenth level. The tenth existence is so great, it has the ninth dimension solely as a divide to it . . . like a bridge for the gap between dimension one through eight and the tenth existence."

"My science class is nowhere near this interesting," Chimera states to Athos.

"Crash in here anytime," Athos answers back.

"Who can enlighten us on what the tenth dimension is?" Indus asks.

A new student buzzes in and sends his answer to Indus's Sphere.

"The tenth dimension of existence is Infinity," the student proclaims. "It is everything, the creation of all matter, the existence of space, the ability for consciousness, the formation of matter, the rules that govern matter and the eighth and ninth dimensions that break normal rules."

"Very accurate," Indus exclaims. "Some interpret this dimension as the realm of the Creator. The tenth dimension is so vast and infinite that the ninth dimension exist as a gulf because nothing less than the ninth dimension can reproduce capabilities of the tenth existence."

Moving a few holograms in his Sphere around, Indus continues his lecture.

"A dimension is a compounding principle," Indus explains. "It forms a foundation relating to existence. Time is distance relative to space. Time travel for our human ancestors on Earth is not yet possible because the laws of Earth physics state that to change or affect an object the object creating the force must be greater than the object it is acting upon. Hue-mans have not yet created a force strong enough to create an effect greater than the fifth dimension." Indus stops to clear his throat. "Um . . . most Hue-mans' mastery of dimensions lies in the fourth existence. There are a few exceptions. Hue-mans who can read minds or move objects via thought have mastered the fifth dimension."

Moving information from his Master Sphere onto the main screen, Indus continues, "An unlocked consciousness gives power over dimensions one through seven. The tenth existence governs dimensions one through eight. The power of the seventh dimension is power over space, movement, time and the formation of matter."

The clock on the main screen nears the 15th degree of rotation. Students slowly begin checking their wristcoms and screens.

"As we bring things to a close, it's important to remember that rules only apply to objects, not thoughts," Indus mentions. "For that reason, consciousness lies in the dimension above rules, which makes it greater than the normal rules and laws of physics. Matter is limited to the parameters of its creation . . . consciousness is like sub infinity. In the ninth dimension, there are rules that govern this dimension however they are very unique rules. These unique rules allow for nontraditional law and physics beyond the norm . . ."

Suddenly, a low humming ping sounds. Students begin sliding the information on their screens onto their wristcoms, and rising from their seats. Chimera remains seated as Athos finishes his upload and begins to stand. On the screen, the notation for the session's lecture, among other notes, reads:

Level 1 = Existence

Level 2 = Matter

Level 3 = Formation

Level 4 = Rules

Level 5 = Consciousness

Level 6 = Time

Level 7 = Space

Level 8 = no rules

Level 9 = Sub Infinity

Level 10 = *Infinity*

Chimera uploads the notes into her wristcom and stands up.

"You ready?" Athos asks.

"Yea, but hold on. I need to ask Indus something," Chimera replies.

She climbs down the seating arena heading toward Indus but before she can reach him he rotates out of the room. Chimera turns back to meet Athos.

"What were you gonna ask?" Athos inquires.

"Nothing, wanted to ask a few more questions," Chimera answers.

On Tychon 4, Lord PrychonGrey is in his study chambers when another Grey approaches his chamber door and announces his presence.

Chapter Three

"Nintius, my trusty subject," Prychon acknowledges. He opens the chamber door. "What brings you to my quarters?"

"Lord Prychon, apologies for disturbing you, may I enter?" Nintius asks.

Prychon nods, and Nintius slowly enters

"Lord Prychon, VengerGrey has a most important message."

"Send him in," Prychon acknowledges.

VengerGrey enters the chambers shortly after, and finds Prychon attaching pieces of his armor.

"It seems you have an important report?" Prychon alludes telepathically.

"Sire, the *Trytech* factory has been raided," Venger tele-communicates.

"Raided!" Prychon yells. "What do you mean raided?"

"Sire, our intelligence suggests Reds did this," Venger announces.

"Speak to me with words!" Prychon exclaims.

"My apologies, sire. Reds appear to be responsible for the raid," Venger repeats.

"I heard you the first time!" Prychon snaps as he raises his hand and reaches out to touch Venger.

As if an invisible force was emitted from Prychon, Venger flies backward and crumples to the ground.

"Assemble the Council, now!" Prychon instructs Nintius.

"Yes, Lord," Nintius acknowledges, as he turns and exits quickly.

Two Greys, who are part of the Elite guard, enter followed by a hovering stretcher. The stretcher de-elevates and the two guards slide Venger onto the stretcher. The stretcher rises up and the two guards exit carrying Venger.

Two degrees later, Lord Prychon and his entourage arrive to the Grey capitol city of Edra for a meeting in the High Council Palace. After landing, Lord Prychon quickly enters the palace and makes his way to the High Council chambers. The palace is massive crystal pyramid and the High Council Chamber is a large upper room atop the pyramid. Lord Prychon reaches the chamber and enters his private area in the upper chamber.

The interior of the chamber is a crystal-like texture with a holographic, iridescent hue. The room appears wall-less and windowless, but a faint amount of opacity reveals the exterior cityscapes of Tychon 4 toward the center of the room lies the council circle. Thirteen members of the Grey Council sit atop oddly shaped chairs, hovering slightly above the ground. Lord PrychonGrey seats himself in the upper chamber that overlooks the council circle. Prychon's chamber is fully enclosed containing only a pyramid-shaped window through which Prychon is visible.

In the center of the council circle is a small device which emits a holographic projection of Prychon that appears to each council member at the same angle.

"As Head of the Grey High Council, I, LumakhodGrey, declare this meeting convened," a Grey at the first seat of the council circle announces. "Lord Prychon, as author of this meeting, feel free to begin."

"Yes, Senator," Lord Prychon begins. "I have received reports of a free Red society in existence, thriving in a region east of here. Automallies, Hybrids and Full-Breeds alike costing! These cretins are believed to have executed a raid on a weapons factory on Tychon 3!"

"Impossible!" several council members declare, glancing at each other in confusion.

"A Red attack on Tychon 3 soil? What evidence of this do you present?" a member of the council questions Prychon.

"Senator Tsuna, I hold a sphere of testimony from AltairGrey," Prychon declares. "Reds are an infection to our society, a plague that cannot be allowed to spread. The mere thought of them disgusts me. Their ideas of expression and creativity are toxic. Their ideas and emotions are irrational and bring instability to the region . . . They must all be eradicated!"

The council nods.

"The current containment force is no longer effective," Prychon announces.

"What do you mean, sire?" one of the Greys questions.

"I am calling for a disband of the Preconditioning Patrol immediately," Prychon orders.

"As advisor to your Lordship, I must urge you to caution any rash decisions," the Alviso states.

"I will not tread with caution, AlvisoGrey," Prychon announces. "I mean to crush any Red uprising immediately. All in favor of this motion, confirm."

Tsuna and the other council members glance at one another.

"Need I remind you that a Red invasion would not only threaten our economy, but the well-being of your family and kin," Prychon warns.

One by one council members nods and taps the left side of Prychon's hologram in front of them.

"It seems an overwhelming majority approve your motion," Lumakhod declares.

Prychon turns to one of the Greys sitting in the third seat to his right.

"Schilark, as head of Red Eradication Patrol, I am tasking you with overseeing the formation of the new Anti Automally committee. This new committee will assemble a new task force and oversee eradication of all non-neophytes. It will be known as the Anti Automally Committee. Consolidate all previous operations from Eradication Patrol to this new committee . . . immediately."

"Yes, sire," Schilark responds telepathically.

"Who will run this committee, Lord Prychon?" another Grey questions.

"My dear Chomora, Tachyon will be lead captain of the Anti-Automally Committee."

Tachyon glances up at Prychon in the upper chamber, surprised at his selection.

"And I tap my eldest nephew SeyfertGrey to be second in charge. I expect quick action, swift resolution. That is all," Prychon declares, concluding his declaration.

"Very well. That will conclude our meeting for today," Lumakhod continues, pressing a button on the council table.

The Grey Council rise quickly with the exception of Alviso and Tachyon, as Prychon exits the room.

Committee of Death

Two lunar cycles pass as Chimera works to get acclimated to AzurNu life. It is the 7th degree and Chimera is inside her sleep pod sitting back in deep thought when she receives an alert on her wristcom. Chimera checks her wristcom and realizes it is a city-wide bulletin: *All Reds report to the Tiberius Hall auditorium immediately for an emergency assembly.*

Chimera readies herself and exits her living quarters on her way to Tiberius Hall.

As she reaches the hall, a large auditorium at the south end of the living quarters AzurNu, Chimera receives another message on her wristcom. Quickly glancing down she sees a message from StarChild.

Are you coming to the broadcast meeting? the message reads. Chimera briefly stops to reply to the message on her wristcom.

On my way now, are you there? Chimera responds, as the crowd of Reds in the halls begin to swell.

Hundreds of Reds fill the corridors, all filing toward Tiberius Hall. Chimera makes her way to main foyer of the Tiberius Hall auditorium, which is even more crowded than the corridors. Thousands of voices fill the foyer, as Chimera looks around to see if she catches a glimpse of any familiar faces. The crowd slowly shuffles into the auditorium and Chimera squeezes her way past the slow moving crowd to a pair of stairs on the right of the foyer. Chimera climbs the packed stairs to one of the upper levels of the auditorium. Reaching an upper level entrance, Chimera pushes her way inside. She is greeted by the red and gold colors of the regal concourse. Inside, the main auditorium is packed with Reds as the ensemble of voices fill the room, louder than outside in the foyer.

"So this is what it looks like," Chimera says to herself. She glances around looking for a row with an available seat, and notices a Red walking down back past her.

"Hey, do you know what's going on?" Chimera asks the passing Reds.

"No idea, must be something big," the Red replies back continuing down the aisle.

Chimera continues on to a row where she spots a few empty seats toward the center. She tries to make her way down the row, toward the seat.

"What is she doing here?" a voice mutters out loud.

"Go back to the surface, outlander!" another voice hollers.

Chimera turns to see several Reds in the rows to her left, glaring at her. Chimera ignores the taunts and continues down the row. Suddenly, a pudgy, brunette Red in the row Chimera is walking down blocks the way, making it impossible for Chimera to pass.

"Is there a problem?" Chimera retorts to the Red blocking her way.

"Yea, you can go back where you came from," the Red declares. "You're one of them, you don't belong here!" the Red scoffs.

Chimera glares at the Red.

"I'm a Hybrid, you Cro-Magnus," Chimera barks. "But even if I wasn't what difference would it make? Automally, Full-breed, we're all Reds!"

"Yea, that's what you think," the Red blocking Chimera indicates.

"She's a marooner, probably doesn't even know her birth kin," a freckle faced Red with curly, ginger-colored hair chimes in.

Chimera begins to clench her fist.

"What, are you gonna hit me, inbetweener?" the Red blocking the aisle remarks.

Chimera begins to step forward when another voice rings out.

"Why don't you leave her alone!" the voice demands. "Just because you're inbred sperma doesn't mean we should have to put up with your narrow mindedness," StarChild snarls, climbing down the aisle and scooting the Red out of the way.

"Ohhhh, the sexy StarChild to the rescue," the second Red remarks.

"Shutup, Conklin!" the Red blocking the aisle orders.

"You shut up, Mangel!" the second Red fires back.

Mangel shoves Conklin, causing her to lose her balance and fall over the row of seats beneath her. She hits the ground with a loud thud.

"C'mon Chi, let's get away from these morons," StarChild suggests as the other two Reds begin arguing with each other. "There's a spot for you over here."

"Thanks," Chimera acknowledges.

"No problem," StarChild replies. "Was just trying to save you the trouble of another fight."

"What makes you think it's any trouble?" Chimera remarks, grinning.

StarChild shakes her head, as she and Chimera make their way down the aisle to an empty seat. More Reds continue to trickle into the auditorium, which is now overfilled. Reds occupy the seats, aisles and even the stairs.

"It's good to see you," StarChild exclaims. "I had to leave early for studies but when I got the emergency bulletin, we all left."

"Yea, I was at quarters when I got the wristcom . . ." Chimera begins.

Suddenly a figure emerges onto the stage and a horn-like hum sounds throughout the auditorium. Reds in the audience begin to direct their attention to the stage but the ambience of voices and screaming can still be heard.

"What's going on?" one Red yells.

"Why are we here, crowded in like this?" another Red hollers. "What is so important?"

The Red on stage begins to speak and his voice fills the auditorium, "Reds of AzurNu, I am LiazoRED. Please take your seats and all your questions will be answered."

The last of the entering crowd file into the auditorium like sea fish, filling any available spaces.

"This is madness," Chimera says to StarChild.

"I know," StarChild replies. "I didn't think I would find anyone in this mess."

"Seriously," Chimera responds. "Did you get my wristcom?"

"No, I didn't," StarChild replies. "What do you think all this is about anyway?"

"We're about to find out," Chimera answers.

Liazo begins again, "Good Reds, if you can decrescendo and lend your attention, OmegaRED will address you shortly."

The remaining Reds take their seats. The sound of voices begins to soften but Reds speaking and questioning each other in confusion can still be heard.

A second, low majestic hum permeates the theater as OmegaRED steps out onto the stage. The crowd becomes silent and stands to their feet. As Omega reaches the center they begin to clap and cheer wildly.

Omega raises his hands. The crowd quiets down again.

Omega begins, "Good Reds of AzurNu, I am OmegaRED, leader of the Red Council as you know. We have assembled you here today in response to a new decree. A new decree that has been mandated directly from the High Grey Council. This decree, which was presented to me today, reads as follows, 'As of sunrise on the current rotation, Lunar Cycle 2057, it is deemed a crime against the Grey principalities and the Tychon Federated Union, for all Reds not reconditioned, to object or abstain from submitting themselves to Grey Enforcement. This crime is punishable immediately, by de-atomization."

Gasps can be heard through the auditorium as a crescendo of voices begin, murmuring, asking questions and expressing disapproval of the decree.

"We ask you stay calm, and not to panic," Omega states. "We are prepared to take all necessary measures to preserve the Red way of life."

"What measures!" one Red yells out. "Our army doesn't stand a chance against Preconditioning Patrol!"

Omega continues, "The previous enforcement squad, which you know as the Preconditioning Unit, has been disbanded. Intelligence reports received, alerted us that the P.P.U. which was created to oversee and monitor all non-Grey inhabitants on Tychon has been dissolved."

"This can't be good," StarChild proclaims, turning to Chimera.

"I bet it has something to do with that raid . . ." Chimera whispers in a low voice.

"I hope not," StarChild mentions. "I knew it was a bad idea though."

Chimera and StarChild continue to listen to Omega as he address the crowd of unsettled Reds.

"Our sources have informed us that the Greys have created a new committee. A committee now known as the Anti Automally Committee. Preconditioning Patrol has been combined into an attack squad for the Anti Automally Committee. Unfortunately, we believe this committee's sole mission is to hunt down and de-atomize any and all Reds that do not surrender by the end of this rotation. As I said before, do not be alarmed. I assure you that our forces will not go quietly into the night."

"What exactly is being done about this new threat?" a Red yells out.

"And how can you assure our safety?" another Red adds.

"At this time, we are congregating to weigh all options for this new threat."

Another uproar of voices begins as Reds begin panicking. The fears of many can be heard as Reds shout questions at the council.

"Congregating?" one Red remarks, rising out of his seat. "A band of neurotic Greys prepare for a campaign of blood and you congregate?"

"We've been underground for seven generations. How could they have known of our existence?" another Red shouts.

"It's because of Automalies," the Red that rose out of his seat declares. "We need immediate transfer of leadership to Full-breed rule!"

Suddenly, a fifteen-foot RED emerges onto the stage.

"That looks like Titan," StarChild remarks to Chimera.

"Yea, he must be here on behalf of the Red Defense Core," Chimera suggests. "To calm everyone's fears."

"Have you no respect for the Commander?" Titan roars. "It's never an acceptable practice to interrupt a public address. Have you all lost your minds?"

"This is crazy!" StarChild exclaims. "What's happening to us?"

"I don't know, but I think I know who would know more," Chimera replies.

"Who?" StarChild questions.

"Sybil," Chimera replies.

"Sybil, curator of Historical Records?" StarChild asks.

"Yea, she knows all about Preconditioning, and what's happening now," Chimera declares, rising out of her seat. "Who knows, it might even help me uncover some info on my father."

"You're going now?" StarChild asks.

"I have to," Chimera replies. "I need to get out of this madness before a riot starts. Something big is coming. The seeds of revolution have been sown. I want to get as much info as possible on what we're up against."

"I understand," StarChild replies. "I'll let you know how the rest of this madness goes."

"Thanks," Chimera states.

She begins down the row and toward the aisle to exit. The roar of voices falls silent as Omega begins to speak again. Chimera reaches the exit and continues out the foyer on her way to the Historical Data and Record library.

Reaching the data library, Chimera slowly enters in. It is a vast room full of circular stations with floating spheres and cylindrical holographic screens above them. Toward the middle of the room, Chimera sees an elderly woman wearing an all white robe adding data to one of the spheres. Chimera moves across the room to the mysterious woman.

Chimera heads over to the woman and introduces herself.

"Greetings, I am ChimeraRed," Chimera announces. "Are you Sybil?"

"Greetings, Chimera," the woman replies. "It appears I am the one you seek. My designation is Sybil, I am head of Historical Records, Data and Information. I do not believe I have previously been graced with your presence, what is your breed?"

"I'm a Hybrid," Chimera responds.

Chapter Four

Sybil raises her hand and holds up her palm to Chimera. Chimera raises her palm as well. Suddenly Sybil steps forward and connects her palm with Chimera's. The two briefly exchange energy before Chimera jumps back, disconnecting.

"What the hell was that?" Chimera questions, confused at what just occurred.

"Such complex energy for such a young pupil," Sybil proclaims. "You are unique. A Hybrid you say, are you certain?"

"What did you just do to me?" Chimera questions.

"Those who are in tune with the certain frequencies of energy can exchange these energies in many ways," Sybil responds. "Tell me, what is it that you seek?"

"What?" Chimera asks.

"You are unique, empathetic, intuitive, curious and strong-willed. No answer is out of your reach so I ask again, what it is that you seek?"

"You can tell all that from touching my palm?" Chimera replies. "What is that like an Automally thing?"

Sybil is silent, as a faint smile becomes briefly present.

"Ok, answers. I came here for answers," Chimera reveals.

"Well of course, you have come to the correct place," Sybil declares. "But it seems something troubles you. You seek answers for clarity, enlighten me?"

"I know a big war may be on the horizon," Chimera begins.

"With this new decree, it definetly doesn't look good. I'm from above the surface. I moved here from Khyber City to get away from war and figure out what happened to my father. Now it seems like war has followed me here. I haven't started my studies here yet and my knowledge of Grey dominion is limited; I wanted to more."

"And what do you intend to do with the information you seek?" Sybil inquires.

"Help preserve our way of life," Chimera answers.

"Hmm," Sybil replies. She looks up into the sky as if searching for something in the air. "To understand the Grey movement, you must first understand the history of the Red."

Walking over to a virtual collection, Sybil scrolls through the master screen before she reaches what she is looking for. Tapping the screen, a sphere rises and Sybil pulls it out.

"Watch this," Sybil states as she hands the sphere to Chimera. "I believe further enlightenment can be found within its viewing."

Chimera takes the sphere and heads to one of the open viewing seats. She settles in, inserts the sphere and sits back. The holographic video begins.

"In the beginning, there existed one species of Hue-mans on planet earth. In an effort find a more advanced yet docile workforce, Grey terrestrials blended their own genetics with this Hue-man species on earth. So not to confuse, frighten or interfere with the evolution and beliefs of this new species, they created a larger version of these Hue-mans called giants to govern the new species."

"Titan," Chimera whispers to herself. "Greys created giants to rule?"

"The creation of Giants was meant to be a transparent arm of Grey rulership," the projection continues. "Giants rained over Hue-mans as gods, reporting to Greys and taking orders from them as well.

"The Grey race that created them were known as the Anteema. This first race they created was called the Sumerians. Hue-mans began to rapidly reproduce and populate. Culture and society began to advance.

"And so, all on Earth worked as designed until a group of Anteema who called themselves the Annu, began to teach and enlighten Hue-mans, against the wishes of Prychon Lucifias Grey, the ruler of the Greys at the time. The Annu taught the people of earth about Astronomy, time, galla, mathematics themselves, as well as through their Annu leaders.

"Occasionally, the Annu would come and visit this primitive but developing race of people. When the Annu came, they would use disguises to mask their appearance. Sometimes they would dress as animal hybrids. For this reason, Hue-mans on Earth began to worship animals, building pyramids, effigies and symbols to honor the star people that visited them with advance technology. When the Annu visited their creations on earth the Hue-mans were in awe of the spacecraft, believing they were divine in nature.

"Eventually, after they had mined a significant amount of resources from the planet and built monuments combining their technology with the simple tools on Earth, the Annu began visiting their creation on Earth less and less. Hue-mans spread to different regions of earth but still retained their belief and worship of the sky people. They built kingdoms in the Asias, Americas and other places.

"When Greys no longer visited their creation on Earth due to expansion on other planets, wars and political issues on Tychon, the Hue-man race flourished on its own. Religions were birthed, and eventually the Annu Giants were no longer gods.

"From about the year 4000 BC to the 1700s AD, Hue-mans continued to develop on their own. Around the 17th century Earth time, a new leader on Tychon had been in power for several lunar cycles. This new leader rekindled an interest in planet Earth and its inhabitants. His name was Prychon Nyt Grey. Seeing how advanced the Hue-mans had become, Prychon Nyt first studied them. At the time there was a shortage of an abundant labor force on Tychon due to war with the Mercurians, which had decimated a large portion of the Grey population. Also destroyed in the war was the genetic information of the Hue-mans the Anteema had created. Of the few original Hue-mans that were brought back to Tychon, all had escaped, were killed during experimentation or died from neglect.

"Seeing an opportunity to rebuild a new work force on Tychon, Prychon Nyt asked his chancellor to develop a program that would rebuild the workforce on Tychon. His Chancellor, Nebulae Grey, began a campaign of abducting Hue-mans from earth. He used DNA and genetic material from the Hue-mans to create Neophytes, a new generation of genetically modified earthlings with altered brains.

"Modern Tychon was born from these Neophyte workers. The Republic flourished, and its army began to be restored to its former glory. It was like this for 26 Lunar cycles. Great change came about, when a group of sympathetic Greys decided to do something about the abduction and enslavement of Neophytes. Creating an underground group known as *The Society for Unenslaved Neophytes* or *S.U.N. of Man*. This secret group began smuggling Neophytes out of laboratories before their minds were altered. A camp was set up east of Tychon 3 which was known as Azur. The majority of the smuggled Neophytes were brought here. The others were kept at the homes of S.U.N. members and masked as servants.

"It was a curious young Neophyte that one day brought the existence of a non-conditioned Neophyte race to the attention of the Greys. The existence of these free thinking Neophytes, which the Greys categorized as either Automallies or Hybrids or Full-breeds, sparked a chain of events that would alter the course of history on Tychon forever.

"The Grey council, Prychon Nyt, his Chancellor, the Bureaucrats and even Grey citizens were at odds as to what to do with these unconditioned Hue-mans. After rotations of heated debate, Prychon

Nyt overruled the Council and Chancellors mandates, creating a decree that allowed freed or escaped Neophytes to live free and unmolested as long as they did not return to Republic zones or interfere with affairs of the Republic. Sadly, before his decree could be mandated into Tychonian law, Prychon Nyt was killed in a mysterious accident.

"Because Prychon Nyt had no heirs, his successor was the first Grey not of royal bloodline. This successor . . . Chancellor Nebula Grey. He changed his name to PrychonGrey. His first order of business was to form a new group called the Preconditioning Patrol Unit to hunt down and retrieve escaped Reds. In any occurrence of resistance, the P.P.U. was authorized to use deadly force and they did so on many occasion. Azure was nearly wiped out and the few surviving Reds fled the region and went underground. They built . . . AzurNu. This holo-video has terminated," the narrator alerts. "Please insert a new sphere."

After finishing the holo-vid, Chimera sits for a moment. Then she jumps up from her chair and storms toward the door.

"Chimera!" Sybil calls but Chimera doesn't respond.

Exiting the library out into the hallway, Chimera heads to her dorm. Stepping into her quarters, she pulls up her wristcom and scrolls through her contacts. Finding the desired contact, Chimera dials the coordinates and her wristcom beeps for a moment before Iona's hologram appears answering the call.

"Hello my love, how are you?" Iona begins, greeting Chimera.

"It was a lie. It was all a lie!" Chimera exclaims.

"What are you talking about?" Iona asks, confused.

"Everything . . . everything you told me," Chimera remarks. "Why and how we got here! It was all a lie!"

"Call me down, love, what was a lie? Tell me what you're talking about, I have no idea," Iona questions.

"What did you think? I would never find out the truth!" Chimera yells.

Just then, StarChild enters in, virtual chatting with her boyfriend.

"Just relax, I can explain everything," Iona pleads.

"There's nothing to explain," Chimera replies. "Let me guess, you thought you were protecting me by not telling me the truth? You should have told me. Who knows what else you've lied about."

"It's not that at all!" Iona cries.

"Uh, is everything ok?" StarChild asks, interrupting her conversation with Dug.

"Yea, I was just hanging up," Chimera snarls.

"Chi!" Iona begins but is cut off by Chimera disconnecting the connection.

Visibly upset, Chimera is breathing heavily. She begins to pace back and forth. StarChild stands near the entrance motionless with her virtual headset still on.

"Uhh Dugey, I gotta call you back," StarChild says cautiously, as she slowly removes the headset.

"I don't understand," Chimera begins. "I feel like I've been living on another planet or something. Like . . . my eyes are being opened for the first time to so much. I don't see how knowing everything I know now, I can just sit back and do nothing."

"What happened?" StarChild questions. "Tell me what's going on."

"I can't right now," Chimera responds. "I have to go."

"Again?" StarChild asks. "Wait, you can't keep darting off like this."

Chimera grabs her magpack and begins to pack several things.

"Can you at least tell me where are you going?" StarChild asks.

"I'll be back," Chimera answers. "I have to do this."

Chimera exits the quarters as StarChild stands confused as to what has occurred.

In the Council wing, members of the Red Council of Action, a special committee created to respond to the Grey threat, meet after the announcement at Tiberius Hall.

"Welcome," Omega greets. "We meet today to discuss what course of action is best for AzurNu and its Red inhabitants. We have been here for a many lunar cycles and plan to remain here. We will not surrender, and we will not be hunted and slaughtered like beasts."

"Our primary course of action should be to strengthen our defenses," Nya suggests. "We're not equipped to handle a full on assault from Grey forces."

"I disagree," Titan proclaims.

"We need to negotiate a truce," another council member suggests. "We are no match for the Grey Army."

"We need to launch an offensive before they attack," Titan interrupts. "Strike them hard before they strike us."

"It's the Red Defense Core, not offense core," a council member declares. "We won't stand a chance."

"How effective would an assault be by the Defense Core?" Nya questions.

"We have alternative forces capable of carrying out such an attack," a Red, dressed differently than other council members, declares.

"Who are you?" a council member inquires.

"What branch of AzurNu authority do you serve?" another council member asks the Red. "I've never seen you before."

"This is MessiahRed. He manages our special interest programs," Omega announces.

"Special interest?" Titan questions. "What use could we possibly have for special interest at a time of war?"

"Any special interest that could help strengthen our defenses is welcomed," Nya argues.

"The Greys would never attack AzurNu," Titan declares boldly. "Even if they did, they would never penetrate our defenses."

"We will strengthen our defenses as well as our offensive capabilities," Omega exclaims. "We will also entertain the option of negotiation. We will leave nothing to chance."

"Negotiate?" Titan retorts.

"There's no way we can negotiate with Lord Prychon," another council member chimes in.

"Always an idealist," Nya murmurs, as the room erupts in debate on the best course of action.

Back at the living quarters wing, Chimera jogs to Tiberius Station and rides the *RedLine* to NorthEnd Station, the zone for the Council wing of AzurNu. After exiting the hover-rail, she make her way down the platform to the council edifice and charges in. As she enters the administration annex, Chimera is greeted by a Red behind a white glowing desk.

"Hello, I am ZettRed. How can I help you?" the attendant at the desk asks.

"I need to speak with someone in Enforcement," Chimera responds.

"Enforcement. I'm sorry, there is no department with that title," Zett remarks.

"I really need to speak with someone from the Council!" Chimera exclaims. "It's very important."

"I'm sorry, that's against protocol," Zett explains. "We can't allow unauthorized entry into noncivil areas."

"What am I supposed to do?" Chimera snaps, frustrated.

"If you fill out a request, a member of our administrative staff will contact you in three to five rotations," Zett declares calmly, as she stares at Chimera with a smile.

"You're sick," Chimera proclaims. "I'm going to see Omega!" Chimera stomps across the room and heads through the hall to the council quarters.

"Excuse me . . . young lady . . . young lady!" Zett exclaims but it's too late.

Chimera is already out of the room and on her way. Heading past the council garden, she turns to the right, toward the General Council room. The corridor is busy with Council Reds traveling to and from the various rooms and chambers. In such a rush, Chimera does not see the Red crossing her path till it's too late. She smashes into the Red, sending the Red to the floor.

"Watch it!" the Red screams to Chimera.

"You watch it, you ran into me!" Chimera remarks.

"Ugh, the nerve," the Red scoffs as she storms off.

Rounding the corner, Chimera reaches her destination. She shoves open the doors, finding Omega still in the meeting with Council of Action members. The room goes silent as Chimera scans around the room, looking for Omega. Locking eyes with him at the head of the table, Chimera motions him with her head.

"I need to talk to you," Chimera announces.

Omega stunned to see Chimera.

Suddenly, five guards suddenly enter the room, with Zett hiding behind them as she points out Chimera.

"You, please come with us," one of the guards commands.

All the council members in the room alternate between staring at Chimera and glancing back Omega as if waiting for something to happen.

"It's ok, she's here with me," Omega instructs the guard. "Excuse me council, I need to attend to a brief matter." Omega rises out of his seat. He slides around the table and heads toward Chimera. Zett and the guards exit one by one.

"Please, let's step outside," Omega instructs. Entering into the corridor, Omega closes the door behind him.

"Tell me, young one. What is it that was so important it couldn't wait?" Omega inquires.

"I'm sorry for barging in like that," Chimera begins. "I know war is coming and I want . . . need to know how I can join Enforcement!"

"Enforcement? War?" Omega inquires, looking around with a confused expression. "I have no idea what you're referring to."

"I can't sit idle anymore," Chimera reveals. "I want to pledge, be a part of Enforcement!"

"What do you mean? What is Enforcement?" Omega questions. "Are you talking about the Grey Army? I don't think your mother would approve of that."

"Look, I know it's an unspoken thing and their existence is supposed to be a big secret, but I know they exist and I know what they do," Chimera explains. "I saw them with my own eyes!"

"Where is all this coming from?" Omega questions. "I thought you came here to complete your studies. Has something happened?"

Chimera pauses. "A lot . . . a lot has happened. I really don't want to talk about it here, but I need your help. Despite what you may believe, I came here to join the fight and be a part of something bigger than me. And to find out what I can about my father. You're one of the only ones I trust here. I know you can lead me to whatever I need to do next."

"Tell me, is everything ok?" Omega inquires.

"It will be," Chimera replies. "But I need your help with this."

Omega becomes silent, putting his right hand on his chin as he walks a short distance away. After several moments, Omega returns.

"What does Iona have to say about this?" Omega inquires.

"It's a decision I have to make," Chimera responds. "The reason we're here, how we got here. Everything she told me was a lie! I went to see Sybil and a holo-sphere explained everything. Who knows what else she's told me isn't true!"

"What did you uncover that was so distressing?" Omega questions.

"The truth that we're not here by choice." Chimera proclaims. "I know this new Grey threat is imminent and the Enforcers are our only chance against slaughter . . . against becoming mindless slaves."

"Tell you what," Omega says. "Visit the Archives library and immerse yourself in our true history. How we were created, and how we fought to preserve our way of life. Then come back and see me."

"But I don't see how . . ." Chimera begins but it is interrupted by Omega.

"Chimera, if you want my help then do this," he explains.

"Fine," Chimera acknowledges. "I'll do it and comback as soon as I'm done."

"Great, now I must return to the council meeting," Omega mentions. "Be well, Chimera."

"Be well," Chimera responds back, as she makes her way across the council garden and back through the entrance of the council wing. On her way out, Chimera sees Zett again. She stops at the reception desk, and then suddenly jumps at Zett startling her. Zett flinches, and knocks a statue off the desk. Chimera grins as she leaves, heading back to the Records and Data library.

Making her way back up to NorthEnd Station, Chimera rides the *RedLine* back to the education wing. After arriving, Chimera approaches the Data Library and stands in front of the door, expecting it to open but nothing happens. Chimera steps back, then steps forward again, expecting the door to open. The door remains motionless. Chimera leans forward to discern a hologram she notices on the wall to the right of the door. The hologram reads "Archive History and Records Library Now Closed."

"Sybil, are you in there?" Chimera calls, tugging at the door.

Suddenly, a female voice says through an intercom, "The Historical Records and Data Library is now closed. Please return tomorrow between the 7th and 24th rotation for service."

"Damn, guess I'll have to come back tomorrow," Chimera mutters to herself. She glances around and then exits, headed back to her dorm.

GENESIS

The next rotation, Chimera awakes at dawn's first light and readies herself.

"I'm gonna head to Mesos's Bazaar," Chimera announces. "I need to pick up a new power converter for my wristcom before heading to the data library."

"Cool, I'm coming with you," StarChild declares, inviting herself.

"If you're coming, I'm leaving now," Chimera states.

"Ok," StarChild acknowledges, rushing to her vanity pod.

Chimera and StarChild head out of the dorm and make their way to Tiberius Station to board the *RedLine* hover-rail. From there, they ride the suspended train to AzurNu Square. The heart of AzurNu and location for the Bazaar, AzurNu Square's corridors, are the veins of the city leading to the various zones of AzurNu. Large holographic monitors, merchants and corridor entrances fill AzurNu square where the Bazaar is located.

Reaching the indoor market within AzurNu, Chimera and StarChild are greeted by a bevy of Reds that fill the Bazaar, shopping for goods, clothes and entertainment. Merchants holler and invite Reds to their shops and the smell of fresh cooked delicacies fill the air as food vendors tempt the appetite.

At the entrance of the Bazaar, is Falls flat, a clear flat dirt area where Reds sit to meet, trade stories and have philosophical conversation. Continuing on through the Bazaar, there is a shop on the left called *Fitted by KevinRed*. Peeking in, Chimera sees a bevy of fancy dresses and high end fashion for Reds.

"Ohhh, looks like they have some new stuff at Fitted!" StarChild exclaims. "I'm gonna check it out."

"Ok," Chimera confirms. To her right, Chimera notices another shop named *Next Level*. Chimera steps in, and finds herself inside a store filled with board games, holographic projection games and other entertainment devices. Chimera purchases a game Virtualization and exits. She makes her way back to Fitted and grabs StarChild, who has two handfuls of clothing. Leaving Fitted, Chimera and StarChild continue on, passing more vendors.

"Foot World, can we go in?" StarChild exclaims. "They have every shoe in the star system there!"

"Help me find *Power One* first," Chimera states.

"Ok, ok," StarChild replies.

Making their way through the crowd of Reds, Chimera and

StarChild move through the Bazaar and reach the Function Junction.

"There, it's over there," StarChild states, pointing to a merchant called Power One.

"Perfect, I'm gonna grab a new converter," Chimera declares.

"Ok, I'm gonna wait for you over there," StarChild mentions, pointing to a vendor named Van-i-T.

Chimera steps into Power One while StarChild walks toward Van-i-T, a merchant of vanity products.

"StarChild," a voice calls as StarChild is about to enter.

"Hey Nexus, right?" StarChild replies, acknowledging the Red that called her.

"Yea, we have Earth studies class together," Nexus confirms.

"Yea, I thought you looked familiar. Hybrid?" StarChild questions.

"No, I'm a Fullbreed," Nexus responds. "You?"

"Yup, Hybrid," StarChild clarifies.

"Doing some shopping?" Nexus asks.

"I am, just here shopping with my bestie," StarChild confirms.

"Yea, that's actually why I called you over," Nexus mentions. "I saw you with another Red, the same one you were with at *Elevated Existence*. I've never seen her before, is she new here?"

"Who, Chimera?" StarChild begins. "Yea, she's been here for a few planetary rotations."

"I thought so," Nexus says. "Is Chimera . . . single?"

"Oww," StarChild gushes, smiling. "Why, you like her?"

"I was just wondering," Nexus quickly replies. "I mean, she's beautiful but I was just curious."

"Well, as far as I know she is," StarChild states. "You should introduce yourself."

"Uh, where is she?" Nexus questions.

"I think she's inside the shop over there," StarChild announces, pointing to Power One.

"I'm gonna be late for class, will you just tell her I said hello?" Nexus remarks.

"How about this, I'll give you her wristcom coordinates. You can give her a call."

"Are you sure she'd be ok with that?" Nexus inquires.

"Yea, she won't mind," StarChild confirms, as she sends the coordinates to Nexus.

"I gotta go find Chimera, I'll see you," StarChild says.

"See you in class," Nexus acknowledges, as he heads the opposite direction.

StarChild returns and finds Chimera leaving Power One.

"Did you get what you needed?" StarChild asks.

"Got it," Chimera confirms. "Did you find anything?"

"Yea, I got something for you," StarChild remarks, grinning.

"What?" Chimera asks.

"You'll see," StarChild states, grinning.

Chimera and StarChild make their way back toward AzurNu Square Station when Chimera notices the Red from the auditorium inside one of the shops. Next to the Red, another Red stares at Chimera oddly.

"Skurtex, what do they sell?" Chimera questions StarChild, referring to the stand.

"Skurtex, stay away from there!" StarChild warns. "They're double-dealing thieves."

"Thanks for the heads up," Chimera confirms. "I'm gonna head to the Data Library right now."

"Ok," StarChild begins. "I've got class. Let's get out of here."

Chimera and StarChild leave the bazaar and part ways as Chimera heads to the library.

Afterwards, she returns to the Data Library. When Chimera arrives at the Data Library, the corridor is buzzing with life. As she approaches the library door, it slides open this time. Chimera walks through the data shelves searching for Sybil once again. After searching several areas, Chimera finds Sybil in one of the studies rooms of the data library. Sybil is again dressed in a white robe with white undergarments. She holds a small, transparent screen.

"There you are," Chimera remarks, approaching Sybil.

"Greetings, again, ChimeraRed," Sybil announces. "I did not expect you back so soon. What information do you seek now?"

"I . . . need everything you have on Neophytes," Chimera explains.

"Neophytes, you say?" Sybil states.

"Yes," Chimera responds.

"Follow me," Sybil states, as she exits the study room and heads to a shelf, where several dataspheres float silently. Sybil taps one of the spheres and then begins scrolling through her screen searching for something.

"You're inquiring as to how Neophytes were created?" Sybil questions.

"Well . . . it was around 46 lunar cycles ago when the descendants of the Anteema began experimenting under the dictation of Chancellor Nebulae Grey. A lab was erected near the Eastern border of Tychon 4 called Deux. Its purpose was to conduct fertilization experiments in an effort to create a new hybrid, super Hue-man worker."

Sybil continues scrolling through her sphere, searching for something.

"What additional information were you specifically interested in?" Sybil asks.

"What were experiments?" Chimera asks.

Before Sybil can answer, a voice out of the blue interrupts.

"Even a Neophyte could answer that," the voice exclaims.

Turning around, Chimera glances up and finds the Red she had bumped into and knocked over at the council wing.

Sybil places her right arm onto Chimera's shoulder to regain her attention and continues.

"You see, in the Grey lab there are three different sectors," Sybil declares. "The first sector handles *extraction* of reproductive material from Hue-mans. The second sector handles *mixing* of Hue-man eggs with Grey genetic material. The third sector known as the *The Farm*, oversees the development of Hue-man embryos from fetus to worker age Neophytes. This third sector is the most critical in Hue-man development."

Chimera nods and then glances back at other Red who interrupted.

"Who is that?" Chimera asks Sybil.

"That, my dear, is Anexichi, daughter of NyaRed," Sybil reveals.

"Nya, of the Red council?" Chimera questions.

"Yes," Sybil answers.

"Is she always so rude?" Chimera inquires.

"If you give her a chance, you may see she's not all that different than you," Sybil responds, glancing back down at her datascreen.

Chimera shakes her head, but Sybil does not notice as she is still searching through the datascreen.

"Does the datasphere have anything on how experiments were done?" Chimera inquires.

"Why yes," Sybil begins. "It appears, the program was broken down into five stages," Sybil begins. "The first stage of Neophyte development after In vitro fertilization is Infant Care. In this step, Hue-man embryos are maintained from fetus to full grown infants. The infants are developed in tubes and monitored by Autonomous robots."

"Robots raising babies?" Chimera questions.

"That is the nature Hue-man development under Grey dominion," Sybil mentions. "The second step is Child Development. Newborn infants are nurtured by Artificial Intelligent bots designed to look and act like adult Hue-mans. These bots which are called pro-creators, feed, communicate with and simulate functions of an adult Hue-man mother."

"No machine can replace the nurturing of a mother!" Chimera proclaims. "Was anything done to stop this?"

"Yes," Sybil replies. "The Suns of Man took a stand to free as many children as possible."

"But what about Reds, why didn't they fight back?" Chimera asks.

"Reds are a peaceful race," Sybil begins. "They were simply not equipped to wage war at the time."

"I don't understand." Why do they destust us so much, what is the really going on?" Chimera remarks.

"Well my youngling, Grey dominion has maintatned a resentment for Reds because we represent a world without absolute control," Sybil explains. "They believe creativity weakens the mind and body. In their eyes, creativity serves no real value, and only weakens the mind. A weakend mind leads to an inferiour species Greys believe."

"I don't understand," Chimera declares. "Without the gift of creation, what else is there?"

"You see, there sole focus is on math, science and the phsyics of the universe" Sybil responds. "Greys believe mastery of these elments is the only true path to superiority".

Chimera shakes her head. "Tell me, what happens after the development stage?" she inquires.

"The third stage is conditioning," Sybil continues. "As Neophytes grow to an age of understanding and comprehension, a campaign of conditioning begins."

"Campaign of conditioning?" Chimera questions.

"Well, children in this stage are taught to obey their so called masters and not deviate from instructions or ask questions," Sybil states. "This conditioning, in conjunction with genetic engineering at the embryo stage to remove higher brain functions, are the foundation of a Neophyte."

"So they're like robots?" Chimera questions.

"Takes one to know one," a voice rings out as Anexichi strolls past the aisle toward the other side of the data library.

Chimera turns to her asking, "Don't you have something else to do than be a pain in the . . ."

"Adolescent Reinforcement is the fourth step in the process," Sybil interjects. "In this stage, pro-creators reinforce the subservient principles and concepts learned in the infancy stage. Once these adolescents are placed in a social atmosphere, they are forced to become part of a larger social structure, instead of developing individually to form personal identities."

"Stripping them of their personalities?" Chimera questions. "I don't understand. Why not just create machines to do the stuff they use us for? We're not meant to live as slaves!"

"Oh, but it gets better," Sybil eludes. "The last step in the process is Confirmation. Pre-adult Hue-mans are intensely reviewed to see if they meet the standards of a Neophyte ready for release from the farm into servitude. If there are any areas that the Pre-adults need to adjust, they are sent back to the reconditioning program run by StarchusGrey. Those that are deemed unfit for reconditioning, are exterminated."

"Exterminated?" Chimera proclaims. "And what happens to the Reds that make it through the program?"

"Neophytes that have been successfully broken are . . ." Sybil begins but is cut off mid-sentence.

"Sent to MakuGrey for barter," Anexichi announces, finishing Sybil's statement. "Is there anything you do knows?"

Chimera turns to glare at Anexichi. "You really can't help but intrude can you?" Chimera snaps. "Didn't anyone teach you manners? You're looking for a serious fight aren't you?"

"I found you, right?" Anexichi replies.

"What's your issue?" Chimera demands. "You've been harassing me since we bumped into each other. You know nothing about me so trust me when I say you don't want an issue."

"I may not know you but I know who you are," Anexichi snarls. "ChimeraRed, the mis-born outlander from above the surface."

"Listen you impure mongrel . . ." Chimera begins, when suddenly her wristcom buzzes with an incoming call. Chimera quickly ignores the incoming call and turns her attention back to Anexichi. She is about to finish her sentence when Sybil interjects.

"Ladies," Sybil declares. "Is this how we communicate nwoadays? I don't quite understand what the quarrel is. Need I remind you both the enemy is above, not here within the walls of AzurNu. I pray you can put aside you differences and be one, just as we were in the beginning."

"I don't understand why everyone here seems to have a problem with me! I haven't done anything to anyone!" Chimera proclaims, as she trudges off and exits the data library.

"Every time I see her she's stomping off, and I've only seen her twice," Sybil announces.

"Urchin," Anexichi mutters as she walks away toward the advance datasphere collections.

"What has become of this generation?" Sybil asks, contining to organize the dataspheres in the aisle.

CHAPTER FIVE

Meanwhile, Chimera returns to her dorm and plops down onto her sleep pod.

 StarChild emerges from the other room.

"Hey, everything ok?" StarChild asks.

Chimera looks up at StarChild, then lets out a long sigh.

"What, what's wrong?" StarChild inquires.

"Coming here was a mistake," Chimera reveals. "I should've never left the surface. I don't belong here, I don't fit in."

"Don't say that!" StarChild states. "You do belong here. It just takes time to adjust! Besides, you're my best friend. What would I do without you?"

"I wish that were all true," Chimera declares.

"It is," StarChild confirms.

"You know what," Chimera remarks.

"What?" StarChild asks.

"I wish I could connect with some music right now," Chimera mentions.

"You want to hit *Elevated Existence* again?" StarChild inquires.

"No, it's not that" Chimera responds. "I just wish I could carry the energy of the music with me."

"That would be cool," StarChild mentions, "music is hard to come by. Why do you think the music spots are all hidden?"

Chimera sighs again. "I'm going to sleep, wake me up when we're there." She closes her eyes and turns her head.

"Chimera, Chimera!" StarChild calls out, but there is no response.

A planetary rotation passes as Chimera continues her research as instructed by Omega. Chimera is in her living quarters reviewing a datasphere when the front door slides open and StarChild pops in.

"Chimera, come with me to the electro-ink parlor!" StarChild exclaims, smiling.

"Um, I don't think I can," Chimera responds. "I have a lot more studying to do."

"C'mon Chi . . . you've been working at that nonstop for the past few rotations. Take a break!" StarChild urges.

"It's super important. I need to do this," Chimera mentions.

"So is this!" StarChild declares. "I'm not gonna stop asking until you come."

"What about Dug, is he busy?" Chimera inquires.

StarChild glares at Chimera for a moment, and then walks over to her. Chimera is seated in a relaxer chair, reading a projection from a datasphere. StarChild reaches down and begins tickling her foot. Chimera shrieks, nearly falling off the chair.

"Star!" Chimera screams.

StarChild darts across the room, erupting in laughter.

"You're in for it now," Chimera yells, hopping up.

StarChild darts for the door and escapes. Chimera gives in and begins the chase. StarChild sprints down the hallway. Chimera is still in full pursuit, as everyone in the hallway watches Chimera chase StarChild. StarChild turns right and toward the end of the hallway she makes another quick left stopping at a hexagonal door across from the holo projection theater on the north end of *Create*. Chimera, who is behind StarChild catches up and grabs StarChild.

"Wait," StarChild pleads. "Before you hit me, let me show you something." StarChild points up at the sign.

Chimera looks up and reads the sound aloud. "E3, what is it?" Chimera asks.

"Only one way to find out," StarChild remarks.

"I'm still gonna get you back," Chimera warns, letting StarChild step in front of her.

StarChild scans her wristcom against a panel on the door and the door spirals open.

StarChild and Chimera enter and are greeted by a second door. As they approach, the second door opens and they are immediately inundated with flashes of light and glowing bodies.

"The electro-ink parlor?" Chimera remarks, peering around.

"I told you you were coming with me," StarChild taunts.

"So you tricked me into coming?" Chimera taunts.

"And you fell for it," StarChild replies sarcastically.

Chimera shoves StarChild, as she glances around. "It's . . . like a planetarium. And is that music I hear?"

"Yup, that's why I wanted you to come!" StarChild announces.

Hard hitting, energetic music grows louder as Chimera and StarChild continue in. The parlor is completely dark inside, as a large spherical light floats at the center of the parlor with dark blue/orange hues. The glow of eyes and versicolored body painted Reds move about the parlor.

"I like the vibe," Chimera acknowledges.

"As expected," StarChild states. "C'mon, follow me."

The two make their way toward a long spacecraft-shaped reception desk where three similar looking Reds sit.

"Chimera, I want you to meet the triplets," StarChild says, pointing to the three identical Reds sitting at the desk. "This is Mai, Tai and Kai Red," StarChild introduces pointing each one out.

The triplets are all dressed alike wearing long sleeve purple suits that stretch up to their necks, and cover everything except a giant circular shape in the chest area with a luminescent color that seems to move and slightly shift colors.

"Welcome to E3, how can we help you?" the triplets say simultaneously.

"Triplicates, this is ChimeraRed," StarChild announces, turning back toward Chimera.

"Greetings, Chimera . . . Greetings, Chimera . . . Greetings, Chimera," the three Reds greet, one after another.

"Greetings," Chimera remarks.

StarChild approaches the reception desk.

"I have an appointment with DagbarRed. I'm just checking in," StarChild replies.

"What degree . . . What degree . . . What degree is your appointment?" the triplets inquire.

"16th degree," StarChild replies.

The three look at their rotation monitors.

"A little late, are we?" they remark.

"Um, I was waiting for her," StarChild mentions, discreetly pointing at Chimera.

"What?" Chimera utters, glaring at StarChild .

"Let us check and see if he's available," the triplets respond, their voices echoing.

Mai taps her headset and initiates a call.

"Hi, your 16th degree is here," Mai begins. "Yes, exactly." She suddenly begins giggling before tapping her headset again and ending the call. Her grin disappears and with a stern face as she announces, "We will lead you to your destination now." Mai points to Kai as Kai rises and shuffles from behind the reception desk.

"Follow me," Kai says, walking StarChild and Chimera past the reception desk into another room.

"Do you know what design you would like to acquire?" Kai asks Chimera.

"Oh, it's not for me. It's for her," Chimera clarifies, alluding to

StarChild.

Kai shifts her attention to StarChild.

"I need to take a look in the gallery to get some ideas," StarChild answers.

"Very well, follow me to the design room and let's take a look around," Kai replies.

StarChild, Chimera and Kai head into the design room, a gallery of floating designs, logos, pictures and Tychonian letters shifting and changing colors. There are several Reds in the room, peering around at the designs.

"Step inside here and disrobe," Kai instructs StarChild.

StarChild steps up to a small platform with a large cylindrical device. It's gold and has a thin door with a small viewing window in it. On it is written *Symbolic Duplicator Model S*. StarChild steps in, and closes the door behind her and undresses. A pants leg and an arm can be seen moving through the cylinder window. Once the moving stops, Kai pulls out a small oval-shaped device.

"Stand still in there, ok?" Kai says into the tiny device in her hand. "Here we go," Kai announces as she presses a button on the device. The cylinder lights up, projected a thick shower of light that can be seen through the tinted viewing window.

"What is that?" Chimera inquires.

"It's a Cloner," Kai explains to Chimera, still watching the machine. It scans you and creates a digital copy of you so you can see what tattoos look good on you.

"Don't move in there," Kai instructs to StarChild. "Almost done."

Within seconds the light stops.

"You can step out now," Kai announces.

After a moment, StarChild shuffles around inside, before opening the door redressed. She steps out, examining her hands and body.

"Now, look over to the left," Kai tells Chimera and StarChild.

As Chimera and StarChild glance to the left, a hologram of StarChild appears on a small round platform, slowly rotating in her under garments.

"Just pick up a design and carry it over to your hologram," Kai explains. "You'll be able to see an example of what it'll look like on you." Kai peeks around the room, retrieves a tribal pattern and carries it to StarChild's hologram. Kai places the design near StarChild's back and the tattoo begins to appear on StarChild's hologram, spreading across her back, with lines glowing and the patterns of the tribal lines shifting.

"Kind of like that," Kai suggests.

"Cool huh?" StarChild asks Chimera.

"Impressive, I'll admit. Is this the first time you've been here?" Chimera asks StarChild.

"I've come two or three times with Dug for his electro-ink, but

I've never been in this room," StarChild replies.

"I'll leave you two to look around," Kai offers. "When you find a design you like, save it in your wristcom and come back and see me."

"Ok," StarChild responds.

"How did you guys even find this place?" Chimera inquires, after Kai exits.

"It's like invite only," StarChild reveals. "Dug got an invite and passed it to me. Now, I pass it to you . . . you should get one."

"Me?" Chimera replies.

"Yea, you should," StarChild urges.

"No, let's find one for you," Chimera remarks.

Chimera and StarChild continue surveying the gallery, checking out the plethora of designs.

"What are you looking for? What type of design do you want?" Chimera inquires.

"I want an animal, something that represents me," StarChild states.

"So like a Desert Vat or a Cave Coy, right?" Chimera remarks sarcastically, with a smirk on her face.

"No, more like a Chimeran Swamp Fish or Chimeran Dirt Bug," StarChild snarls.

Chimera laughs, as she continues checking out the gallery. Coming across something, she hollers, "Star, I think you might . . ."

Chimera is in the process of turning around when she stops,

noticing another figure behind her that's not StarChild.

"You again?" Chimera barks.

"It's Anexichi," Anexichi retorts.

"I know what your name is and I don't care," Chimera professes. "What are you doing here? Why do you keep popping up everywhere?"

"I was here getting some electro-ink done, but that's none of your business," Anexichi remarks.

Just then, two of the Reds in the room make their way past Chimera, Anexichi and StarChild.

"A fight, they must be Automallies," one of the Red mutters as they pass toward the exit.

"What did you say?" Anexichi snaps, shifting her attention to the passing Red.

"Your kind always looking for a fight," the Red mentions. "It's sad."

"Our kind?" Chimera interjects. "We're all Reds."

"That's what you think," the Red snaps.

"I am sick and tired of this class nonsense!" Chimera shouts. She raises her arm about to strike the Red.

"I think we've all had a really long rotation and maybe need to hit the Zen lounge," StarChild interrupts, stepping between Chimera and the provoking Red.

"Come on, let's go," the second Red urges.

"Good idea," Anexichi scoffs. "Listen to your friend and walk away before it's too late."

"I agree," Chimera adds.

The second Red pulls the proving Red away and continues on, exiting the room.

"Are you like a fight magnet or what?" StarChild asks.

"That would explain a lot," Anexichi remarks.

"Come on, we're on the same side," StarChild suggests.

"I didn't think anyone was on her side," Chimera replies, alluding to Anexichi.

"Look, let's squash all this," Anexichi offers. "Whatever happened, happened."

"Why would I do that?" Chimera retorts.

"Because you both seem stubborn as hell," StarChild answers. "And this feud will never end."

Anexichi stands for a moment looking at StarChild then back at Chimera.

"I . . . guess I can be the diplomatic one being that it's is in my blood," Anexichi declares. Anexichi reluctantly holds up her palm, then closes all but her pointer, middle finger and thumb.

"So we might have gotten off on the wrong foot. Maybe we can put aside whatever differences we have for now," Anexichi offers.

Anexichi stands with her hand up, offering a truce.

Chimera stares at Anexichi for a moment, and then turns. "I'm outta here. I'll wait for you to get your ink done," Chimera remarks, exiting the room.

"That girl is always storming off," StarChild states.

"So I heard," Anexichi replies sarcastically.

Chimera heads to the lounge area of the parlor. The music is still playing louder now that Chimera is near its source. There are several lounge seats with several Reds seated. Chimera takes a seat, leaving a large gap in the center of the lounge chair. She begins writing notes in her wristcom.

StarChild later emerges, with a large grin.

"Where'd you go?" StarChild questions. "I wanted you to pick one out with me."

"I know, I'm sorry," Chimera answers. "I really don't like her. I needed some space."

"She's actually not that bad," StarChild defends.

"Oh no, not you too," Chimera states motioning her disapproval. "Did you find one?"

"Yea, I found a really cute one!" StarChild remarks. "It's a Dyloidian Lepidot. Dug's gonna love it!" StarChild gushes.

"Disintegrate me now," Chimera retorts, rolling her eyes.

Suddenly, one of the triplets appears from the front of the parlor.

"StarChild, are you ready?" the triplet questions. "Dagbar will see you now."

"Yea I am, Kai. I hope that little disagreement earlier didn't scare off any of your patrons," StarChild states.

"Kai . . . I'm Tai," the triplet says. "And what disagreement are you speaking of?"

StarChild glances at Chimera, confused.

Chimera shrugs her shoulder.

"Nevermind," StarChild declares. "C'mon, Chimera, I'm up."

Tai leads the way as Chimera follows StarChild into one of the electro-ink rooms, a dark room with an application char, walls made of projection screens and a glass tank filled with electric fish.

"StarChild, you can lie right here face down in the application chair," Dagbar instructs. "And uh, what's your friend's name?"

"Chimera, her name is Chimera."

"Rad, nice to meet you, Chimera," Dagbar states.

 Chimera nods. "So how long does this usually take?" Chimera asks Dagbar.

"It depends on the design of course but it looks like your friend's getting a Dyloidian Lepidot so it should be about uh, 6 degrees," Dagbar declares.

"Six degrees?" Chimera and StarChild both inquire simultaneously.

"I'm totally joking," Dagbar mentions. "We should have her inked up and out of here in a degree or less."

StarChild sighs.

"Rad, so triplets gave me your simulation, you want to keep it these colors.

StarChild nods.

"Is this your first tattoo?" Dagbar asks.

StarChild nods again.

"I'm honored to be your first. You're gonna love it," Dagbar brags, chuckling as his head bobs up and down.

Chimera rolls her eyes.

"Rad, let's get this thing started shall we?" Dagbar declares.

StarChild settles in and Dagbar picks up his tattoo machine. He selects the colors and presses a button. A device above StarChild's chair projects an outline of the tattoo onto StarChild's back. Dagbar begins electro-inking.

Chimera watches as Dagbar slowly inks the Dyloid onto StarChild.

The music continues on, blasting a steady evolution of sound that keeps the mood energetic. The sound of the Electro-tattoo machines hums beneath the upper frequencies of the music.

"Where can I get something to snack on?" Chimera asks Dagbar.

There's a food machine to the right of the lounge, just hook a left when you go out that door, a right and then another right when you get to the lounge," Dagbar instructs.

"I'm gonna go get something to eat, you need something?" Chimera offers to StarChild.

"No, I'm good," StarChild professes. "How does it look so far?"

"No peeking, you'll have to wait and see," Chimera states. "I'll be right back."

StarChild huffs.

"You know, I could use a . . ." Dagbar begins, but as he looks up he notices Chimera has already left the room.

Chimera purchases a snack and heads back to Dagbar's ink studio.

"Excuse me," a Red calls.

Chimera continues on her way, headed back to StarChild.

"I can't help but notice you have a series 3 wristcom. Those are legendary, impossible to find!" the Red declares. "If you don't mind me asking, where'd you get it?"

Chimera looks up to see a shorter, awkward looking Red.

"I'm sorry, who are you?" Chimera asks.

"Rude of me. I apologize," the Red says. "I'm Draconis. I ask a lot of questions, sometimes prematurely."

Chimera hesitates for a moment, "It's fine. It's a limited edition Tech series 3, the last model they made."

"Wow, where on Tychon did you get that?" Draconis inquires.

"It was given to me from as a gift from my mother."

"Wow, she must have been really important," Draconis says.

An alert sounds on Chimera's wristcom before she can respond. She glances down, and begins to type on her wristcom.

Draconis remains, waiting for Chimera to finish.

"Uh I heard you arguing earlier. Someone giving you a hard time?" Draconis questions.

Chimera looks up from her wristcom. "No, it's one of those wrong place wrong time things," she responds.

"Speaking of wrong place wrong time, what do you think of the new decree from this new Anti Automally Committee?" Draconis jeers.

"I think it's a load of rubbish of course," Chimera answers. "They've been trying to eradicate us for rotations. Only difference is we can finally fight back now."

"You think so?" Draconis asks. "But there are whispers of resistance."

"Yea, like I said, now we can finally fight back," Chimera explains.

"I meant resistance to rulership of the Red Council," Draconis clarifies. "That could create instability and make it impossible to fight the Greys."

"I haven't heard of any whispers of dissolution," Chimera states.

Draconis is about to reply when StarChild emerges, finished with her tattoo. Chimera does not notice her, as she is facing Draconis and her back is toward StarChild.

"Hey, you ready?" StarChild asks, shoving Chimera with her hips.

"Yea, done already?" Chimera remarks. "Seems like you just started."

"It's been a degree," StarChild responds.

"How was it?" Chimera asks.

"I'm kinda sore," StarChild replies, her voice sounding a bit distressed. "Let's head back to the dorm."

"Ok," Chimera confirms, as she turns to Draconis. "Good meeting you. I gotta jet."

Draconis glances at Chimera with an odd expression, as if he were hoping to continue conversation.

"Can I . . . have your coordinates?" Draconis asks as Chimera begins toward the exit.

"I'll see you around!" Chimera exclaims as she and StarChild turn the corner.

"Ohhhhhh, new boyfriend?" StarChild inquires, with a smirk on her face.

"Very funny," Chimera replies, not amused by StarChild's suggestion.

"I wouldn't get too comfortable, especially when another Romeo has his heart set on you!" StarChild warns.

"What do are you talking about? Has that ink gone to your brain already?" Chimera remarks, feeling StarChild's forehead.

"You know who I'm talking about," StarChild proclaims. "Nexus, the one we ran into in the corridor a few rotations ago?"

"What about him?" Chimera replies quickly, as the two enter the main lobby to exit the parlour.

"Well . . . he was asking about you," StarChild explains.

"And?" Chimera leads, trying to extract more information from StarChild.

"And . . . he's been asking if you were single, so I gave him your wristcom coordinates," StarChild admits.

"You what?" Chimera exclaims.

"I did you a favor, you're welcome!" StarChild responds.

"Now I owe you for two times!" Chimera snaps, as StarChild begins to sprint out of the exit.

"Kill me now, thank me later!" StarChild responds as she darts away, her back to Chimera while she laughs to herself.

"Why would you do that?" Chimera hollers to StarChild, speed walking after her.

"Because he's kind of cute," StarChild states. "Besides, he might be perfect for you."

"I'm not interested in getting to know anybody," Chimera warns, continuing with StarChild out into the main corridor outside the parlour.

"You'll never know till you try," StarChild retorts.

Suddenly, there is a beep on the AzurNu intercom system as an announcement begins.

"All Reds 19 lunar cycles and older, report to the Citizenship Bureau to sign up now for active duty. Enlist in the Red Defense Core and fight to protect AzurNu. The Grey threat is imminent. Enlist now!" the message declares, as it concludes.

"Are you gonna sign up, seeing as you like fighting so much?" StarChild taunts, as she and Chimera reach the door of their dorm.

"Oh, I'm signing up. Just not for the Defense Core," Chimera declares, as she enters the dorm.

"What does that mean?" StarChild asks.

Chimera proceeds into the room, leaving StarChild outside.

"Wait, what does that mean, seriously?" StarChild hollers, but Chimera is silent.

Three planetary rotations pass. Chimera is in the den of her quarters alongside StarChild who is playing Wala, a two person virtual game in which opponents try to guess the other players choice of word association for a given object. Chimera is studying in the same room.

"You know. I think you and Dug spend more time using technology to communicate than actually being together in the flesh," Chimera declares.

"Not true!" StarChild exclaims. "You're just jealous because I have a beau and you're still single."

"O yes, clearly," Chimera retorts. Suddenly her wristcom beeps as she receives an incoming call.

"I don't recognize this frequency," Chimera tells StarChild.

"You should answer, might be important," StarChild suggests.

Chimera contemplates, as her wristcom continues to sound. She retrieves a small device from her wristcom and places it in her ears. On the final ring, she answers.

"Hello," Chimera begins.

There is pause as the mystery caller on the other end speaks.

"Yea, this is Chimera," Chimera says to the caller.

StarChild quickly pauses her game with Dug and darts over to Chimera.

"Who is it? Who is it?" StarChild questions impatiently shaking Chimera.

"Hold on," Chimera whispers, motioning for StarChild to stop pestering her.

"It's him, isn't it!" StarChild exclaims.

Chimera shakes her head in denial. StarChild grabs Chimera's arm and toggles a button on Chimera's wristcom, placing the call on loudspeaker mode. The voice on the other end becomes audible.

"Did I catch you in the middle of something?" the voice questions.

"I was studying for my symbology exam," Chimera mentions.

"Oh, ok. I just wanted to com you and say hi," Nexus begins. "StarChild gave me your coordinates so I wanted reach out."

"It is Nexus!" StarChild shouts in excitement.

Chimera glares at StarChild as she hops up and moves away from StarChild heading to the other room quickly.

"Who's that?" Nexus questions, hearing StarChild's voice.

"Nobody, it was an A.I. bot," Chimera answers back, as StarChild follows Chimera to the other room, grinning.

"I saw you at Elevate and wanted to talk to you . . . but didn't get the chance," Nexus admits.

"Really?" Chimera says.

"Yea, how was it?" Nexus inquires.

"It was good. My first time there," Chimera confirms.

"Curious- what'd you like best about it?" Nexus asks

"I . . . really liked the music," Chimera answers.

"The music?" Nexus reiterates.

"Yea, the music," Chimera responds. "I've never been to a place like that."

"I know what you mean," Nexus replies. "Tell me, what music creators do you like?"

"I haven't heard a lot of music yet. I really don't know creators by name," Chimera explains. "What about you? What creators do you like?"

"Well . . ." Nexus begins, "I dig ElectraRed and MeridianRed. Their music is super smash."

"It's so hard to find music here. I don't think I've heard their sounds," Chimera admits.

"Really?" Nexus questions. "It's really good."

"To be honest, I haven't heard music from any of the creators you mentioned," Chimera reveals.

"You have to!" Nexus proclaims. "I'll have to play you some of their songs. I have a feeling you'd really like it."

"I'd like to hear some," Chimera responds. "Something about the music I heard at Elevate . . . it sparked something in me."

"Yea, I know the feeling. Aside from music, what else are you into?" Nexus asks.

"Umm, I've never really thought about it," Chimera replies. "I'm usually so busy. I guess . . . feeding my brain and my stomach . . . and anything fast."

"Nice, me too!" Nexus exclaims. "I'm always trying to feed myself. I'd love to feed you sometime."

Chimera laughs.

StarChild, who is still in the room listening, begins to snicker

"You know, Dug is still waiting for you on Wala," Chimera reminds StarChild.

"Shoot!" StarChild exclaims, as she sprints out of the room back to her game.

"Uh, you sure no one else is there?" Nexus asks.

"Sure," Chimera replies.

"You know, it's like you dropped out of the sky," Nexus mentions. "Where are you from?"

"I'm . . . from the surface," Chimera mentions. "I guess you can say I kind of did drop from above."

Nexus begins laughing. "Oh wow, an above grounder! I would have never guessed. What region and what was it like?" he inquires anxiously.

"I'm from Khyber City, east of AzurNu," Chimera replies. "It was different."

Chimera and Nexus continue conversing for a third of a degree. Suddenly, Chimera glances at clock in the room and realizes the time.

"I'm sorry, Nexus, I actually have to get back to studying," Chimera announces.

Suddenly, StarChild reenters the room.

"Still on the com I see," StarChild taunts.

Chimera glares at StarChild.

"There's a holo-show coming up, you should consider coming?" Nexus offers. "ElectraRed is performing."

"Yea, maybe," Chimera mentions. "I'll see."

"Smash," Nexus replies. "Well, it was really good talking to you."

"Thanks," Chimera responds.

"Good night," Nexus mentions.

"Same to you," Chimera replies ending the call.

"Ohh, someone has a date coming up!" StarChild jeers.

"Not at all! I don't do dates," Chimera clarifies, as she moves back to the other room to resume studying.

At the main Mind Reconditioning facility for Reds on Tychon 3, newly appointed SeyfertGrey arrives aboard a transport with two other Greys. He dons a metallic silver spacesuit with a black robe. After exiting the transport, Seyfert descends to the detainment level of the facility.

"Welcome to the detainment level," a Grey guard announces to Seyfert. "What brings you to the Reconditioning locale?"

"I'm here on behalf of the Anti Automally Committee," Seyfert declares. "I must obtain information from one of the detained Reds, seized from the Zayin region."

"Do you have an authorization order?" the guard asks Seyfert.

Seyfert reaches down, and pulls his robe back, revealing a triskelion-shaped melee weapon known as a yang blade.

"Right this way, sir," the guard confirms nervously.

Seyfert passes through an air lock and enters the detainment level, a large, dome-like, area with hundreds of cells. Each cell is enclosed by a laser security field.

A group of Grey civilians move through the third level of the detainment cells taking a tour of the facility, which is a frequent tourist attraction for Greys.

As Seyfert exits the airlock, he heads to the control center of the detainment prison

"Bring me class A prisoner 115 in cell 777," Seyfert instructs one of the watchkeepers in the control room.

"Yes, commander," the Grey confirms as he presses several buttons on the screen ahead of him.

Two Grey-like droids known as Underseers emerge from a pit below ground, carrying staffs. They are each numbered, the first number 66 and the second number 49. Resembling Greys in features, the Underseers are the main workforce of the detainment level. They handle day to day operations, which include feeding detainees, escorting them to and from their cells and maintenance of the facility.

Reaching the ground level, the Underseers head toward cell 777. Without warning, the ground begins to tremble in intervals. Suddenly, a massive droid emerges from behind a wall, standing in the center of the area. Known as the Overseer, the droid resembles an Underseer but is one hundred times larger. The main source of security on the detainment level, the Overseer roams detainment maintaining order, supervising the Underseers and ensuring prisoners remain obedient,

The Overseer monitors the two Underseers as they arrive at cell 777. There are two Reds inside the detainment cell: one a male and the other female.

"Swift, I think they're coming here for us," the female Red declares.

The Underseer marked 66 places a small hand sized globe through a small opening of the cell security field.

"Detainee 115, hold this device firmly to activate your shackles," the droid instructs.

"What's happening? Am I being sent to reconditioning?" Swift asks the Underseer, ignoring the command.

"Swift, no, don't go!" the female Red pleads as she grabs his arm.

"It will be ok, Ataja," Swift proclaims. "I will return."

"Step forward and grasp the sphere immediately," Underseer 66 repeats as it takes a step forward. "Prisoner 114, step back and do not interfere," it adds, pointing its staff at Ataja.

"Don't go, I don't want you to go!" Ataja cries out as she embraces Swift tightly.

"I'll always be here for you," Swift promises. "No matter what happens."

A loud growl rings out, as the Overseer stomps over to cell 777.

"Step forward and place your hands on the shackle sphere," the Overseer's deep voice booms. "Your compliance is mandatory."

Swift continues to comfort Ataja.

Suddenly the security field is deactivated and the two Underseers approach with staffs drawn.

Swift positions Ataja behind him, shielding her.

"Exit the cell now, detainee 115!" The Overseer commands as its voice shakes the walls.

"I will see you soon," Swift whispers as the Underseers approach. Swift raises his hands up in compliance. When Underseer 49 reaches out to grab Swift, he grabs its staffs and redirects it toward the other Underseer, electrocuting it. Underseer 66 falls to the floor as Swift sprints out of the cell. He looks right then left, and begins running to dart left toward an elevator as an alarm begins to sound.

"The tour is over. Take the visitors to the gift shop," Seyfert snaps to the watchkeeper, as he watches Swift dart across the stairwell.

"I'm gonna make it," Swift says to himself as he nears the elevator.

A large crash suddenly throws Swift off balance, as the Overseer slams its hand down blocking Swift's path. Swift tries to get up and run the opposite direction but the Overseer grabs him, squeezing him tightly.

"I . . . can't . . . breathe," Swift mutters, stuck in the tight vice of the Overseer.

Seyfert and the other Greys continue watching on.

The Overseer places Swift in a containment cube and three more Underseers arrive to carry the containment cube off to the interrogation level.

As Swift is carried off, another Red in detainment begins to chant, "Live red, live red, live red." Soon after, several other reds join. Ataja begins to chant as well and soon, what seems like the entire detainment level begins chanting "Live red, live red, live red."

CHAPTER FIVE

"Silence them!" Seyfert declares. "I'm going to the interrogation level!"

On the interrogation level, Swift is released from the cube and placed into an examination chair.

"You'll get nothing from me," Swift assures the Underseers.

Seyfert then enters the room. "We'll see," he projects telepathically to Swift.

"Get out of my mind!" Swift hollers, wiggling in the interrogation chair.

"Your mind is the least of your worries," Seyfert warns. "You will soon experience pain like never before."

Seyfert unsheathes his yang-blade and begins to cut Swift Red. Screams of pain are suddenly muffled by the closing of the door, as Seyfert continues to torture Swift.

Two degrees later Tachyon arrives at the Reconditioning facility and immediately heads to the detainment level.

"Where is prisoner 115?" Tachyon inquires with one of the entry guards.

"Ah, sir . . . he's currently under interrogation," the guard who assisted Seyfert reveals.

"Interrogation by who?" Tachyon asks.

"Sss . . . Seyfert, sir," the guard answers.

"Under whose orders?" Tachyon questions.

The guard is silent, as the second guard quietly points to the first guard.

"Execute him!" Tachyon orders one of his soldiers, referring to the guard who authorized Seyfert.

"But I . . ." the first guard pleads, as he is carried off by two of Tachyon's soldiers.

Tachyon storms up to the interrogation rooms, checking each room for SwiftRed. After checking several of the rooms, Tachyon finally finds Swift still strapped to the torture chair. He is motionless.

"Seyfert!" Tachyon exclaims.

THIS IS WAR

Two small, four-legged creatures called Speros sit in a cove off the coast of Paradisium, an undeveloped island East of Tychon 4. The sound of waves crashing along the shoreline is carried by the coastal breeze. Without warning, two foreign spacecrafts appear out of thin air. The two crafts are composed of a short shaft with a cockpit, a wing-like stabilizer above the shaft and two small anti-gravity power plants that power the craft. The two animals quickly scurry under a fallen tree. One of the crafts begins to project a beam that displaces the air in a large three-dimensional circle. Suddenly a massive hexagonal craft appears.

Inside the heagonal craft, a scally reptile like creature motions to another creature. "Begin the attack," the creature commands.

Pieces of the hexagon begin to break off and transform into smaller spacecrafts. The smaller spacecrafts that have broken off begin to move inland toward Tychon 4.

Back on Tychon 3, Prychon is in his quarters. It is pitch dark however there is slight movement in the darkness. Without warning, there is a knock at the door. As Lord Prychon arises and moves toward the door, the solid door becomes a one-way holographic window. The one-way door screen reveals Nintius outside the door.

"Lord, I bring corresondence from Racheon," Nintius projects.

There is a pause then Lord Prychon telepathically replies, "This best be of urgent nature. You're disturbing my private study."

After several moments, Prychon approaches the door and it opens. Two spiral-like devices stand sentry guarding the entrance to Prychon's quarters. As Nintius moves forward to enter, one of the spiral-shaped sentries extends a door-size laser field that blocks Nintius.

"Hand me the cube," Prychon instructs.

The shield emitted from the sentry deactivates and Nintius hands Prychon a small cube. Prychon takes the cube and returns back to his quarters as the door slides closed behind him.

Back inside, Prychon slides his hand over the cube and it lights up. Prychon is instantaneously transported into a room filled with several Greys who monitor a three-dimensional screen. On the screen is a holographic recreation of the hexagonal craft that appeared on the beach in Paradisium.

Several Greys are seated at a round table to the left of the screen. All Greys in the room don a triangle with a sphere at the top, the Grey Army symbol.

A hologram of Prychon' appears on an elevated platform adjacent to the table of Greys. One of the Greys immediately turns as Prychon transports in.

"Sire," the Grey says.

All the Greys at the table rise, performing the royal greeting.

"Racheon, why have you summoned me?" Prychon questions.

"Lord, the Corrillians have launched an attack," Racheon explains. "They are traveling inland toward Tychon 4. Our defenses are already active and we are dispatching a force to intercept the intruding forces."

"Deploy everything, crush them!" Prychon exclaims.

"A significant portion of our forces are undergoing retrofitting of our new weapon systems," Racheon projects. "However, we are dispatching all available forces to intercept."

"Don't speak of it, show of it!" Prychon demands. "I will arrive shortly."

Back at the beach, the smaller Corrillian spacecraft that descended from the hexagon continues to fly inland, passing the southern tip of the Tychon 4 region. The crafts streak across the sky. In Prychon City, the capital of Tychon 4, Grey inhabitants peer up into the sky, taking notice of the foreign craft. They glance up in dismay, covering their eyes from the bright glow of Tychon's two suns, as the crafts fly pass. One of the crafts descends toward the city and is immediately disintegrated by an unseen force field protecting the region.

The Corrillian crafts arrive in Tychon 3, the Grey industrial region. After reaching Tychon 3 airspace, the crafts begin to slow. Hovering above the anti-aircraft forcefield, the crafts assemble in small groups. One by one, the crafts each release backpack-sized devices covered in a liquid, slime-like material that floats down slowly and penetrates the forcefield.

Immediately, the cities sentry defense weapons begin rising from underground. The sentries propel a plasma material toward the incoming objects. Several of the backpack devices are destroyed as others make it through the forcefield and assemble into a new spacecraft.

The newly formed crafts made of the backpack pieces retract a diamond-shaped cannons. They then fire at the factories and structures filled with Neophyte workers. Explosions rip through buildings and structures as neophyte workers flee in every direction. The inferno engulfs everything in its path as screams from human workers ring out. The sentry pillars maintain their rate of fire striking any targets that come into range, as the Corrillians continue there assault on the city.

Small, silver spheres soon arrive to the city amidst the violent battle and begin projecting trace lasers onto the Corrillian crafts.

Back at the operations control facility for the Grey Army, Lord Prychon arrives in the flesh. He, RacheonGrey and other members of the Grey Army quickly asses the situation, monitoring the defense efforts.

"Vector spotters on site," one of the Greys in the control room acknowledges.

"Slaughter them!" Prychon angrily exclaims, watching the battle unfold from the screen of control room. "And where is Captain Cauelem? "Our mighty Grey Sky Force should have already intercepted those nefarious thundertrolls!"

At the battlefield on Tychon 3, the carnage escalates. The Corrillian crafts are still targeting Grey structures, when the ground suddenly opens. A large trapezoid-shaped mechanism brandishing the Grey Army symbol arises, floating on a black platform. The bottom panel on the mechanism expands outward revealing a displacement of heat riveling that of a small sun. Without warning, the trapezoid fires several bursts of concentrated heat, which destroys all crafts targeted by the Grey vector spotters.

"Commander Cauelum on site," a Grey inside an arriving flying saucer announces. Dozens of more with the Grey Army symbol streak in, engaging the Corrillians. The Grey saucers fire plasma lasers and the Corrillians crafts fire back, as a fullscale battle ensues.

"Switch the blanks" Cauelem instructs.

The saucers begin firing a sonic weapon that produces an ear deafening subsonic bass. From the sound burst, an energy field is emitted that destroy all the Corrillian crafts within range.

Inside one of the structures, a young Grey peers out the window as the city burns. Grey and Corrllian crafts streak acorss the sky as fires and plums of smoke bear witness to the destruction.

Cauelum leads the fight as he and the Grey Sky Force go on the offensive, attacking the Corrillian invaders with a barrage of weapons. Moving his saucer at the speed of light, Cauelum shoots down four Corrillian crafts in a matter of moments. Rising up toward space to reposition himself and gain the advantage, Caulem diverts back toward the main concentration of Corrillians, shooting down three more crafts. A Corrillian quickly positions itself behind Cauelum but before it can fire, Cauelum accelates away at the speed of light.

Forcing the Corrillians into a tri-lateral disadvantage, Grey Sentries defend from the east, the trapezoid heat ray forms a scorching barrier on west and Cauelum's Grey Sky Force strike from the north and south. The battle begins to shift in favor of the Greys as a significant portion of the remaining Corrillian crafts are.

In response to the shifting tide of the battle, the Corrillian crafts begin to drop several small discs. The discs float in midair for a few moments before moving toward the defending Grey spacecraft. The small discs slip under the Grey saucers and enter into their power duct. Any suacers that the discs enter begin to slow before implode abrubtly. The Corrillian crafts continue dropping what appears to be hundreds of more discs in an effort to regain control of the battle.

In the Grey war room, Lord Prychon and Racheon watch as the Grey Army tries to maintain the upper hand.

"I want them all annihilated!" Prychon orders. "Finish it Racheon."

"Yes, Lord," Racheon responds. "Release the Hypersonic Rotators immediately!"

"Dispatching," one of the Greys in the war room confirms.

On the battlefield, the carnage rages on. Several more Grey saucers arrive and release metallic balls. As the balls activate, rotating lasers swirl around the metallic surface at hypersonic speed. The lasers rotate in all directions, resembling an electron orbiting an atom. The balls attack the Corrillian crafts, obliterating them on contact. Cauelum and the Grey force form a wall, push the invaders towards the rotating destroyers.

The battle continues as the strength of the Grey Army clashes against the deadly Corrillian attack force.

"The enemy is retreating," a Cauelum announces. "We are traveling to the source, six units follow me," he instructs as he moves away from the battle.

"Understood, Commander Cauelum," another Grey pilot in one of the saucers acknowledges, as he breaks away from the battle. Four more Grey saucers follow as Cauelum's ship slices through the air behind the retreating crafts.

"Cowards!" Lord Prychon declares, still in side the control room.

After arriving at the beach, Cauelum and the other pilots spot the Hexagonal craft.

"It's a Corrillian Hexasphere," Cauelum declares. "We must summon the Hydro-Electrofier."

Several pieces of the Hexasphere break off and begin toward the flying saucers in intercept formation.

"Transferring coordinates of primary target now," Cauelum declares as he maneuvers and shifts his saucer in an orbital pattern above the beach.

Within moments, a gigantic circular disk with a circular gap in the center, slowly rises out of the water. As it surfaces, ocean water flows over the brim and down the sides of the disc, revealing Tychonian symbols and the Grey Army crest engraved on its exterior. Inside the disc, three inner circles begin to rotate as a loud powering up sound becomes audible.

Inside the disc, three Greys stand in the control cabin, manipulating a large holographic sphere.

"Launch to coordinates *40°45'45"N 73°58'27"W*," a Grey inside the disc orders.

Following the command, a large circular stream of water begins gushing upwards, propelled by the disc. The sizzling sound of electricity emminates from the disc as a jetstream of water rises up high into the sky. The large stream of ejected water begins falling back down to the surface forming a wall of electro-charged water. As this charged water reaches the hexagonal ships, it disintegrates them. The Hexagonal ship begins to retreat. A new vortex of air appears in the sky as the Hexasphere craft slowly disappears through an air portal, as quickly as it had entered.

Back in the Grey control room, Prychon slams his fist onto the table.

"Those heathens!" Prychon projects.

"Sire?" Racheon questions.

"No hostile forces to be deployed in Tychonian space. That was the treaty the Corrillians swore by," Prychon replies.

"What shall our response be Lord?" Nintius asks.

Prychon pauses. "Swift, merciless and deadly," he responds. "Convene a tribunal immediately to prepare."

"Under what order shall the tribunal be convened?" Nintius inquires.

"War," Prychon snaps.

Several rotations pass and on AzurNu, Chimera and Nexus continue to speaking more frequently.

It is the 17th degree and Chimera is inside her dorm writing in her holpad. StarChild is once again on her headset with Dug. Chimera looks up and suddenly her wristcom rings. A bit startled, Chimera looks down and a slight grin slides acorss her face. She turns off the holopad and retrieves a round sphere from her desk. She places the sphere onto her right ear and presses a button, triggering a thin transparent visor in front of Chimera. A live capture of Nexus appears on the transparent visor and Chimera begins speaking.

"Hey Nexus," Chimera answers.

There is a pause.

"Yea, I'm good. How are you?" Chimera asks.

Another pause.

"I was studying for Earth Studies, you?

As Chimera turns up the volume, Nexus's muffled voice becomes slightly audible.

"Um, I kind of have a lot to do . . ." Chimera reveals

"Trust me, it'll be worth it," Nexus declares.

" . . . I mean, I could use a break," Chimera admits. "I've been studying nonstop for rotations. Where are you going?"

"It's a surprise," Nexus announces.

"Surprise?" Chimera asks.

"Yes!" Nexus confirms. "And I know you're gonna really like it."

"I not a fan of surprises," Chimera reveals. She thinks for several moments. "Alright, I'm in."

"Smash!" Nexus exclaims. "You can meet me at *Create*, in front of the Holoprojection theater at the 21st degree. We can go together there."

"I'll see you," Chimera confirms as she ends the call.

"Ohh, was that who I think it was?" StarChild questions grinning from cheek to cheek.

"It was nobody. I'm gonna freshen up," Chimera replies, trying to keep a straight face.

"You two have been talking a lot! What happened to all that talk about you not being the dating type?" StarChild retorts.

"It's not a date!" Chimera proclaims. She heads to her vanity pod, a large grey and black pod designed for showering and changing attire.

Chimera presses a button on the right side of the pod and it opens. Chimera steps inside and undresses. A small drawer opens inside the pod, and Chimera places her bio suite in the drawer. After placing her suit in the drawer, it closes.

"Bath cycle," Chimera announces firmly.

"Bathing cycle initiated," a voice confirms inside the pod.

Suddenly, water can be heard from inside the pod, as it begins to rinse Chimera. After a few moments, the water ceases.

"Dry cycle," Chimera proclaims.

"Drying cycle confirmed," the command system confirms.

A power up sound begins as a slight burst of heat radiates from the pod.

It continues for a few instances, before the pod powers down.

"Dry cycle complete," the voice from the pod declares. "Thank you for using Hygiene Acceleration Systems."

The drawer inside the pod opens once again and Chimera begins to dress. When she emerges shortly after, Chimera is dressed in a uniquely shaped black skirt, lenticular holographic mid cut top and black overcoat.

"Thirty seconds, that's an all time slowest record," StarChild jokes, watching Chimera exit the pod. "Long rinse cycle, all dressed up? Obviously this nobody you're going to see is someone special."

"I have no idea what you're talking about," Chimera responds, as she heads to the food receptacle and opens it, pulling a beverage out. She walks back to the vanity pod and checks herself out in the mirror.

"You look good," StarChild confirms.

Chimera makes an odd face and then heads toward the door.

"I'm gonna step out for a bit. I'll be back soon," Chimera declares.

"So you're not gonna tell me who this mystery guy is?" StarChild asks.

"What makes you think it's a guy?" Chimera replies.

"Because I heard his voice, alien girl!" StarChild exclaims.

"I'll be back," Chimera responds. "Once again, you forgot about Duggy on hold, StarGirl," Chimera remarks.

"O shoot!" StarChild shouts, putting her headset back on.

Chimera exits the dorm as the door slowly slides closed behind her. She travels through the hallway to Tiberius Station. From there, she rides the *RedLine* hover-rail to *Create*. After exiting the hover-rail, she enters the *Create* zone, which is heavy with foot traffic being the 18th degree. Studies are complete for the day and Reds that work the first shift have already completed their cycle.

Chimera makes her way toward the projection theater. She stops near the entrance. She looks down at her wristcom and is about to call

Nexus when suddenly she feels an arm grab her shoulder. Startled, she turns around and almost elbows the mystery guest in the throat.

"Hey it's me!" the mystery guest exclaims.

"Nexus . . . you startled me!" Chimera remarks.

"Sorry, wanted to surprise you," Nexus responds.

"It's ok," Chimera replies. "I thought someone was following me on my way over here, so when you grabbed me I didn't know who it was."

"Weird. Well, I got you these, hopefully they'll make up for it," Nexus jokes as he hands Chimera a handful of efflorescence.

"Aw . . . thank you," Chimera responds. "So how do we get to wherever we're going?"

"It's a secret, remember?" Nexus reminds Chimera. "I'm not gonna tell you."

Nexus places a digital blindfold visor onto Chimera.

"Really?" Chimera asks, grinning.

"Trust me," Nexus declares, as he leads Chimera through a corridor into a cave. In the cave, they then enter another passageway that curves under the entertainment wing of AzurNu. They continue on until they reach another large cavernous opening.

Arriving at the destination, Nexus deactivates Chimeras blindfold. Chimera opens her eyes.

"Whoa, is that a . . . stadium?" Chimera exclaims, looking up at the massive structure before her.

"Yea. Here, here's your entry bracelet. Put this on," Nexus

instructs as he slides a white bracelet on Chimera's right wrist. The bracelet begins to glow.

"I like," Chimera responds.

The stadium entrance spans the entire front of stadium. There are blue translucent circles around the floor of the entrance. Reds fill the cavern, waiting in line to enter the stadium. As Reds step forward onto the glowing circles, rising discs of light appear and scan them. Afterword, a number appears on their entry bracelet.

"This is a crazy surprise!" Chimera exclaims.

"Knew you'd like it," Nexus admits.

"What are we seeing?" Chimera inquires.

"There are a couple creators performing," Nexus announces. "ElectraRED is here to perform Indigo!"

"Is that the creator you were telling me about?" Chimera asks.

"It is," Nexus replies. "Are you ready?"

"Yea, let's rock!" Chimera answers.

Chimera and Nexus step forward onto one of the blue translucent circles and are scanned. After the scan, a path of new translucent circles appears, leading toward one of the entrances of the stadium. Chimera and Nexus travel up the glowing circles and enter the stadium.

"Here we are," Nexus says, as he and Chimera enter the stadium. "Our seats should over there."

"Got it," Chimera confirms. "Is there a place to maybe get something to eat here?"

"Of course," Nexus responds. "You're hungry?"

"Yea, I haven't eaten anything in a few degrees," Chimera states.

"Um there are a few concession areas here," Nexus confirms. "We're kind of late, so I'm gonna check in first, and then I can grab us something to eat if you want."

"No worry," Chimera says. "If you want to check in, I'll grab something to eat really fast and meet you at our section."

"I can get it for you," Nexus offers.

"No problem," Chimera answers. "I'll grab something really fast and be right back."

"Are you sure?" Nexus asks.

"Yea go ahead," Chimera suggests. "I'll be right back."

"Alright, well at least take some credits," Nexus urges reaching his wristcom out toward Chimera.

"It's fine, I've got it," Chimera responds.

"I insist," Nexus persists. "It's the least you can let me do. The concession area is down that corridor and to the right. You can meet me at our section after you grab food."

Before Chimera can walk away, Nexus taps his wristcom against hers and transfers credits to her.

"I'll be back," Chimera confirms, as she turns and heads down the busy walkway. The bustle of Reds anxious to reach their seating areas fills the stadium air with excitement. Chimera continues down the crowded walkway, searching for the concession area.

"That was a right and another right?" Chimera mutters to herself.

The crowd begins to fade away as Chimera continues searching. The sound of muffled bass becomes audible as the roar of screams and cheers is faintly heard.

"Ok, I'm about to miss the beginning," Chimera declares. "Let me just gonna ask somebody."

Chimera walks until she sees a Red standing alone near three pillars.

"Maybe he'll know," Chimera says to herself, walking up to the Red. "Hi, do you know where I can find the concession area?" Chimera asks. "I've been looking for a while now and I'm gonna miss the show."

The stranger pauses, then slowly turns. It is an older Red.

"You see that entrance, over there?" the Red asks pointing to a hallway. "Go through there and you'll reach a hall. Enter the RED double doors at the end of the hall and you will find what you are looking for."

"Thank you," Chimera acknowledges.

She turns and heads in the direction suggested by the Red. As Chimera enters the hall, she notices the area is unusually quiet. She finds the double RED doors and makes her way through them.

As she passes through, three soft chimes are heard, followed by a voice prompt that says, "Thank you, please stand clear of the door." The area is dark and unlit.

"This can't be right," Chimera to herself as she turns around. "I'm more lost now and I'm gonna miss the show!"

She begins back through the RED doors when she feels an arm on her shoulder again.

"I thought I told you I don't like being startled, Nexus!" Chimera exclaims.

As she turns around, she sees a dark figure and hears a quick sound before she blacks out.

Chimera awakes, partially suspended in midair, above a round platform. Her pupils adjust to the light and her sight becomes clear.

She floats in a room in which everything is red from the floor to the ceiling. In the room, there are three golden statues of phoenixes, the national symbol of Reds.

Coming to, Chimera notices a row of Reds in front of her, also suspended in midair. As she regains control of her muscles, she turns her head and sees more Reds afloat in the room. Near the entrance across from Chimera, she sees two Reds with weapons standing guard. Several drones hover about the room.

The other Reds that float beside Chimera begin awaking.

"Where am I?" one Red murmurs.

"What just happened?" other Reds question.

Suddenly, a larger platform to the right of Chimera lights up. On the platform stands a Red in an all black space armor. The Red has a small blue cape and a Red phoenix is visible on his chest armor. The Red begins to speak.

"My name is Lead Master GhostRED. I am a Recruit Training Officer for Enforcement, more specifically the training instructor for tactical recruits. Across from me on the adjacent leadership platform is Lead Master RavenRED."

Chimera looks to the left. There, stands a tall slender female RED in black and gold space armor.

GhostRED continues, "She is the Recruit Training officer for the intelligence division. Raven reports to LuminoRED, the Intelligence Commander for Enforcement. I report to SphinxRED, the Tactical Commander. Sphinx and Lumino report to Quintari, Second in command to the Head of Enforcement, General ShadowRED.

"We here at Enforcement are the Alpha and Omega for the fight against extermination. Titan and his Red Defense Core have been preparing to fight battles but we are the force that will win the war," Ghost warns. "We're gathering the intelligence, weapons and resources to even the playing field and to give our outnumbered race a chance."

"I knew enforcement was real," Chimera whispers to herself. "But how the hell did I end up here?"

"What are you going to do with us?" one of the Reds who floats next to Chimera asks. "Why are we here?"

"You will all address me as Lead Master sir when you speak to me, is that clear?" Ghost announces.

"Yes, Lead Master sir," the room confirms.

Chimera is late to respond and confirms, "Yes, Lead Master sir," after the other Reds.

"To answer your question," Ghost begins, "and the question that is on all of your minds, you are here because you were chosen to be part of the secret enforcement training program."

The recruits in the room begin murmuring in excitement.

"For the next three planetary rotations you will be physically, emotionally and psychologically tested. When you reach your breaking point, you will be pushed even harder. We are here to gauge if you are fit to be one of the few, elite members of Enforcement."

There is more chatter as the recruits anticipate the upcoming training for Enforcement.

"Quiet!" Ghost orders. "It is important to note that I am not here to befriend you. I am here to provide you with the skills and the training to turn you knuckle dragging bottom feeders into viable prospects of Enforcement."

A large door adjacent to the middle phoenix statue suddenly opens and another RED enters.

"Attention on deck," Ghost announces.

The Red stops in the center of the room and the platform he is standing on elevates.

"I am Quintari, second in command for the Enforcers. Most of you will never see me again after this recruitment process ends. There is one complete platoon of twelve enforcers and another near complete platoon of ten, representing the core of Enforcement. There are twelve of you here, six recruits for Tactical team, six recruits for the Intelligence team. Once training has concluded, one of you from each group will be chosen to stay and become an Enforcer. You will eat, sleep, breathe and train here at enforcement headquarters. Those of you currently enrolled in studies will also complete your coursework here. Are there any pressing questions before we begin?" Quintari inquires.

The room is silent.

"Very well," Quintari declares. "All of you recruits remove your wristcoms now. From this moment forward, you will no longer be in contact with anyone outside of this program. Communication with your family and acquaintances will be taken care of. Anyone who wishes to leave, step down and exit now."

Quintari pauses for a moment and looks around the room. None of the Reds move or speak.

"Very well, remove your wristcoms and place them on the rack of the collection drone," Quintari commands as one of the drones hovers down toward the recruits.

"When will we get them back, Commander sir?" one of recruits asks, sounding a bit nervous.

"For most of you, sooner than later," Quintari answers.

Chimera and all the other Reds hurriedly unlock their wristcoms and remove them from their wrists. The drone flies by each Red, as the recruits place their devices on a rotating tray connected to the drone.

"I will swear each of you in, and then GhostRED and RavenRED will take over," Quintari remarks. "You will break off into your two training groups and your recruitment training will begin."

Quintari presses a button and circular holograms the size of a hand appear next to each platform.

"Each of you will place your hands on the circle in front of you. Your oath will appear in a holographic textbox triggered by your palm. Read the statement in the textbox to make your pledge of covenant."

The oaths begin on the left side with a Red who identifies himself as PhazeRed. The next, a recruit named VadenRed.

The oaths continue, and it is with the fourth Red that Chimera hears a familiar voice.

"I, AnexichiRed, swear by the seal of the Great Phoenix."

Chimera glances to her left and confirms it is Anexichi, the Red from the library. Chimera shakes her head and sighs quietly.

The oaths continue as the last Red on the left side begins.

"I, IscariRed, swear by the seal of the Great Phoenix of Tychon that I will support and defend the ideology of Red beliefs against all aggressors . . ."

Without warning, a loud buzz sound rings out followed by an alarm.

"Anomaly detected. False declaration . . . Anomaly detected. False declaration," the voice continues to alert as two drones fly over to Iscari, the same Red that questioned Quintari about the wristcom. Iscari stops his declaration and glances around in confusion.

"Please step down, place your hands in front of you and follow to the nearest exit," the drone commands. "Please confirm compliance."

The two sentries near the door shift their attention and point their weapons directly at Iscari.

"What's happening? What's going on?" Iscari asks, raising his hands as if to announce his innocence.

Chimera and the other recruits watch as Quintari glances at Ghost. The command speaker system continues its alert, "Anomaly detected, false declaration. Anomaly detected, false declaration . . ."

The drone in front of Iscari repeats its command, "Please step down place your hands in front of you, and follow to the nearest exit. Please confirm your compliance."

"The drones are programmed to repeat a command three times," Ghost declares. "You're on your second command, I wouldn't let the third arrive."

Iscari is motionless for several more moment. He quickly steps down and places his hands in front of him. One of the drones is about to shackle him when Iscari suddenly sprints toward one of the doors. The two sentries power up their weapons but one of the drones fires an electric charge at Iscari. The electrical charge strikes Iscari in the back and he stops mid sprint, falling to the floor. He lays on the ground unconscious as several additional Reds enter the room and carry Iscari out.

"He'll survive," Ghost announces. "Let this be the first lesson of many. Lying, cheating or insubordination will not be tolerated. Once again, if you do not believe you have what it takes to complete this program or are not here with the correct intentions, leave now. The consequences far outweigh the embarrassment of walking away."

Ghost looks around, giving the recruits a final opportunity to discharge themselves. Quintari stands silently behind Ghost.

Chimera's side of the room begins their oaths with a recruit named CaitiffRed. Chimera is next.

Chimera raises her palm to the circle and reads her oath, "I, ChimeraRed, swear by the seal of the Great Pyramid of Tychon that I will support and defend the ideology of Red beliefs against all aggressors, alien and Hue-man. That I will be honorable and truthful, swearing allegiance to the Anti-Republic under the Golden Phoenix of Enforcement; that I will obey all orders of Enforcement leadership and Red Command; and most important of all, I will not disclose what I do, see or hear at Enforcement, so help me infinity."

After their oaths, groups are announced. Chimera and five other recruits are chosen to stay with Ghost while the other six remaining recruits will train under Raven. In Chimera's group are CaitiffRed, SyrexRed, PhazeRed, EchoRed and InxRed. Anexichi is chosen for Raven's group.

"Here is the breakdown," Quintari explains. "All debriefings will be held here in the red room. All recruits will be trained in six areas."

As the recruits move into their groups, Chimera and the recruits for GhostRED are sent to the changing chamber. After changing to her training suit, Chimera and the other recruits return to the red room to begin their training.

"Alright recruits, play close attention," Ghost states. "There are the six levels of training here at Enforcement. The first step is the *Recon Training Level*. You will be using a training space that alternates close quarter and long distance scenarios. In this level, you will learn to improvise, gather intelligence, retrieve objects, plant devices and practice infiltration techniques."

The recruits nods as Ghost continues.

"After Recon, you will move to *Combat Training*," Ghost begins. In combat training, you'll learn to attack and defend yourselves with melee weapons as well as with no weapons at all. After the Combat Room, you will move to *Weapons and Explosives Training*. At this level, you will be trained and tested on weapons and incendiary devices within Enforcement's arsenal. This is the most dangerous training level and you will need to take the utmost precaution. You will start with theory, followed by nonlethal laser tagging battles before graduating to firing live weapons."

Chimera begins to grin to herself. The other recruits appear anxious as well, and ready to begin.

"After Weapons and Explosives, will be the *Automation/*

Intelligent Systems and Tech Training, " Ghost reveals. At this stage you will learn some of the complexities of our computing systems. You will also learn how to navigate the advance technology of A.I Systems. From Weapons and Explosives, you all will be trained to operate heavy duty vehicles and light spacecraft."

"That's what I'm here for," one recruits to the right of Chimera mumbles.

"The last area you will train is . . . Terrestrial Influence."

Chimera and the recruits look at one another in confusion.

"Politics, Lead Master sir?" one of the recruits questions.

"Negotiations and Influence," Ghost snaps. "In this phase, you will study Red philosophical beliefs, learn to mediate surrenders and utilize level 5 mind control to influence others to disclose information or obey commands."

"Now that's what I'm here for," another Red proclaims proudly.

"If there are no questions, we can begin," Ghost announces.

And with that, Chimera and the other recruits begin. They train vigorously in the six program phases, for two planetary rotations of hard training pass. Chimera performs well in her group, however the highest scoring recruit is CaitiffRed with a ranking of 94%. Chimera is second, at 91%, scoring less in symbols and programming. The recruits continue training for two more planetary rotations.

It is a cold Tychonian morning, around the 5th degree when a wake up signal sounds. Chimera is startled, sitting up to confirm the alarm.

"All recruits, please report to the red room in half a degree," the command speaker system announces.

Chimera rises out of her bunk pod and stretches. Being the only female in group A, Chimera has the dorm entirely to herself. Chimera readies herself in the dorms less advance vanity system and exits. Stepping into the hallway, Chimera joins the other Reds who are also exiting their dorm rooms. Chimera begins down the spiral walkway toward that leads to the briefing room. On the way down, Chimera catches a glimpse of Anexichi who has been in group B for the duration of training. The two exchange glances, and then Anexichi approaches Chimera.

"Hey wait a sec," Anexichi calls.

Chimera stops, but does not turn to face Anexichi. Instead, she turns her head but stands in the opposite direction.

"Look, I was a jerk to you and I know it, I'm sorry," Anexichi admits. "How I acted was out of line."

Chimera looks at Anexichi for a moment and then nods. She continues on her way.

"Is that an acceptance of my apology?" Anexichi hollers as Chimera walks away.

Chimera turns around to glance at Anexichi, then continues on her way down the staircase.

Entering the red room, Chimera is headed toward her platform when one of the escort drones leads her in a different direction. She sees Caitiff ahead of her stepping through a door into an unknown room. The drone leads Chimera toward the same door. When Chimera reaches the door, the drone scans a control panel nearby. Chimera enters and is greeted by a massive room filled with blue and purple lights.

"What is this place?" Chimera asks.

Above Chimera, there is a simulated sky projected onto the ceiling, that replicates the days rotation and gives the appearance of the sky outside. On several screens in the room are displays of key Grey targets in the Tychon Federated Union.

The room itself is centered around a gigantic magnetic blue glowing sphere with the phrase "Globotron" written on it. There are a group of chairs attached to a track that leads to the Globotron. Several more chairs are attached to the Globotron with some of the Enforcement recruits already seated in them.

"Please take a seat and your chair will activate," the drone commands Chimera.

"Activate?" Chimera asks.

There is no response from the drone.

Chimera steps up and sits down in one of the chairs. The chair begins to slide backwards toward the Globotron. As she approaches the glowing sphere, Chimera rises as the anti gravity power of the seat turns on. Still in her seat, Chimera floats toward the Globotron and her magnetized chair attaches to it. Her seat slides over to align with the other chairs already attached and locks into place.

GhostRED enters the room and walks toward the sphere. He slowly ascends, disappearing inside the Globotron. He reappears, rising through the top of it on a small disc platform. On this platform, Ghost stands behind an angled podium. As Ghost completes his ascent to the top of the Globotron, Echo is the last recruit to attach. One of the clocks on the screens reads 5.5 degrees, the call time for the briefing. A short alarm sounds. Just as it finishes, another recruit enters in.

"You're late recruit, Inx," Ghost says.

"Yes sir, I am regretful," Inx admits. "I did not hear the first alarm."

"All the other recruits did. Is there an issue with your auditory process?" Ghost asks.

"No sir," Inx responds.

"I should hope not," Ghost responds. "Because of your tardiness, you will not be participating in today's exercise."

Inx drops his heads and sighs loudly.

"Please exit my briefing," Ghost proclaims. "And be on degree next time."

Inx is escorted out by one of the drones.

"Commence," Ghost declares.

Suddenly, the sound of a generator begins and the Globotron

starts to rotate. As the speed of the Globotron increases, a ring around the sphere appears. On the ring sits holograms of Tychon 2 and 3.

"Today is especially important," Ghost announces. "It will be your first live mission and will be executed in Grey territory."

A rise of voices can be heard as the recruits gush with the excitement of their first mission.

"In approximately one degree, you will board a transport and take off to rendezvous at a location two clicks east of Tychon 2. This is a reconnaissance mission gathering intelligence on the convoy for RothGrey," Ghost announces.

"RothGrey, as you know, is the wealthiest Grey on Tychon. The majority of his wealth was acquired by forcing the Tychonian Federated Union to purchase Hue-man slaves from his business consortium, rather than creating them. He created a monopoly by banning Grey governance or any other private company, the option to synthesize Hue-mans."

"RothGrey is responsible for the assassination of Prychon NytGrey," one of the recruits adds.

"Not true!" Caitiff blurts out.

"That's enough," Ghost interjects. "Listen up to the mission specs. Your objective today is to perform reconnaissance. I repeat, it is a recon only op. We will not be engaging the convoy should we encounter it. Our primary objective is to confirm the accuracy of the intel we received, study the convoy and assess their level of armament.

We will view the target from a safe zone to avoid detection. Team B will be launching spotter droids to survey the area. Team A you will be providing support and protection for team B. CaitiffRed, you have excelled across the board in training and are at the top of your class. You will lead team A for this mission. Remember, the intel we retrieve today will help eradicate the biggest threat to our society. Are there any questions?"

One of the recruits raises his palm.

"Yes, recruit Syrex," Ghost acknowledges.

"Lead Master sir, what type of weaponry will we be using for this mission?" Syrex asks.

"As this is a recon operation, you will be armed with series Z stun rays," Ghost acknowledges.

"And what if we are attacked, sir?" Syrex adds.

"Then you have failed your mission, and you would not need a weapon anyway," Ghost responds. "Training Officers Raven and I will be armed. Field Officers Sphinx and Lumino will be supervising and armed as well."

Syrex steps back into line.

"Each of you will operate in two person teams," Ghost reveals. "One recruit from team A and another from team B. Once you retrieve your recruitment wristcom, you will find your partners info under the sync tab. Connect with them immediately, and then meet Sphinx in the gear room for equipping."

Chimera and the other recruits' chairs retract from the Globotron and return back to ground level. After unstrapping themselves, the recruits head to the gear room to prepare for the mission.

Stepping inside the gear room, Chimera begins to assemble her gear assigned for the mission. She grabs black and white battle armor, a combat helmet, Level 6 stun ray, an Enforcer wristcom and a military grade magnetic backpack. As she is about to leave she notices an unmarked equipment box. Opening it, she discovers anti gravity incendiaries. Chimera glances around the, as the other recruits are retrieving their gear as well. Chimera is about to drop three of the incendiaries into her pack when RavenRED enters.

Caught off guard, Chimera accidentally knocks some of the gear on the tables onto the floor.

"Finding your gear ok?" Raven asks.

"Yea, I am," Chimera confirms, grabbing the last of her required equipment. Chimera then heads to the loading dock, logging into her new wristcom on the way to check the sync tab.

"Looks like my partner is PhazeRed," Chimera announces, as she checks the wristcom.

Chimera continues to the flight docks of enforcement. After reaching the docks, Chimera finds PhazeRed.

"Hey Chimera, looks like I'm partnered with you," Phaze mentions.

"Yea, you're pretty lucky," Chimera remarks.

Phaze laughs, shaking his head.

On the docks, there are two ships on deck; one chartered for group A recruits and the other for group B.

"Group A, you're in Zeta ship. Group B, you will be flying in the Nuance," a voice over a loudspeaker announces.

"I didn't think I would get paired with you," Phaze whispers to Chimera. "Are you nervous?"

"Not at all," Chimera replies. "I'm anxious to get to the surface."

"Hopefully not too anxious," Phaze responds. "You don't know what's out there."

Chimera and Phaze board the waiting ship, a bell-shaped disc 40 meters long. There are two rows of seating inside the ship. An inner and outer ring that face downward toward the floor of the ship.

"Welcome to the Zeta," a crew member at the door announces to Chimera.

As Chimera steps up, a crew member holds a device up and scans her.

"Recruit 7, strap in seat 9c," the crew member says to Chimera.

Chimera moves over to seat 9c, climbs in and plops down. The straps of the seats immediately retract securing Chimera.

The rest of the recruits from team A board, are scanned and take their seats. The training officers are the last to board, as Ghost seats himself in the inner seating row. The recruits stare at Ghost admiring his battle armor.

"I can't wait to get my heavy battle armor," Syrex proclaims proudly.

A portion of the dock begins to ascend, carrying the Zeta and Nuance up to the sub-surface level.

Chimera listens as the pilots in the cockpit communicate with the flight tower awaiting clearance to launch.

"Zeta, this is tower 317, contact departure."

"Departure this is Zeta 1, ready for takeoff," one of the pilots announces.

"Zeta 1, depart base mountain Charlie. Sky's clear, board is RED, you're cleared for launch."

"Tower 317, copy," the pilot replies.

As the platform comes to a stop, Chimera glances out the translucent walls of the ship.

"The launch pad is inside a mountain?" Phaze asks.

"What better camouflage?" Syrex responds.

The front of the mountain changes opacity as the Zeta rises.

Passing through the camouflage field, the Zeta reaches cruise altitude and hurls forward toward its destination. The Nuance lifts off and follows.

THE ALIEN THREAT

Onboard the Zeta, Chimera and the other recruits' chairs begin to slant forward, facing the ground. Chimera watches the terrain speed by through the pellucid floor. The arid dry beds of Tychon 1 rise and fall as the ship passes over the regions mountain formations and valleys. It is nearly silent onboard, aside from the low hum of the ship edging through the sky.

"How long is the ride?" Syrex inquires aloud.

"A little less than half a degree," one crew member remarks. "This baby's supersonic. She'll get us there quick."

"Destination in proximity," a voice suddenly announces over the ship's audio projection system.

As the Zeta and Nuance cross the border into Tychon 2, the terrain transforms from dry desert to the chrysillium crystals, sky high structures and transport circuits that fill the horizon. The Zeta begins to slow and descends rapidly into a field of chrysillium, a collection of massive crystal-like pylons. The field is a quarry for chrysillium, a commodity on Tychon mined for construction.

The Zeta comes to a rest alongside the Nuance ship in an excavated area of the fields. Before the ship powers down, the crew and officers are already unbuckled and out of their seats.

"As your seats moves to the upright position, exit immediately," the voice on the ship's intercom announces.

"Let's go recruits," Ghost commands after the announcement. "Mission info will be displayed on your headset, lined to your new wristcom. Team positions, rendezvous points, objectives and call signs will also be listed. Follow your overlays to your waypoints. In the event that you see the target objective, relay your position right away and contact me or Lead Master Raven. We will head to your location and take the reins. Do not engage the target under any circumstances. I repeat, do not engage your targets!"

"And what do we do if the convoy never shows?" Syrex inquires.

"Once you complete your tasks, or if the target does not arrive by the designated rally time, head to the extraction point for pickup," Ghost proclaims. "Do I make myself clear?"

"Clear, Lead Master sir," Chimera and the other recruits reply.

"Move out," Ghost orders.

Chimera is the first to unbuckle and exit the craft. She waits outside the ship for Phaze, who exits after Caitiff and Syrex.

"C'mon, let's go," Chimera urges Phaze, as she powers on her headset.

Chimera and Phaze begin northwest, following the headset overlays to the objective point. Chimera leads the way, as they trudge past the chrysillium field, climbing over some and under others.

"This chrysillium provides the perfect camouflage but is a pain to walk through," Phaze admits.

"I'm getting some interference on my headset," Chimera mentions to Phaze. "I think it's the crystals. Our first rendezvous point is west of here but my headset is switching between west and north."

"My NavMap is saying north," Phaze declares.

"Let's keep west," Chimera urges.

"But my Nav is showing we're off course," Phaze warns.

Chimera ignores Phaze's suggestion and continues heading west. After a fourth of a degree of walking, Chimera and Phaze stop at a small clearing.

"This should be our mission point," Chimera announces, looking around.

"My headset is telling me this is the wrong location," Phaze responds. I don't think we're in the right spot."

"I'm gonna reset my headset and check," Chimera declares.

"Where in the wrong location. We've gone too far west," Phaze announces.

As Chimera's headset comes back online she checks her overlay.

"Dammit! I think you're right" Chimera exclaims. "We must have . . ."

Suddenly, the sound of heavy footsteps ring out.

"Shh, movement right," Chimera whispers to Phaze as she motions for him to crouch down. Chimera crouches as well and pulls out her stun ray. Out of the clearing comes a figure in black, white and red armor.

"It's CaitiffRed!" Phaze reveals.

Caitiff emerges, accompanied by Syrex.

"What are you doing in this zone?" Chimera asks.

"That's no way to address your captain," Caitiff retorts.

"You're not captain, you're a recruit leader!" Chimera answers back sharply.

"This is our mission rally point. What are you doing here?" Caitiff questions.

"Chimera let's go," Phaze suggests.

As Phaze begins to lead Chimera away, another figure appears from the sprawl of oversized crystals. Chimera begins to draw her stun ray when Phaze signals her to stop.

"Look, it's Anexichi and Rex," Phaze points out.

Anexichi approaches with her recruit partner.

"Confirmed, we are definitely in the wrong location," Chimera admits.

Chimera turns and begins to walk back in the direction she and

Phaze came from.

"What are you doing here?" Anexichi questions.

"We were just leaving," Chimera replies.

Chimera gets a few steps in when her headset starts to beep.

The words "Proximity alert! Target in range!" flash on Chimera's headset.

"Chimera, are you seeing this?" Phaze questions.

"Yea, you're getting it too?" Chimera questions.

"I, I'm getting it to," Caitiff stutters.

"Me as well," Anexichi confirms, looking up in the sky.

In a matter of moments, a small fleet of ships exit hyperspace and appear over the chrysillium field, slowing as they pass over.

"I'm seeing seven, eight, nine ships," Chimera announces.

Three small triangular spacecraft hover in front of two medium sized tube-shaped crafts. The ships are dwarfed by a colossal insect looking craft with two layers of wing like attachments. Behind the largest ship are three more small triangular spacecraft. Caitiff, Phaze and the other recruits freeze.

"Alright, recruit leader, what do we do?" Anexichi questions Caitiff.

Caitiff remains quiet, watching the massive ships pass overhead. He begins to shake.

"What do we do Caitiff? Our objective is in sight!" Syrex hollers.

Without warning, Caitiff turns and darts off, running away from the field.

"Take cover, take cover!" Caitiff hollers back to the recruits, as he flees the.

Chimera and the others look at each other in disbelief.

"Did he just leave us?" Phaze asks.

"I think he did," Anexichi remarks.

Watching the middle of the convoy fly overhead, Chimera turns back toward Phaze and Anexichi and rises up.

"Alright, here's what we're gonna do," Chimera begins. "Everybody stay low and move out of the clearing, slowly. The chrysillium is our cover. I'm turning on visual tracking so we can get a holo-vid of this. Phaze, since there's no radio reception here, you double back out of the fields and contact Lead Master Ghost. Let him know the objective is in the area."

Chimera turns to Anexichi.

"Anexichi, once you get reception you contact Lead Master Raven, tell her to alert Intel Enforcement to run comm intercept for data." Chimera instructs. "Echo, you can run like your partner Caitiff, or secure the perimeter."

Phaze and Anexichi stare at Chimera and then each other for a moment.

"I . . . I'll stick with you and keep the perimeter clear," Rex states.

"What about you?" Phaze questions. "Are you going to be ok?"

"Go!" Chimera exclaims as she flips a switch on her headset. "My objective is to observe and assess Roth's transport for weaknesses". Syrex and I will keep visual contact."

Anexichi and Phase head out of the clearing and begin out of the chrysillium field.

"Anyone near coordinates 40.42.45N, 74.00.22W, L33 beware that the target is in the vicinity," Chimera announces. "I'm placing an overlay marker on my position."

Chimera continues surveying the convoy, observing Roth's ship. Chimera is looking up and does not notice Phaze sprint past her. Still looking up, Chimera doesn't see Anexichi charging right at her until it is too late. Anexichi slams into Chimera, sending Chimera to the ground in a similar fashion to the previous incident at the council wing.

"What the heck!" Chimera screams. "I thought we were past this and now you attack me in the middle of a mission?"

"Chimera!" Rex exclaims as he returns, pointing behind Chimera.

Chimera is busy scolding Anexichi. Chimera reaches down and grabs Anexichi about to strike her when she hears a growl. Phaze grabs Chimera and helps Anexichi up.

"We have to get out of here!" Rex screams, pointing to something.

Just then, two creatures emerge from behind a row of crystals and step into the clearing, growling.

"Iridescent Vexors!" Phaze yells.

The iridescent colored Vexors, four legged predators of the Tychon 3 region approach. Two more Vexors enter the clearing as Chimera helps Anexichi up, followed by three more bringing the total to eight.

"Looks like a hunting pack!" Chimera warns, as the four recruits huddle together. "Be very still and follow my lead," Chimera whispers. "They're scent based hunters."

Chimera begins to slowly step backward. The Vexors sniff the air. As the recruits retreat, Phaze trips and falls backwards. His stun ray is in hand and when he hits the floor his weapon discharges.

"Zuuuuush" the stun ray sounds as it shoots a beam into a chrysillium pylon.

The Vexors begin charging in the recruits' direction. Chimera tries firing her stun ray at the charging creatures but the Vexors dodge her shots. One of the Vexors jumps in front of the pack, approaching quickly. Searching around for an alternative, Chimera looks down and notices a broken off piece of chrysillium. She picks it up.

The lead Vexor reaches the recruits eyeing Anexichi. Shifting to an attack stance, the Vexor leaps at Anexichi. Chimera jumps forward in front of Anexichi and strikes the Vexor with the piece of crystal knocking it to the ground.

"Thank you," Anexichi declares to Chimera.

"Don't thank me yet," Chimera responds. "Let's get out of here first."

The recruits begin running as Chimera tries firing again at the Vexors with her stun ray, which proves ineffective.

"These stun rays are useless!" Chimera confirms. "Stay close, I've got an idea."

Chimera, Anexichi, Phaze and Rex run through the fields dodging and climbing over crystals.

"What's the plan?" Phaze questions as they continue sprinting out of the field. "We only have stun rays, they're gonna pop in front of us any second!"

"That's it!" Chimera exclaims. "Gravity poppers, we'll use gravity poppers!"

"But we don't have any!" Rex mentions. "We only have these useless stun rays."

"I . . . took some when nobody was around," Chimera admits, her voice bouncing as she runs full speed away from the approaching Vexors.

"Nice!" Anexichi exclaims.

"I don't think that's a good idea," Phaze warns. "I'll attract too much attention."

"What other option do we have" Chimera asks. "They're gaining on us."

"Anexichi, reach into my magpack and grab a grenade!" Chimera shouts.

As the recruits sprint through the fields, Anexichi opens Chimera's bag and tries to retrieve one of the gravity grenades.

"It's kind of hard to get with you shaking up and down," Anexichi says to Chimera.

"I'd love to slow down . . . but that's not really an option right now!" Chimera responds, her voice fluctuating with the steps of her sprint.

"Alright, I got one!" Anexichi exclaims, pulling out a small round blue ball with several glowing lights inside. "Now what?"

"Set it for grid mode!" Rex instructs.

"How do you do that?" Anexichi asks.

"Let me see it!" Rex commands.

Anexichi tosses the device to Rex. He presses several buttons on the device and a small glowing green square grid is projected from the device.

Just then, one of the Vexors leaps onto Phaze and knocks him to the ground. It begins to growl and bite Phaze, whose armor takes the brunt of the attack.

"Toss it here!" Chimera commands to Rex, as she stops to aid Phaze. "The rest of you take cover!"

Rex tosses the grenade to Chimera and then heads to safety with Anexichi. Chimera twists the side of the grenade and throws it toward the Vexors. Chimera presses a button on her boots and her boots light up. After a few seconds, there is a flash followed by a loud implosion.

Chimera grabs Phaze, as the area becomes gravity-less and the Vexors are sent sailing into the air. Chimera holds Phaze by the arm as he flies into the air as well. Her boots keep her anchored to the ground until the effects of the grenade subside and the Vexors come crashing back down to earth. The implosion disrupts the surrounding gravity field causing the area to shake.

"Nice!" Anexichi congratulates as the recruits come to Chimera's side.

Suddenly, two of the escort ships break away from the rear of the convoy, which was past the fields nearing the city limits of Tychon 3. The escorts begin to turn around, heading toward the explosion.

"Uh, guys, looks like we might have a bigger problem now," Rex proclaims, watching the escort ships from Roth's convoy as they begin to approach.

"Everybody, run! They haven't seen us, yet we need to get to those caves over there," Chimera orders, pointing to a small opening to the right.

"I told you grenades were a bad idea!" Phaze exclaims as Chimera and Rex help him up. They make break for it running faster now than before. The recruits' armor scrape and clank against the crystals as they race across the field. A third ship breaks from Roth's convey and begins toward Chimera.

The first of the three of the ships reaches the chrysillium fields.

"Shoot, I think we're made!" Phaze hollers.

"We have to make it to the cave!" Chimera exclaims. "And stay low!"

Chimera and the others dart to the mound of uprooted crystals that form a cave-like shelter trying to remain out of sight. They reach the mound, and hunker down under the crystals, hoping to avoid being spotted.

One of the ships hovers directly above.

"Did they see us?" Phaze asks.

"Quiet!" Chimera warns. The recruits remain hidden, as the Grey ships lurks close.

"Look, over there!" Anexichi points out.

Chimera turns and sees Caitiff huddled down nervously under another fallen crystal.

"Caitiff!" Chimera shouts.

He doesn't respond, and Chimera calls again, "Caitiff, over here!"

Caitiff hears Chimera and glances toward her.

"Chimera?" Caitiff hollers.

"Yes, come quick!" Chimera directs.

Caitiff is hesitant, but eventually trudges over to Chimera.

Anexichi and Phaze crawl over to Chimera's position where Caitiff approaches crouched and still shaking.

"Why did you leave us?" Phaze asks.

"Everybody, quiet," Chimera whispers. "The crystals should

block them from tracking us but they may send drones."

Caitiff looks up and sees the ships searching. One of the ships emits a beam of light that scans the area. The ship then resonates a pinging sound.

"This is not good," Phaze whispers.

"No no no," Caitiff cries. "We have to get out of here!" he pleads as he rises up.

"Caitiff, wait!" Chimera exclaims.

Ignoring Chimera's advice, Caitiff turns and tries to sprint away again.

"It's not clear ye . . ." Chimera begins, but before Chimera can finish her sentence the ship lowers a turret from its bow. The turret turns toward Caitiff and fires a laser that hits the ground. The blast throws Caitiff into the air, and he falls back down with a loud thud. The ship remains for a few more moments, before flying off.

"You guys, stay here I'm gonna check on Caitiff!" Chimera demands.

"Rex is a med in training, he can help," Anexichi announces.

Chimera and Rex run to Caitiff dropping to the ground to check his pulse. Caitiff lies on the ground motionless. His armor damaged and cracked in several places.

"He's still alive," Rex proclaims. "His leg is in pretty bad shape, but he's still alive."

"It, it hurts," Caitiff mutters, writhing with pain.

"You're gonna be ok. Stay with us," Chimera reassures.

Anexichi and Phaze arrive accompanying Chimera and Rex.

"We need to get out of here so we can call for an evac," Chimera suggests.

Rex reaches in his pack and grabs a tube of blue gel. He spreads the gel across Caitiff's wounds and the wounds begin to coagulating.

"Let's get out of here so we can radio for help and get to an extraction point," Chimera says.

Chimera, Rex, Anexichi and Phaze lift Caitiff and carry him out of the chrysillium fields. Reaching a clearing, they set Caitiff down as Rex continues tending to his wounds. None of the recruits notice two of the other escort ships quietly slipping by directly above. One of ships lowers its turrets, similar to the first attack. The turret turns toward the recruits and begins to power up.

Chimera rises and the recruits watch as Chimera stands over injured Caitiff. Two Grey ships hover overhead, preparing to fire.

Inside one of the escort ships, a Grey speaks through a holographic intercom.

"Five more Reds in sight, orders?" the Grey in the cockpit inquires.

Chimera removes her helmet, looks up to the sky and closes her eyes. Suddenly there is a loud boom, but not from above. Chimera opens her eyes.

"Look!" Phaze exclaims.

Out of the clouds, emerges the Nuance with its bay door open. Inside, Sphinx and Syrex stand. The Nuance fires plasma rockets and sonic atomizers at the Grey ships, striking them. One of the ships is crippled and comes crashing down. The Zeta then appears, joining the fight. The Zeta descends and lands in an open area to the right of the field as the Nuance remains above in a defensive position. As the bay door opens, Ghost appears.

"We received your message from Syrex!" Ghost hollers.

Sphinx and the other Enforcers in the Nuance continue combat with the remaining Grey ships. The second Grey ships is struck and fires back, hitting the Nuance in the rear before it also retreats into the distance followed by the third ship.

"Is everyone ok?" Ghost asks, stepping off the Zeta.

"Caitiff's injured. I think the rest of us are ok," Syrex replies.

Medreps exit the Zeta, coming to assist Caitiff. They remove his armor and provide Caitiff with oxygen.

Ghost approaches Chimera, looking around at the chaos.

"What happened?" Ghost inquires.

Chimera is silent.

"Prepare for extraction," Ghost proclaims. "We'll discuss this back at AzurNu."

The Medreps carry Caitiff aboard. Chimera and Anexichi limp back onto the ship carrying each other with Phaze right behind them.

Ghost also reboards the ship.

Within moments, the Zeta is airborne and heads east back toward AzurNu.

Onboard, all are silent as the Zeta quietly flies home. After landing, the recruits are sent to the medical infirmary for examination. All the recruits head to the infirmary, except for Chimera.

Noticing she is walking toward the opposite direction, Ghost calls to Chimera, "Have the medics at the infirmary check you out before you head to debriefing, recruit."

"I'm fine," Chimera replies back.

"Fine?" Ghost snaps. "No, you're not fine! That's the problem. It seems you think you can decide which commands to follow and not follow. You seem to think you can make your own rules, as with today's mission."

"That is not the case at all, Lead Master sir," Chimera responds.

"The rules of engagement were to initiate no contact under any circumstance!" Ghost explains.

"But sir," Chimera begins.

"Quiet," Ghost exclaims. "This is not a discussion! You were given specific instructions. This was a reconnaissance mission. You were not to jeopardize your position, your team's position, or the mission! Because of your actions, one recruit is severely injured, our asset has been compromised and you were almost de atomization."

Chimera is silent.

"You are hereby placed on probation," Ghost announces. "Any further failure to adhere to the commandments of Enforcement, will result in your removal from the program. You are dismissed for now."

Chimera returns to her dorm, skipping the debriefing. She lies in her bunk, writing in her holopad. Suddenly, there is a buzz at the door. Chimera hops down, and opens the door.

"May I enter?" Sphinx asks.

Chimera nods, and walks back to her bunk.

"You missed the debriefing," Sphinx states.

"Yea, I just needed some time," Chimera responds to Sphinx.

"Are you ok, recruit?" Sphinx questions.

Chimera nods again

"Anexichi told us what you did," Sphinx says. "I know having to choose between following orders and saving a life is no easy decision."

Chimera is silent for several moments. "I, I need to clear my mind. How can I request a temporary leave of absence and get permission to visit Infinity?" she asks.

"In half a planetary rotation, all recruits will be allowed provisionally exit of Enforcement grounds," Sphinx answers. "You will be allowed to visit the general areas of AzurNu for four rotations."

"Really?" Chimera questions.

"Really, recruit," Sphinx answers. "Keep your head high and your low profile low. I see infinite potential in you." He then turns and exits Chimera's dorm. After the door closes, Chimera returns to her bunk and lies down again.

Half a planetary rotation passes as Chimera trains harder than ever. Since the RothGrey mission, Chimera begins to build a relationship with Anexichi. Caitiff is expelled from Enforcement for deserting his team. Syrex is paired with PhazeRed and in Phaze's place, Chimera is chosen to sync with Anexichi.

Chimera and Anexichi begin speaking and realize they have more in common than in difference. Being synced together in training, Chimera slowly befriends Anexichi.

Another half a planetary rotation passes and the recruits' four rotational freedom arrives.

The day of the provisional release, Chimera is in her dorm cleaning her gear when there is a ring on the audio speaker system. The ring is followed by an announcement.

"Enforcements recruits, following the completion of this announcement, your four rotation leave will begin. You will be permitted to travel anywhere within AzurNu. You must be back by the 30th degree of the 4th rotation. Failure to do so will eliminate you from the program. There is a hidden room that shifts its location every three degrees. When it is time for you to report back to enforcement you will receive a message with the location of the secure room. You will receive detailed instructions on how and when to enter the room. All recruits must return their Enforcement wristcoms prior to exiting the grounds. Your personal wristcoms will be returned to you temporarily. If asked, you are to instruct your acquaintances and family that your absence was due to mandatory quarantine. Do not discuss anything Enforcement related, either in person or via your wrist communicator. Should you fail to adhere to this command, you will be eliminated from the program and may also be sent to detainment, depending on the nature of the information you leak. We are watching. Now, you will all report to the briefing room for your wristcom and exit pass. When your *temporary identification device* or T.I.D is scanned in and you receive your personal wristcom, you may exit. Thank you for your cooperation," the announcement concludes, and another ring sounds.

Chimera hurries to the briefing room as instructed. She leaves her enforcement wristcom and a drone brings Chimera her original wristcom. After exiting, Chimera turns down the hall toward the exit location when she sees Anexichi.

"Hey," Anexichi remarks.

"Hey," Chimera responds

"What do you have planned for your leave?" Anexichi questions.

"Me? . . . meditate," Chimera responds. "I'm gonna go to infinity and meditate. Maybe connect with some friends. What about you?"

"I'm actually gonna stay here at Enforcement," Anexichi admits.

"What, you don't have friends or family that wanna see you?" Chimera inquires. "What about Nya?"

"I haven't been here at Enforcement long enough to miss her," Anexichi says, laughing a bit.

Chimera chuckles.

"Do you miss your mother?" Anexichi questions. "You haven't spoken to her since you've been here at Enforcement."

"It's been longer than that," Chimera reveals. "We had a fight before I came here. We weren't on good terms . . . I haven't spoken to her since."

"Wow," Anexichi says. "Don't you want to at least let her know you're ok . . . and make sure she is? Existence is short, you should never take the ones that matter for granted."

"So why don't you take your own advice and visit Nya?" Chimera jokes.

"I . . . need to prepare for the big test coming up," Anexichi responds.

"Very responsible," Chimera states. "Well, I'm gonna go. See you in a few rotations?"

"Yea," Anexichi proclaims. "Take care."

The two raise their palms to each other and then part ways. Chimera heads to the processing room. She is met by an agent who places a visibility helmet on her head, disabling her from seeing or hearing anything. Chimera is then led onto a gravity mover, a small hovering platform. The gravity mover hovers Chimera down a corridor to a hidden exit.

Chimera is placed in another room, where she feels some vibration that lasts a short while. After the vibration ceases, her helmet unlocks. Chimera removes it and looks around. The room is dark except for a small door panel with a tiny tube protruding from it.

"Please breathe into the tube," a voice in the room instructs.

Chimera approaches the panel, takes a deep breath and exhales softly. A beep rings out as the word "Accepted" appears on the screen of the panel.

The door opens, and Chimera finds herself in a very narrow hallway. She continues forward and reaches another door. Her body is scanned and the door opens. Chimera exits the hallway and sees other Reds shuffling back in forth. She's once again across from the stadium where she was kidnapped.

Chimera quickly turns and walks back toward the *RedLine* station. After reaching the *Create* Station, Chimera heads to Infinity. Outside of Infinity, the water inside the gravity pool circulates slowly as it floats. Near the entrance of Infinity, there is also a sculpture of the infinity symbol, adorned in gold. The front facade of Infinity is a glass-like material, revealing the three interior levels of the facility.

Being the latter part of the planetary rotation, there are a fair amount of Reds shuffling to and from Infinity. Chimera approaches and stops at the gravity pool, letting the water, which is believed to be mystical, cleanse her hands. She then walks to the entrance of Infinity.

As Chimera enters, she passes through a changing field. Her clothes are instantaneously transformed to white leggings and a white long-sleeved top.

After crossing the changing field, Chimera walks to the entryway of the second floor. A sign at the entryway reads "Meditation Level." At the entryway, small cloud-like cushioned platforms carry Reds up and down the meditation deck. Chimera steps atop one of the clouds and is gently carried up to the meditation floor. Reaching the top, Chimera steps off the platform onto the meditation level.

Catching wind of the change in scent, Chimera takes a deep breath.

"I missed that smell of Sychar trees and ibus flowers," Chimera announces, exhaling.

"You know the air here is ten times more pure here than anywhere else here at AzurNu," a stranger with a long white beard proclaims to Chimera. She glances around to see if there is another Red the stranger was speaking to.

"Excuse me?" Chimera questions.

"It's the purest air in AzurNu," the stranger repeats. "The purer the air, the purer the mind. It's the only way to reach singularity."

"Thank you for that invaluable information," Chimera acknowledges, as she slowly steps away.

The sound of meditation music plays faintly throughout the floor. There are hundreds of tent-like domes setup for Reds to meditate in. Each tent is lit with a red or green light atop the roof: green denoting available, red denoting occupied.

Chimera steps into a green lit tent, kneels down, closes her eyes and begins to clear her mind. After relaxing her thoughts, she begins to meditate. Chimera remains in mediation for two degrees.

After reaching an elevated state, Chimera returns to her regular consciousness and slowly opens her eyes. She reorients herself and stands up, stepping outside the tent. She walks toward the cloud platforms to descend. Stepping back onto a cloud, Chimera is lowered to the first level where she steps into the main lobby. Chimera is heading toward the exit of infinity when a voice calls her from behind.

"Chimera!" the voice calls.

She turns around, recognizing the voice.

"Athos!" Chimera exclaims. "How've you been? We haven't seen each other in forever."

"Yea, you just kind of disappeared," Athos says. "What happened?"

"Well I," Chimera begins, and stops when she notices the bearded stranger from upstairs approaching.

"What?" Athos questions, turning around.

The stranger passes and continues toward the exit.

"Nothing," Chimera begins. "I thought I saw something."

"Oh," Athos replies.

"Like I was saying, you wouldn't believe me if I told you,"

Chimera eludes.

"Try me," Athos replies.

Just then, the stranger crosses Chimera's path once again.

"Just my luck, I was placed on a mandatory quarantine for examination," Chimera explains, watching the stranger fade into the crowd.

"What, did you have some sort of virus?" Athos jokes, stepping back.

"Of course not!" Chimera exclaims. "It was a mandatory examination, like tribunal duty. Everybody has to do it at some point."

"Really?" Athos asks. "I've never heard that."

"Yea," Chimera replies. "They confirmed my body is cleansed. I was here making sure my mind was cleansed now."

"Makes sense," Athos responds. "Well I'm glad you're released now."

"Same here," Chimera answers back. "And what about you, what are you doing here again? I bumped into you here last time."

"Me, I come to the Dedication level every day. I usually finish up around this degree," Athos explains. "That's why I was surprised to see you here."

"Understandable," Chimera acknowledges, looking around to see if the stranger returned.

"Were you waiting for someone?" Athos questions.

"Huh?" Chimera asks, too distracting to hear the question

Athos chuckles a bit. "Are you ok?"

"Yea, yea I'm good," Chimera confirms. "I just have a lot on my mind."

"Well I actually brought a close comrade of mine," Athos begins. "Hopefully you don't have too much on your mind. I wanted to introduce you to him."

"Maybe after I head back to my dorm and freshen up," Chimera offers.

"Well that's actually him right there," Athos announces, pointing behind Chimera.

Chimera turns to see a tall Red with green eyes approaching.

"Chimera this is PhoenixRED," Athos announces. "Phoenix this is ChimeraRed. Phoenix is part of the Tychon Broadcasting Group. He's a creator."

"Tychon Broadcast Group?" Chimera asks.

"Yea, we create," Phoenix declares.

"What do you create?" Chimera inquires.

"Music, art, stories, culture . . . everything that defines Reds," Phoenix states.

"I dig that," Chimera responds. "You look a little familiar, have I seen you before?"

"Um, most likely not," Phoenix replies. "I live south of Azure in the Techno region. At TBG headquarters, I rarely make it over here to AzurNu. Athos's been pressing me to check out a creator he told me about so I had to make it over."

"What's it like over there?" Chimera questions. "In the Techno region?"

"Fun, different, creative . . . It's like a whole other planet," Phoenix remarks.

"And with a lot less politics than AzurNu," Athos adds

"But why separate from AzurNu?" Chimera questions. "I'm just curious, can't you do here what you do there?"

"Three reasons," Phoenix begins. "Number one, AzurNu has everything except the main ingredient . . . Individuality. There are too many rules and uniformness here, not enough individuality."

"Yea, the equalization system here is pretty unfortunate," Athos chimes in.

"Equalization?" Chimera inquires

"Yea, every AzurNu citizen earns an equal amount in any occupation program," Athos replies. "It's a noble gesture, but just doesn't work."

"Fair enough," Chimera admits. "What's reason two?"

"Number two is risk," Phoenix announces. "If we're all here, what happens if AzurNu is destroyed, or if a virus spreads?"

"Good point, especially since she's just been quarantined," Athos jokes.

Chimera shoves Athos. "Alright, and what's the third reason?"

"Foundation," Phoenix answers. "We've built so much at

Broadcast central that it wouldn't make sense to pick up and leave."

"I definitely get it," Chimera states.

"And the whole *Sol Exitus* things," Phoenix adds. "Feels a bit like detainment."

Chimera laughs.

"You should come down," Phoenix offers. "They usually don't let outsiders in, but you have a personal invitation from me or Athos."

"I appreciate the invite," Chimera acknowledges.

"Actually, you should come tonight," Phoenix adds.

Chimera thinks for a moment.

"I can't . . . not tonight at least," Chimera replies. "But thanks for the invitation."

"No problem," Phoenix responds. "It was great meeting you. I'm gonna get out of here. We're headed back to Broadcast Central."

"It was nice meeting you as well," Chimera answers back. "Maybe I'll see you again . . . and take you up on that offer."

"Definitely," Phoenix replies.

"Ok Chi," Athos says. "I'll see you later, be well"

"Be well," Chimera replies to Athos

Athos and Phoenix disappear into the crowd.

Chimera walks to the exit. As she is about to pass the changing field her wristcom rings. She looks down and an angry expression slides across her face. Chimera ignores the call and continues out of Infinity. She heads out into the courtyard and continues on her way.

"I need to get a good meal and some rest," Chimera mentions to herself.

Heading out of the *Create* zone toward *GRUB*, Chimera suddenly remembers something. "Nexus!" she exclaims.

On her way to the hover-rail station, Chimera pulls up her wristcom and dials Nexus. After a few rings a voice answers on the other end.

"Hello?" Nexus answers.

"Hey, how . . . are you?" Chimera asks.

"I'm good," Nexus responds. "Why do you sound like that?"

"Sound like what?" Chimera inquires.

"Like you're about to say something bad," Nexus responds.

"Well . . ." Chimera begins. "I know I haven't talked to you since the stadium and . . ."

"What do you mean?" Nexus questions. "We spoke earlier today!"

"We did?" Chimera asks confused. "I mean, yea I know we did but . . . we haven't talked since then.

"Who's been talking to everybody while I was gone?" Chimera mutters to herself, covering the receiver on her wristcom.

"What was that?" Nexus asks.

"I didn't say anything," Chimera declares.

"I'm just confused," Nexus states. "We talked about this before and like I told you, it's fine. You've been a little different since the stadium. I haven't seen you, and every time I talk to you since then, it's been different. "

"Different in what way?" Chimera asks

"Errr . . . I don't know," Nexus mentions. "Distant I guess."

Chimera begins to grin. "Yea yea, everything is good. I've just, been in quarantine."

"Is everything ok?" Nexus questions

"Yea, everything's ok," Chimera acknowledges.

"Well, what are you doing tonight?" Nexus inquires. "I want to see you."

"Tonight?" Chimera begins. "I kind of have to catch up on a lot of stuff."

"What about tomorrow, mid rotation?" Nexus asks.

"Tomorrow?" Chimera begins. "That would maybe work, except I have a meeting with the Citizens Bureau for my residency."

"And in the evening?" Nexus asks, sounding slightly frustrated.

"Evening?" Chimera says, thinking for a few moments. "Um . . . that might work if I don't have a meeting with Omega."

"You know, I'm really trying to make this work," Nexus proclaims. "If I shouldn't, just let me know."

"It's not that," Chimera explains. "I'm really not good at all of this, and like I said, I have a lot going on. Things I can't really talk about."

"I understand," Nexus mentions, "but that's what I'm here for."

"You just have to trust me," Chimera states.

"I do!" Nexus declares. "That's why I wanted to take you to my secret spot tomorrow. Somewhere I know you'll like."

"Secret spot where?" Chimera asks.

"I can't tell you, or it wouldn't be my secret place," Nexus teases.

"Urg," Chimera grunts. "I hate surprises!" she replies, grinning. Nexus chuckles.

"Well I gotta go," Chimera exclaims to Nexus through her wristcom, entering the hall of *GRUB*. "Comm me tomorrow."

"Ok, talk to you tomorrow," Nexus replies.

Chimera ends the call and steps up to one of the ordering queues of *GRUB* called Sukura. In the Sukura, circulating holograms of various food items pass on a revolving conveyor with a hollow tube in the center.

Chimera scrolls through the Sakura before selecting an order. Touching the hologram of her food choice, the cuisine slowly materializes in the tube. Once it's complete, Chimera grabs her meal and heads to her dorm. When Chimera reaches the door, she takes a deep breath and enters.

CHAPTER EIGHT

A Rift In the Stars

The room is empty with no sign of StarChild. Chimera seats herself at the supper table and begins eating her meal. After finishing up, Chimera plays Virtualization, a board game where digital atomic elements are given to players who try to create an object greater than their opponents. After finishing, Chimera readies herself for bed. It is about the 29th degree and all is quiet, as the time nears the last degree of the day.

"I have a long day ahead tomorrow, I'm gonna call it a night," Chimera says to herself.

She heads to her sleep pod and sets the sleep setting to number four. Afterwards, she climbs in and closes the door. A light mist of chemicals is released inside the pod and within moments Chimera is fast asleep.

It is the 2nd degree of early morning when Chimera is awakened by a ruckus outside her pod. She opens her sleep pod to find StarChild stumbling into the room with Dug holding her up.

"Is everything ok?" Chimera asks.

"Yea, everything is ok, she's just had too much Zile," Dug responds.

"Oh, now juu wanna to talk to me?" StarChild mumbles, slurring her words.

"What do you mean?" Chimera asks.

"You dis-o-ppear for rotations and hardly speak to me," StarChild begins. "Now you wanna talk?"

"StarChild, you're not yourself right now, I think you should get some sleep," Dug suggests.

"No, she needs to heer this!" StarChild exclaims.

StarChild turns back to Chimera.

"You're supposed to be my bestest friend, but we don't even hang out n-e more! You're so focused on everything else and then you disappear! You forgot I'm the one that's been here for you since day one!" StarChild exclaims.

"It's not like that, Star," Chimera remarks. "Things have been crazy and then I had mandatory quarantining."

"I've had a lot going on too, but I didn't cut you out," StarChild snarls.

"I never meant to neglect you," Chimera declares. "O infinity, I sound like a mother right now. Look, I just had some other things I needed to take care of."

"Oh . . . so now the truth comes out!" StarChild proclaims. "I just don't matter anymore!"

"Star, that's not what I'm saying," Chimera clarifies.

"No, that's exactly what you . . ."

"Babe, I really think you should get some rest and talk about this tomorrow," Dug urges, interrupting StarChild.

"I want to talk about it now, before she disappears for good!" StarChild demands.

"What is that supposed to mean?" Chimera questions.

"It means maybe your priorities are off," StarChild states.

"Maybe we're going in different directions!" Chimera replies. "I really need to find myself and my place here. I don't think you know what it's like to be a stranger among your own kind. You've always been here for me, I'm not saying you haven't, but I just need time to figure everything out"

"Are you breaking up with me?" StarChild asks sarcastically.

"I think we should go, c'mon StarChild," Dug pleads, trying to lead StarChild away.

"No, it's ok. I'll go," Chimera interjects, as she grabs her wristcom, magpack and boots and storms out of the room.

Chimera heads to the other end of the living quarters and stops at dorm 425. She buzzes the panel and waits. Inside, Athos checks the x-ray door scanner and sees Chimera through the door. He opens the door.

"Hey, what's going on?" Athos whispers.

"Hey Athos, sorry to wake you up," Chimera remarks. "StarChild is flushed and we got into it. I really don't want to go back."

"Don't worry about it, come in," Athos offers. "You can take my sleep pod."

"It's fine, I'll crash on the floor," Chimera says.

"It's ok, I'll sleep on the floor," Athos mentions.

"No, I don't want to trouble you," Chimera explains. "I just needed a place to crash."

"You're not troubling me at all . . . and I'm not going to let you sleep on the floor," Athos proclaims. "So you might as well set the sleep pod to your preference and make yourself comfortable. Can I get you something to eat, drink?"

"No, I'm good thanks. Have a long day tomorrow. I really just need to get some rest."

"Fair enough," Athos mentions. "Holler if you need anything."

"What about you? Where are you gonna sleep?" Chimera inquires.

"I'm gonna grab some sleep gear from the closet and probably catch some sleep on the tarpit," Athos states.

"Tarpit?" Chimera asks.

"Yea, the ground," Athos clarifies.

"Got it," Chimera confirms.

"Have a good night," Athos bids.

"Good night, thank you again, Athos," Chimera replies, still clutching her bag.

Chimera awakes around the 5th degree. Athos is sitting on the ground, watching a hologram on his projection system.

"You're still up?" Chimera questions, rubbing her eyes.

"Yea, I don't sleep much," Athos answers.

"I know what you mean. I had a pretty weird dream last night; it was hard for me to get back to sleep," Chimera mentions.

"What was the dream about?" Athos inquires.

"I had a dream that AzurNu was attacked," Chimera explains.

"I'm glad it was just a dream," Athos confirms.

"Me too," Chimera agrees. "Is it okay if I freshen up in your vanity pod?"

"Of course, go ahead," Athos responds. "Just set it to silent mode. I don't want to wake anyone in my dorm."

"Ok," Chimera whispers. She sets the pod to silent and then quietly steps inside. She freshens up and changes, emerging in an all black jumpsuit.

"Feeling colorful I see," Athos retorts.

Chimera laughs. "Thanks again for letting me stay the night and offering me your sleep pod. I think you're the nicest Red I've met here."

"It's no problem," Athos mentions, blushing a little. "Are you leaving now? It's still early."

"Yea, I have a busy day today," Chimera answers back. She bids Athos farewell and then exits the dorm.

Stepping into the main corridor, Chimera begins to walk. She circles the entire living quarters area several times in deep thought. It is almost the 8th degree when Chimera leaves the living quarters wing aboard the *RedLine*, headed to NorthEnd Station. Entering the Council zone, Chimera meets with the Bureau of Foreign Affairs regarding her residency status at AzurNu.

On Tychon 3, Lord Prychon sits with SchilarkGrey in his solar room, a white and grey room with egg-shaped seats, a large oval desk in the center, a wall of tiny Unupentium cubes and metallic lined windows that overlook the city.

"I want all conspirator Reds found and detained," Prychon says to Schilark. "Nintius contains the holofile with all subjects. AuroraRED is a priority. And the escaped youngling. Do what you have to, and get me Luna and Mercury Grey."

"The bounty hunters?" Schilark asks.

"Correct, I want all subjects alive," Prychon declares.

"I will do my best, Lord, but Seyfert is a savage. He kills and maims for the thrill of it. It will be no easy feat to acquire these subjects with Seyfert alongside. I think Tachyon is best suited to accompany me on this request."

"You will need Seyfert's talent," Prychon assures. "Take them both, I trust you will be successful in your quests. That is all."

Just then, another Grey arrives. "Sire, Racheon is here with updates on the progress of the Grey Army," the Grey announces.

"And who might you be?" Prychon inquires.

"I am your new messenger KatoGrey," the Grey reveals.

"Very well, Kato, invite Racheon in," Prychon confirms.

"Good day, sire," Schilark bids as he makes his way to the exit. "It best be good news," Schilark whispers to Kato as he passes.

"And Schilark," Prychon begins.

"Yes sire," Schilark replies, turning toward Prychon.

"Have all subjects, save those I specifically mentioned, brought directly to detainment once they are captured," Prychon commands.

"Yes my Lord," Schilark replies and continues on to exit.

Racheon then enters, greeting Lord Prychon. Prychon turns and begins toward the other side of the room.

"What news do you bring for me this rotation, Racheon?" Prychon questions.

"We're seeing moderate victories in the Keplex system, sire," Racheon proclaims.

"You come bearing news of moderate victories?" Prychon remarks, turning to Racheon.

"Sire, the Grey Army has completed their retrofits on our primary units," Racheon explains. "They are now ready for battle. I assure you these reinforcements will provide much needed support to our forces. Also of notable report, our Galactic scouts have reported a large presence forming in the Zeta Reticula system."

"Corrillians?" Prychon questions.

"More than likely, sire" Racheon confirms. "Another attack may be imminent."

"Have you spoken with Altair?" Prychon asks.

"Yes sire," Racheon confirms.

"Is the new weapon ready then?" Prychon snaps, as he glances at a golden hourglass resting on one of the rooms' tables.

"Not yet, sire," Racheon replies. "Without the blade of Kybon, progress has been . . . delayed."

"Do not talk to me about what we do not have," Prychon snarls, snatching the hourglass off the table. "I need results now! You are leader of the magnificent Grey Army. Your duty is to decimate all that oppose. To do this we need weapons; weapons far greater than our enemies."

"This is no doubt true, sire . . . however, perhaps our efforts would be best spent enhancing our current weapon systems instead of seeking a mystical blade that exists in the mind of a Necromancer?" Racheon suggests.

"She is no necromancer!" Prychon retorts, quickly turning to glare at Racheon. "You will be well to watch your tone, Captain."

"My apologies, sire, I mean not to offend," Racheon states. "Please understand, overseeing war with the Corrillians as well as with Reds is no easy feat for me or the Grey Army. The Reds are not as weak as you believe them to be."

"The Anti-Automally Committee will handle the Reds," Prychon confirms, turning away from Racheon again.

"At the expense of the Army?" Racheon argues. "Soldiers of the committee are taken from my regiments . . . as well as ships and weapons for this crusade. I beg you to."

"Thank you for your report, Captain," Prychon interrupts before Racheon can finish. "That will do for now."

"Yes," Lord Racheon confirms, as he turns and exits.

On the outskirts of Tychon 1, sits a secret RED refugee reserve. The rotation nears the 18th degree as Reds of all ages prepare for supper inside the reserve.

As the evening degree grows closer, four Grey saucers arrive, stopping near the factory.

Inside one of the saucers, Seyfert and Caulem survey the area through a holographic screen aboard the saucer.

"Release the reconnaissance device" Seyfert orders.

Caulem manipulates the holographic screen and moments later a drone is released from the saucer. The drone floats down and scans the area. After its scan, the drone floats enters the factory through a smoke-shaft. Gliding into the main floor of the factory, it activates a transparent outer-skin becoming seemingly invisible. The drone makes its way through the factory, scanning all the inhabitants of of the reserve. Seyfert and Caulem monitor the scan of the drone, as it makes its way through the factory, examining the inhabitants.

"It Appears our source was accurate" Seyfert declares

"No sign of her here" Caulem announces.

The drone completes its scan, and floats back up the chimney stack, returning to the saucer.

"Very well, proceed with eradication Seyfert declares"

"Eradication?" Cauelum responds. "Our orders are to capture, kill only those who offer resistance."

"Kill them all," Seyfert declares to Caulem. "A.A.C command units, terminate all Reds on site" Seyfert instructs the other ships, over the saucers transmission system.

"Confirmed" the pilots of the other three saucers confirm as they begin to prepare their weapons.

Inside the factory, the peace of supper is shattered as Grey saucers begin firing on the factory. Streaks of lasers slice through walls and obliterate Reds as they try to scurry for cover. Several Reds try to fire makeshift weapons at the saucers in defense, but their weapons are no match for the saucers.

Inside the saucer, Seyfert grins, as the reflection of Reds being slaughtered on the monitor in front of him reflects inside his eyes.

A final shot from Seyferts seals the reserves fate, as the laser strikes a generator inside the factory and explodes. The resulting explosion ignites a chain reaction that causes the entire factory to erupt into flames. Screams of Reds are suddenly silence as the factory walls crumble down.

Seyfert glares at the holographic screen in front of him, waiting to see if any movement is visible.

"We are done here" Caulem announces, as he maneuvers the saucer up into the clouds and slowly hovers away.

After the remaining three saucers also depart, a young Red emerges from underneath a pile of fallen rubble, tattered and full of dirt. Still clutching a small toy, the child peers around at the once vibrant reserve, which is now silent.
"Mommy, daddy?" the child calls out, as she hugs the toy tightly.

Back at AzurNu, it is the 15th degree when Chimera emerges from the Foreign Affairs Bureau.

"That was extremely entertaining," Chimera remarks sarcastically.

From the Affairs Bureau, Chimera heads to the other side of the council wing to visit OmegaRed's chateau.

Chimera reaches the chateau and presses a button located to the right of the large gold entrance. As the door opens, Chimera steps forward into the courtyard. Between the courtyard and the main entrance is a moat. Chimera steps forward and looks down. The moat drops a few kilometers down to the heated core of AzurNu. Chimera is greeted by a narrow walkway, which is the only means of crossing the moat. Midway across the walkway, stands a guard station with an automated weapon turret. Two protector drones float about, guarding the entrance of the chateau.

"This should be fun," Chimera remarks, looking at the oddly shaped structures ahead of her.

Past the courtyard, Chimera spots Omega's compound comprised of a collection of cubes stacked on top of one another. The cubes are made of an organic, glass-like material that displays projections and information onto the walls of the cubes. There are three cubes stacked on the right and three on the left and one large cube in the center.

Chimera approaches the walkway, which is not yet extended. This leaves Chimera unable to cross the moat. Chimera steps through a security scanner at the foot of the walkway and is immediately scanned.

"No weapons detected," a voice alerts.

The security platform fully extends, allowing Chimera to enter. She walks across the walkway away from the courtyard and to the entrance of the chateau.

Reaching the entrance, the doors open and Omega greets Chimera. He is accompanied by two protector drones.

"So good to see you, Chimera," Omega announces.

"Good to see you too," Chimera responds, noticing a golden necklace holding a pendant with three vertical lines. As she glances at the necklace, Omega tucks it into his shirt.

"And where have you been might I ask? I haven't seen you in rotations."

"I've . . ." Chimera begins. "Nevermind, long story. This place is awesome though!"

"Here, let me give you the grand tour," Omega offers as he turns and begins to walk. As they enter center cube, TitanRED exits, accompanied by several soldiers. He glares at Chimera on his way out.

"What's wrong with him?" Chimera asks, referring to Titan.

"Don't pay him any mind," Omega states.

Chimera follows Omega past the front desk into the lobby.

"This is the grand lobby," Omega announces, with his arms spread open in grandiose manner. "This is the focal point, the entrance to my world. It's breathtaking, isn't it?"

"I've never seen anything like it," Chimera replies.

"The room up there on second floor," Omega announces, pointing to one of the cubes, "is the executive meeting room. That's where all the council members meet when we're not in the council wing."

Omega leads Chimera to the cube underneath the executive meeting room.

"PD - 7, PD - 17, cancel protection detail," Omega commands.

"Command confirmed," the two drones acknowledge.

"Activate patrol protocol," Omega instructs.

"Activating patrol protocol," the drones confirm, as they hover off back toward the main lobby.

Omega leads Chimera to a uniquely shaped red door. He puts his palm to the door and it opens.

"Welcome to my suite," Omega announces.

The suite is a large, open room lit by soft blue hues. There is minimal furniture in the room, but a cylinder-shaped piece of furniture with small white and black rectangles on it catches Chimera's eye.

"Is that a pianotron?" Chimera asks.

"Yes, yes it us," Omega declares proudly.

"I didn't know you play?" Chimera questions.

"I don't," Omega replies, chuckling a bit. "I just love the way it looks."

Chimera steps up to the pianotron and studies it. "Do you mind?" she asks.

"Go right ahead," Omega offers. "It hasn't been played for rotations."

Chimera begins to play several notes on the instrument. Powerful, choral sounds emanate from the instrument. Chimera takes a seat and becomes engrossed, attempting to arrange a set of melodic chords.

"Not bad, not bad," Omega announces, clapping his hands.

"You've played before?"

"This is the first time I've seen one up close," Chimera admits.

"Here, check this out," Omega suggests. He presses a button on his wristcom and the pianotron begins to play.

Omega's private quarters boasts a breathtaking view of AzurNu, visible from the left side of the cube. As the pianotron plays in the background, Chimera stares at the view.

"Come, there's more," Omega states, as the music begins to fade away.

Exiting the suite, Omega leads Chimera to the right side of the chateau.

"You see that that room to there?" Omega asks.

"Yea," Chimera answers.

"That's the broadcast center, where we make all our subterranean broadcasts. The room on the right is the staff quarters and above that is the executive guest suite. If you ever need a place to lay your head, you have an open invitation."

"I wish I would have known that yesterday," Chimera remarks.

"What makes you say that?" Omega asks.

"Nothing," Chimera replies. "Thanks, but I think this place is probably too fancy for my taste."

Omega chuckles, continuing the tour as he leads Chimera down another hall. "Well moving on, to the left over there is our very own library, and to the right is our executive control and communication room for AzurNu."

"What do you do there?" Chimera questions.

"We have the ability to control any and everything on AzurNu in that room," Omega responds. "The lights, irrigation, defense systems, even the oxygen levels."

"Wow," Chimera replies.

"No worry, it's in good hands," Omega assures. "And that room up over there, that's my office. That's actually where we'll be meeting, let's head up."

Chimera and Omega travel up a pair of stairs to Omega's office.

"Come in, come in," Omega exclaims.

Chimera follows Omega into the room.

"Judging by the dark attire you're wearing and the look in your eyes, I can tell you have a lot on your mind," Omega proclaims.

"Well," Chimera begins, "I wanted to come connect with you so I could thank you for that thing you did."

"What thing?" Omega asks.

"You know, the thing," Chimera repeats as she nods her head at Omega.

"I have no idea what you are talking about," Omega answers.

"Right . . ." Chimera responds smirking

"Can I ask you something?" Chimera questions.

"Of course, fire away," Omega replies.

"What is it like?" Chimera begins. "Being leader of AzurNu?

Knowing everybody depends on you and looks to you?"

"Well it's not easy," Omega admits. "Sometimes you must make decisions that extend beyond regret. It is a commitment that consumes you. It ceases to become something you do, and becomes something you are. It's a great sacrifice."

"Do you worry?" Chimera inquires. "Worry you'll do something wrong?"

"I worry about a lot of things," Omega answers. "The shortage of food, the threat of attack, the survival of my people. The key is to remain rational in time of crisis; to be brave in the eyes of your people even when the odds seem insurmountable and the danger is so real you can taste it."

"I like danger," Chimera replies. "I don't mind insurmountable odds. What I don't like is this feeling like an outsider. Have you ever felt like you don't belong among your own kind?"

"Every day," Omega remarks. "As an Automally, I am part of the enemy some Reds think. Can I be honest with you?"

"Please do," Chimera urges.

"The reality is there are no Automallies, no Hybrids, no Reds, no Greys . . . It's all an illusion. No matter where you're born, how you're re-born . . . or what planet you're from . . . we're all citizens of the universe. We're all connected."

Suddenly Chimera's wristcom rings. She looks down seeming agitated by the call. She ignores it, and returns her attention to Omega.

"Somebody bothering you?" Omega questions.

"No, it's Iona," Chimera responds. "We haven't spoken since the day I found out she lied to me."

Omega shakes his head. "Forgiveness is paramount. Sometimes the ones who love us the most, are the ones that hurt us the most . . . trying to protect us. She needs you more than you think."

"Needs me? How would you know?" Chimera questions. "She's always been so sure about everything."

Omega takes a deep breath. There is a long pause. "I know because . . . we used to be connected."

Chimera gasps, "What? Not true!" "Many rotations ago, before I was the Red I am today," Omega states. "Back when I still had a normal life."

Chimera is silent as she stands up. She walks to the other end of the room. Then she turns back toward Omega. "Why didn't she ever tell me?"

"I made her promise never to speak of it," Omega admits. "I wanted you and me to have a genuine connection, untainted by the past."

Chimera asks, "Tell me you're not my . . ."

"No," Omega interject.

"Do you know his name?" Chimera adds.

Omega is silent.

Chimera returns to the other side of the room and sits down next to Omega. The two begin to talk as Omega speaks with Chimera about the history of AzurNu, his connection to Iona and Tychon.

Several degrees past and it is the 20th degree when Chimera receives another call on her wristcom. She looks down and answers.

"Are we still on for tonight?" a voice asks, emitting from Chimera's wristcom.

"Yea, yea we are," Chimera replies as she glances at Omega shaking her head.

"Alright, I'll send you the coordinates," Nexus proclaims.

"Ok, be well," Chimera concludes, ending the call. She stands to her feet. "I didn't even realize how late it was. I got so caught up, I have an engagement I have to get to."

"Well I won't hold you," Omega says.

"I have one more question for you," Chimera mentions.

"Shoot," Omega acknowledges.

"What will become of AzurNu? Will we survive?" Chimera asks. "Why stay here, why not just go to Eden?"

"The future is not written," Omega proclaims. "Every day, the things we do build our tomorrow. We are exactly where we should be; when one star falls another rises. That's the way it was and will always be."

Chimera nods. The two bid farewell and Chimera is about to exit.

"Chimera, wait," Omega calls. "There's one more thing before you go. I have something for you."

"Something for me?"

Omega walks to the corner of the room and retrieves a small grey box from a chest. He brings the box to Chimera and hands it to her. Chimera opens the box, revealing a metallic bracelet with a small cube attached to it. On the top of the cube are three horizontal lines.

"It's beautiful. What is it for?" Chimera asks.

"This bracelet is a symbol; the key to you unlocking your gift," Omega explains. "It has been passed down for many generations to heirs of gifted nature. It was given to me by a very close friend, and now I entrust it to you."

"Thank you, Omega. I am forever grateful for the void you fill," Chimera states, seeming to hold back.

Chimera and Omega share a long embrace before bidding farewell again as Chimera heads out.

In a rush, Chimera stops at her dorm to grab something and then hurries to the coordinates Nexus sent her. She arrives at the location, an industrial space near the underground farms of AzurNu. Being the 20th degree, the corridors and hallways are filled with Reds walking to and from.

The location is a cycle jump, a parking hub for Reds to store their hoverbikes. Looking around, Chimera spots Nexus, waiting, next to a yellow hoverbike. He wears black pants with cushion-like attachments on the knees and thighs, and a black jacket.

"Hey!" Chimera announces.

"There you are!" Nexus exclaims, walking over to her. Nexus hugs Chimera before stepping back to admire her. "I see your intention was to match with me," Nexus says jokingly.

Chimera grins, and turns her head, watching several Reds pass.

"You look great!" Nexus says.

"Thanks," Chimera answers, smiling slightly. "So, what's the plan?" Chimera asks.

"Well, we're headed to the mouth of AzurNu. We'll exit from there. Have you ridden before?" Nexus inquires.

"A little bit," Chimera responds.

"Well, if you hop on my cycle, I'll take you to the really cool place I wanted to show you," Nexus offers.

"Sounds good, can I bring a friend?" Chimera questions.

"Uh, sure," Nexus states, sounding confused.

Chimera walks over to one of the cycle jumps, an automated retrieval system with parking racks for hoverbikes. She presses a button on her wristcom and a small disc emerges from the wristcom. She inserts the disc inside the panel of the cycle jump and waits. The large rubix cube-like system rotates one of its rows up, then two of its rows to the right, bringing one of the racks to the retrieval door. Chimera steps forward and pulls out a black oval case from the retrieval door. She places the case on the floor, presses a button on it with her foot and steps back.

The case suddenly expands and shifts into the midsection of a hoverbike. A seat and tail section materialize, followed by a bar that rotates laterally, forming a handle bar. A matte black hoverbike emerges after the transformation, powering on as it begins to hover.

"You ride?" Nexus exclaims, dumbfounded.

"Just a little," Chimera answers, winking at Nexus. "How else do you think I got here?"

Chimera hops onto her cycle.

Nexus stares at Chimera for several moments. "Wow, I'm impressed."

"You should be," Chimera proclaims. "But you said the mouth of AzurNu, are we leaving the city?"

"Just for a bit," Nexus announces. "Do you have a *Sol Exitus* point you can use to leave?"

"I do," Chimera responds.

"Are you ok with using it for this ride?" Nexus questions.

"I don't mind," Chimera replies. "But I should probably stop at my dorm again."

"You need something?" Nexus asks.

"More like need to drop off something. I didn't know we were leaving, and I shouldn't take it out the city."

"It's alright, they never search," Nexus confirms.

"Are you sure?" Chimera inquires. "I really don't feel like getting sent to detainment today."

"Yea, totally . . . you're good," Nexus promises. He hops on his hoverbike and then reaches down pulling out a pair of visor glasses. He puts the glasses on and then turns to Chimera.

"Follow me," Nexus instructs, as he presses a small button on his visor.

The glasses emit a light, scanning the contour of Nexus's head. A rubber like material begins to cover the 3-D scan of Nexus's head. After a moment, it hardens forming a helmet. He revs his cycle and begins to hover toward the mouth of AzurNu.

Chimera puts on her visor, activates it and begins to follow Nexus. The two reach the mouth of AzurNu, the city's exit dock for civilian Reds and non-aircraft transportation. At the exit, there are several exit passageways, each manned by a security guard station. Chimera and Nexus approach one of the security stations.

"Purpose for travel?" the guard inquires.

"Visiting a family member in the outer corridor," Nexus explains.

"Number of Reds in your party?" the guard asks.

"Two," Nexus declares, turning back to glance at Chimera.

The guard stares at Nexus for a bit, then looks at Chimera. "Alright, you guys just pull to the side for a sec and we'll have you on your way."

"Pull to the side, why?" Nexus questions.

"Random security check, nothing to be concerned about," the guard discloses. "Unless you're hiding something."

Chimera glares at Nexus who glances back at Chimera nervously.

"I think . . . I forgot the gift I was bringing for my agnate," Nexus announces, looking down into his bag.

"Not to worry, you can grab it as soon as we finish up," the guard proclaims. "Remove your bag please."

Nexus removes his bag and the guard checks it, shuffling through the contents. "Alright, you're good to go . . . please pull forward so I can check your guest next," the guard orders, waving Chimera forward.

Nexus pulls forward, as Chimera doesn't move.

"Ma'am, I'm gonna need you to pull forward," the guard reiterates.

"She's good she doesn't have anything," Nexus explains.

"I'm still gonna need to check," the guard repeats.

Chimera removes her bag and leans forward to hand it to the guard when she accidentally touches the throttle and accelerates into Nexus, bumping his hoverbike and dropping her bag. She hops off her bike and retrieves her bag. She then hands it to the guard.

"What's wrong with the younger generations these days?" the guard mumbles as he begins to search the bag. Suddenly a ruckus begins to the right of them as another guard begins yelling.

"We got a smuggler," the guard in the lane to the right of

Chimera and Nexus yells as a hoverbike speeds in past the guard station.

"Here you go, Miss," the guard exclaims handing the magpack back to Chimera. "You guys are free to go," he adds as he hops on a vehicle similar to a hoverbike and speeds of in the direction of the intruder.

Chimera and Nexus stare at each other for a few moments, and then erupt in laughter.

"Nice work," Chimera congratulates.

"Thanks, I thought crashing into me was a nice touch," Nexus adds.

Chimera laughs.

"Seriously, I have no idea how we got that lucky, but let's get out of here," Nexus instructs.

Chimera and Nexus ride through the passageway toward the exit elevators and wait for the door to open. After it opens, they hover onto the elevator. The elevator rises to the sub-surface level and stops. From there, Chimera and Nexus approach the exit transport system. Resembling a transparent rectangle floating on a track, the transport closes and begins to float silently away from the city.

Reaching the exit of AzurNu, there is a small monitoring station. Chimera and Nexus ride past the station to the exit door. The Red at the monitoring station opens the gate and the two ride onto the exit platform. As the door closes behind them, it is relatively dark except for a faint blue light. After a few moments, the blue light switches to red and a voice on an intercom announces, "Please stand clear, doors opening." After a short pause, a flood of light enters as the door to Tychon opens. Chimera and Nexus hover out into the warm Tychonian evening.

Nexus leads the way, hovering at a moderate pace. The two ride across the barren Tychonian desert keeping a watchful eye for potential threats. It is the 19th degree and the sun is setting. Two of the planet's moons peek above the horizon and the sky shines a reddish orange color as daylight slips away.

"Have you been this direction before?" Nexus asks, opening his visor and hollering over the sound of the wind rushing past their hoverbikes.

"You know I can hear you through your helmet comm right?" Chimera asks sarcastically.

"Yea, I knew that," Nexus retorts, adjusting the mouthpiece on his helmet as he closes his visor.

"And no, I haven't been this far north," Chimera responds. "I've been south, but never this way."

"This area is pretty uniform, mostly rock formations and mountains," Nexus explains. "Easy to get lost,"

"I see. I better stay close then," she mentions, as she opens up the throttle on her hoverbike and roars past Nexus. He opens up his throttle and tries to catch up with her.

"Where you going? You're supposed to be following me!" Nexus exclaims through his helmet.

"You gotta keep up!" Chimera declares.

"You don't even know where we're going," Nexus remarks, taunting Chimera as he weaves back and forth on his hoverbike, pretending to change directions.

Chimera eases off the throttle and lets Nexus reclaim the lead. The two ride for a third of a degree as the geography begins to change from bedrock to sand.

"We should slow down, there are a lot of ridges and desert combs in this area," Nexus warns.

Suddenly, Chimera receives a proximity alert on her hoverbike display. Looking down, she sees a large group of something approaching from the south. Before Chimera can utter a word, Nexus calls out to Chimera.

"Are you seeing . . ." Nexus begins.

"Yea," Chimera answers before Nexus finishes.

Chimera slows down and then comes to a complete stop. She hops off her cycle and turns on the telescopic view on her visor to get a look at the approaching objects. Nexus stops a bit ahead of Chimera, noticing she dismounted her hoverbike.

"What are you doing? Let's get out of here!" Nexus urges.

"I think you should take a look at this," Chimera suggests.

Nexus scrambles to turn on his telescopic view. Finally he activates it and sees the approaching objects are within meters of him.

Dozens of hoverbikes zoom by, almost knocking Nexus off his bike. Most of the bikes rush past before one stops near Chimera.

Turning on his intercom, the rider asks, "Are you guys ok?" through the loudspeaker in his helmet.

"Yea . . . what's going on?" Chimera questions. "Where's everybody going?"

"It's cycle night," the rider responds. "We're headed to Jupiter's crater. You're welcome to follow," he adds before accelerating off with the rest of the group.

"Let's follow them!" Chimera exclaims.

"But what about our . . ." Nexus begins.

Before he can complete his sentence, Chimera is back on her hoverbike, revving it.

"C'mon!" Chimera hollers at Nexus on her helmet comm, as she speeds off to catch up with the other riders.

Chimera and Nexus follow the group on a high-speed ride through the treacherous terrain of "No Redsland" till they arrive at an indentation in the ground.

As Chimera approaches a huge open space in the middle of the desert it becomes apparent that the indentation is a crater.

Seeing the Red that previously stopped and offered the invitation, Chimera grabs his attention and waves him over. The Red approaches.

"Hey, thanks for the invite."

"No problem," the Red responds. "I'm GeoRed by the way."

"I'm ChimeraRed, and this is Nexus," Chimera introduces.

"Good to meet you guys," Geo mentions.

"I've never heard of this place. Why is it called Jupiter's crater?" Chimera asks.

"Some debris from Jupiter drifted over and crashed down from space a long time ago," Geo explains. "Formed this impact crater."

"Who would have guessed?" Nexus retorts.

"Hover crews converge here at the crater once every planetary rotation to show off, hangout and do tricks with their hoverbikes," Geo reveals. "We customize our bikes and helmets to make them our own."

As Chimera glances around, one helmet catches her attention. It's the head of a Grey with Red facial tattoos.

Chimera and Nexus remove their helmets and watch as hoverbikes buzz back and forth with riders trying to outdo one another. One rider rides with his helmet off, vying for attention trying to top everyone else.

"I think I know that Red," Chimera acknowledges.

"That show off?" Geo remarks, pointing at the rider Chimera was referring to. "That's Solar. He's always looking for attention."

Solar notices Geo pointing at him and spots Chimera. He suddenly begins to increase his efforts to show off even more, jumping atop his hoverbike and riding it while standing.

Chimera and Nexus continue watching the cycle night spectacle when Chimera receives a call on her wristcom. So caught up in what was going on around her she nearly misses the call. Looking down, at the last beep, she answers.

"Give me a second," she says to Nexus. "I gotta take this." She moves away to a quieter location.

"Hello," Chimera answers.

"Greetings, Chimera," a voice on the other end begins.

"Omega?" Chimera exclaims. "This is unexpected."

"Listen very closely, Chimera, this is very important," Omega declares.

"Ok," Chimera acknowledges.

"I'll be brief, Chimera. I want you to meet an acquaintance of mine," Omega announces.

"Who?" Chimera asks. "And what's this about?"

"I just need you to trust me," Omega answers. "Time is of the essence. I'm going to send you coordinates, and you will meet with Liazo my chief communication officer at that location."

"Omega, I'd love to help, but I'm not in AzurNu right now," Chimera reveals. "And I'm not alone," she adds.

"I know," Omega replies.

"Really?" Chimera asks.

"We don't have a lot of time," Omega reiterates. "I need you to head to the coordinates I'm sending. This is very important."

"Ok, but what about Nexus," Chimera inquires.

"For your own safety and his, its best if you're alone," Omega warns.

"Is everything ok?" Chimera remarks.

"Everything is fine," Omega confirms. "I have to go now Chimera. We'll speak again shortly, safe travels and be well."

"Be well," Chimera states.

Chimera ends the call and heads back to Nexus.

"Nexus . . . I'm so sorry about this, but I have to go," Chimera remarks.

"Have to go?" Nexus exclaims.

"Yea," Chimera answers. "I was just contacted. Something came up and it sounds like it's urgent."

Nexus pauses for a moment.

"Do you realize, every time we've been out together, you've bailed on me?" Nexus asks.

"Nexus, it's not like that!" Chimera exclaims.

"If you never wanted to go out you could've just said that. It would've been a lot easier," Nexus remarks.

"Like I said it's not that . . . you have to believe me," Chimera explains. "I wish I could tell you everything, but I can't. It was Omega. Something really important came up."

"Omega, leader of the Council Omega?" Nexus inquires.

"Yea . . . Omega," Chimera replies. "I would explain but I have to go. I'll comm you, ok?"

"Um, alright." Nexus responds, "I'm not sure what to say."

"I'll explain everything to you as soon as I can." Chimera confirms. She hops on her hoverbike and puts her helmet back on. She loads the coordinates from Omega into her nav system and speeds off.

Solar is doing another trick atop his hoverbike. Seeing Chimera ride off, he becomes distracted and falls off his bike, landing on the ground.

Chimera continues toward her destination, slowing down several times to check her heading and surroundings.

"Is someone following me?" Chimera asks to herself, believing she notices something behind her. She glances to her rear periodically.

As Chimera passes the outer limits of No Redsland, she enters the border to Tychon 2. Approaching the coordinates, Chimera comes to a stop in front of an abandoned power conversion station. The station is an old, rundown facility, with rusting coverings. Chimera hops off her cycle and begins to search the area, cautiously.

Being the 21st degree, the sun has set and it is relatively dark. Suddenly a figure in the shadows moves. Chimera quickly removes her bag and retrieves a weapon. A Grey emerges from the shadows. Chimera aims the weapon at the Grey.

She is about to fire when a voice from behind her yells, "Please holster that weapon!"

Chimera turns to see Liazo appearing from behind one of the adjuncts of the power station.

"What is this?" Chimera questions, with her weapon still pointed at the Grey. "If this is a trap, you've got a fight on your hands."

"It's not a trap," Liazo declares. "Just calm down, Chimera. This is CorumGrey, who Omega wanted you to meet."

"Impossible, it's a Grey!" Chimera screams.

"Yes, but he's not like the others," Liazo explains. "His name is Corum and he is a representative for a high ranking member of the Grey Council and part of the rebirth of the S.U.N. They are secret supporters of Red coexistence. Corum has something he wants to communicate with you. You'll need to let him telecommunicate with you."

"Tell me this is dream," Chimera states. She stares at Liazo and Corum, as they stand before Chimera, waiting.

"This is too much!" Chimera states. "I won't do this!" she exclaims as she hops on her hoverbike. She powers it on.

"Chimera, wait!" Liazo calls. Omega wants to speak with you.

Liazo walks over to Chimera and hands her a small round speaker connected to his wristcom.

"Hello?" Chimera answers.

"Chimera," Omega begins. "I need you to trust me on this. You may not understand this, but I want . . . need you to trust me. We have the opportunity to do something that's never been done. Please do what Liazo and Corum ask of you. If not for me, for all Reds on Tychon."

"Are you really gonna put the weight of the entire Red race on my shoulders?" Chimera asks.

"Only because I trust you," Omega declares. "I can't think of a better choice on all of Tychon than you, Chimera."

Chimera is silent for several moments. "So, what do I have to do?"

"Corum will accompany you to a new location where you will be given instruction," Omega explains. "You have my word that you will be safe. Liazo will see to it personally. You do trust me, don't you?"

"I do," Chimera replies.

"Then please do not leave, you can do this," Omega urges.

"Ok," Chimera responds as she hangs up the call. She remains on her hoverbike, motionless. Then, she revs up the engine and cuts off the power. Chimera dismounts the hoverbike and walks over to CorumGrey.

"Just try and clear your mind," Liazo instructs.

"Easier said than done," Chimera replies.

"Greetings, Chimera," Corum begins to project telepathically. "I am CorumGrey, speaking on behalf of a technology master and great influencer of Grey governance."

"Wow, I can hear your words in my head!" Chimera exclaims.

"I can hear yours as well," Corum says to Chimera telepathically. "We believe we have something that will revolutionize life here on Tychon. Something we've been working on for many planetary rotations. We're on the brink of completing development but there is something that eludes us. An element to the equation that's missing. My employer has commissioned me to search for a lifeform with a more creative perspective to add the last piece of the puzzle. Omega believes that piece is you . . ."

"I doubt that," Chimera thinks.

"You disagree," Corum questions, reading Chimera's thoughts.

"I hate to break it to you, but uh . . . I was the worst in my symbols and equations course," Chimera states. "I'm no prodigy."

Liazo approaches her.

"Chimera, Omega was wise in his selection of you for this project. You must consider this if there is to be a revolution," Liazo declares.

"Revolution?" Chimera questions.

"Yes," Liazo responds. "Reds are being slaughtered by the hundreds each rotation. Greys have crossed Jacob's rift and are searching for Reds as we speak. Since the new decree was announced, it's been a bloodbath. Nomad camps, settler cities, even neutral separatist reservations have been massacred. If we do not fight now, there will be no Red race in the future."

Chimera contemplates her decision. "If I do this it will only be under one condition," Chimera announces as she closes her eyes for several moments, before opening them. "If I ever need something, you'll return the favor."

"Ion has already prepared retribution terms with Omega," Corum proclaims.

"Those are my terms, take it or leave it," Chimera replies sternly.

Corum glances at Liazo, who shrugs his shoulder.

Corum presses a small round clock-like device on his arm and begins speaking Tychonian. After a bit, he presses the button again and returns back to Chimera.

"We accept your terms," Corum projects to Chimera telepathically. He then hands her a holographic card. "This card contains the secret location to teTrad. It will also provide you access into the facility. You will travel in one of our ships that will be arriving shortly. You must leave your weapons onboard. Will you comply?"

"This is really out of my element, and there are too many unknowns," Chimera says. "But if this is our chance to build a new tomorrow, yes, I accept."

"Very well," Corum responds.

Within moments, a mid-sized tube-shaped craft arrives overhead, kicking up sand around the power station as it lands.

"We must move quickly," Corum telecommunications, heading toward the ship as its bay door opens.

Chimera turns to Liazo and bids him farewell. Then she boards the ship.

"Welcome to the Gallant," Corum projects to Chimera, as he motions for her to take a seat. The bay doors close and the ship lifts off, elevating quickly.

On Tychon 2, RothGrey stands pensive inside one of his massive business structures on Tychon 3. As he stands, viewing a map of Tychon, another Grey quietly enters.

"You summoned?" the Grey inquires, closing the door behind himself.

"Yes," Roth projects to the Grey telepathically. "Come, Mercari," Roth instructs, motioning for the Grey to come closer.

Mercari shuffles over to Roth, who is still examining the map.

"What do you see when you look at this map?" Roth asks Mercari telepathically.

Mercari studies the map for a bit. "All the business interests your syndicate operates here on Tychon?" Mercari remarks.

"No," Roth answers. "This map represents opportunity. I did not build this empire by putting affiliates in power and letting them do what they please. There is an order to the process, obligations to fulfill, a hierarchy to this system."

"I understand," Mercari states.

"When this hierarchy is disregarded new pillars must be laid," Roth declares. "Lord Prychon is not using our banking credits to fund the war with the Corrillians. Even more beguiling, I've heard talk of him ushering in backroom deals with other resource providers. His pillar must be replaced!"

"And so it will be," Mercari replies. "How can I be of assistance?"

"I would like you to set a private meeting with Lumakhod of the Grey Council," Roth declares.

"It will be done, my Lord," Mercari confirms.

THE CLUE

After completing the secret mission for Omega and Corum, Chimera returns back to the power station where she boards a Red transport back to AzurNu. Chimera makes her way to her living quarters. Entering, Chimera finds the dorm is empty once again, with no sign of StarChild. Undressing, she retires for the night, exhausted from the day's events.

The next rotation, Chimera awakes later than usual. After grabbing a snack she retrieves her wristcom and dials Nexus. There is no response.

"Alright, I need to study for that enforcement exam," Chimera says to herself.

She places a datasphere from her collection onto her SphereReader. As a projection appears, she begins to study. A few degrees pass as Chimera continues her review, preparing for the exam. It is the 11th degree when Chimera pauses to look at the time. Checking her wristcom, she notices a message from Athos.

I need a break, I think I'm gonna exercise a bit here in my dorm, Chimera writes to Athos.

Exercise, you should come to the Bethesda Complex, Athos writes back. *Best place to work out. They have everything you can think of.*

I haven't been yet. Is it usually really crowded this degree? Chimera responds to Athos's message.

Let's check it out, Athos offers.

Alright, why not, Chimera answers. *Where should we meet?*

I'll come to your dorm. We can go from there, Athos instructs.

I'll see you soon, Chimera answers. She puts her wristcom down and turns off the datasphere. Scooting out of her seat, she changes, grabs a rehydration beverage from her refrigeration box and exits the dorm.

Outside, she waits for Athos. When he arrives, they make their way out of the living quarters wing and board the hover-rail. They travel to Bethesda Station, the location for the Fitness Arena.

"Here we are," Athos proclaims as the exit the *RedLine* and arrive at the complex. "Welcome to the Bethesda Complex, the largest underground sports arenas on Tychon!" Athos exclaims in an announcer-like voice.

Chimera laughs.

The two enter the complex under a large entrance bridge and pass a holo-statue.

"So tell me, why come here to AzurNu if you have residency at

Broadcast Central?" Chimera asks.

"AzurNu is ripe grounds to find new creators," Athos answers. "And also spread our message."

Chimera nods

"I'm still finishing my studies as well," Athos adds. "AzurNu has the best lecture agents on Tychon."

As Chimera and Athos continue under the bridge, a large statue catches Chimera's eye.

"Who is that?" Chimera asks.

"That statue is BethesdaRed," Athos states. "He's the most famous athletic figure of AzurNu. The only Red to win the Unupseptium medal three times in a row at the Olympiad games."

"And where is he now?" Chimera questions.

"He lives in Regence, section A of living quarters," Athos replies. "He keeps to himself, no one really sees him."

The two continue into the complex.

"If you need to stretch, those are stretching rooms there," Athos acknowledges, pointing to several rooms on their left. "You can lift weights or just float around in the gravity rooms over there."

"Sounds fun," Chimera remarks.

"They are," Athos confirms. "And past the Gravity rooms are the infinity pools if you want to take a dip. There's also a magnetic climbing wall and a gravity track."

"And what's above the climbing wall?" Chimera asks.

"Above the climbing wall is Tarragon, the Holoball stadium," Athos declares. "C'mon, I want to show you something."

The two continue on through the complex. "This is Hellion stadium. I'm sure you've heard of it," Athos states.

"I have," Chimera confirms. "Isn't it where they play Gidden?"

"Yea, the whole arena is magnetic so they can glide from side when they hit the opposite team's homebase sphere with their sphere."

"Cool," Chimera says.

"There are Gidden practice courses on the ground level if you ever want to lose against me," Athos jokes.

"I'm gonna head to the warm up rooms and warm up for a bit," Chimera mentions to Athos.

"Alright, I was gonna work out in the gravity rooms but I'll join you," Athos proclaims. "I'll beat you in Gidden after."

Chimera grins. As she and Athos head back to the warm up rooms when once again, there is a beep preceding a message on the broadcast intercom, "All Reds 19 lunar cycles and older, report to the Citizenship Bureau to sign up now for active duty. Enlist in the Red Defense Core and fight to protect AzurNu. The Grey threat is imminent. Enlist now!"

"Are you gonna sign up for the Red Defense Core?" Chimera inquires on the way to the warm up rooms.

"Being a soldier is not really my forte," Athos admits. "I'm a lover, not a fighter. I'd rather join the Red Council and help influence change with my words than with a weapon."

"That's powerful," Chimera states, as the two reach the warm up rooms.

After a quarter of a degree of stretches and warm ups, Chimera and Athos heads to the Gidden practice course. After trying Gidden for the first time and falling a few times, Chimera and Athos exits the MagLev course.

"Thank you for that, Athos," Chimera states. "I think I got enough physical prep in. Gonna get back to studying."

"Sounds good," Athos confirms. "I'll see you soon."

"See you soon," Chimera replies, as she heads toward the exit.

On her way out, something catches her eye.

Approaching a Red nearby, Chimera asks, "Hey what's that area down there?"

"That? *NearbyUnderground*," the Red responds. "The heat springs spa heated from the nearby volcanoes. Good for skin and stress release."

"Thanks," Chimera remarks. "I think I'll check it out."

Chimera begins toward the heat spring. Entering a cave-like structure, she finds herself in a lobby full of iridescent bathing clothes, storage pods and waiting seats made of rock. In the center, is a path that leads down deeper into the cave.

"This is really cool," Chimera says.

Following the path, Chimera descends down into another subterranean area. Lush trees and vegetation surround several heated spas filled with clear green water. Chimera turns, about to exit when she spots another Red. She turns her head and begins back up the path trying not to make eye contact.

"Chimera, ChimeraRed is that you?" a voice exclaims.

Chimera continues, pretending not to hear but the Red catches up to her and taps her on the shoulder. Chimera turns.

"Hey," she acknowledges, continuing up the path.

"Hey, funny I should run into you again," the Red says, following Chimera.

"Yea, Draconis right?" Chimera replies glancing back for a moment.

"Right!" Draconis exclaims. "I haven't seen you in a while. How are you?"

"Fine," responds Chimera. "Kind of in a rush."

"Oh, me too," Draconis responds. "You leaving?"

"Yea on my way out now," Chimera states.

"I'll walk up with you," Draconis answers back, inviting himself.

"That's really not necessary," Chimera mentions.

"I insist," Draconis comments as the two head up the stairs toward the lobby.

"So, where've you been?" Draconis question.

"I've been around, tycho busy," Chimera explains.

"I know what you mean," Draconis replies. "Things have been crazy here since the new decree. What did you think when you heard?"

"What do you mean? It's nonsense of course, why?" Chimera inquires.

"Well . . . Is it really?" Draconis states. "When you think about it, Greys created us for a purpose. Technically we're Grey property."

"Property?" Chimera shouts, stopping. "What do you mean property? We're Reds! Beings with thoughts, ideas, emotions!"

"Yea, that's not what I meant," Draconis replies to Chimera. "Take enforcement, for example."

Chimera glances around to see if anyone other than Draconis is nearby. "It doesn't exist," Chimera confirms.

"Either way," Draconis begins. "We hear stories of Reds disappearing, covert missions to assassinate Greys and stuff like that"

"Greys kidnap and de-atomize Reds every day," Chimera snaps. "Enforcement is not the enemy."

"But that's exactly my point," Draconis replies. "What makes us any different to them then?"

"What makes us any different?" Chimera answers. "We're defending ourselves for one. We're not going over there searching for-" Chimera stops. "We're trying to protect our way of life. Look, I'm not gonna have a philosophical debate down in the heat spa cave."

"I'm just saying, don't you think there's another way?" Draconis inquires.

"Why are you asking me?" Chimera answers. "Shouldn't you be asking the Red council?"

Chimera and Draconis finally make it to the exit and Draconis stops

"I mean . . . with all the politics and laws here, how are we even free?" Draconis whispers

"You do realize you don't have to be here," Chimera declares. "You're free to move to a separatist reserve if you like." Chimera looks down at her wristcom. "Sorry but I really have to go," she states as she turns and exits.

On Tychon 3, RothGrey arrives at the Grey Council's palace to meet with LumakhodGrey, the secret meeting set up by MercariGrey. Amongst the other attendees of the meeting are MakuGrey, a wealthy industrialist turned banker who made the bulk of his Tychonian fortune selling Hue-mans to Grey rulership; IonGrey, the wealthy Grey who dominates the Alien Technology realm; FarroGrey, another member of the Grey Council; and RothGrey's assistant Mercari.

"Welcome members of the Illumination Consortium," Lumakhod begins. Lumakhod turns to RothGrey. "What projections do you have for us today, vault master Roth?"

"Your High Council, I come to you with great urgency this rotation. Lord Prychon has been less than cooperative in his order of power. Many resources have been lost, many Greys killed and the state economic affairs is ghastly."

"What are you suggesting?" Lumakhod inquires.

"Your rulership, we need a more progressive Prychon," Roth announces.

Chatters begins amongst the other attendees, as they begin to speak on Roth's suggestion.

"Quiet down!" Lumakhod instructs, as he turns to Roth. "Was this not the assessment you provided for Prychon Nyt? And at your advisement, Lord Prychon was placed in power? To restore Tychon to profitability and its former glory? And expand beyond the Zeta Reticulum limits," Lumakhod declares.

"Yes, your rulership, however I believe we were deceived by Lord Prychon. I believe he is unfit to restore Tychon to its former glory."

"How blithe," Lumakhod responds. "It was your unsatisfactory assessment of Prychon Nyt that led Lord Prychon to power. Now you decree he is unfit for rule as well?" Lumakhod asks Roth.

"Your rulership, he has been conducting meetings in secret, disobeying the council of Alviso and . . . his temperament is a risk to the stability of Tychon," RothGrey declares.

"Temperament, secret meetings?" Lumakhod begins. "Are these the forthright issues that dilute your faith in Prychon, or perhaps is it a more personal matter?"

"Your rulership, the reasons I've provided are the truth," Roth confirms.

"Yet I've heard whisper of your vote of no confidence in Lord Prychon being rooted in the fact that he refuses to rely on credits from your banks to fund war with the Corrillians," Lumakhod announces.

The other members of the council begin chattering again.

"What doth members of the consortium have to say?" Lumakhod asks.

"We have received no alarming proof of no confidence in Lord Prychon," MakuGrey remarks. "Perhaps this is a more personal matter."

"It has nothing to do with credits, I assure you," RothGrey defends.

"So you say," Lumakhod remarks. "We will hold a vote in five rotations for confidence of leadership. For now, this meeting is adjourned," Lumakhod orders. "Dismissed."

Following the meeting, Roth meets with Mercari after all members of the consortium have exited.

"We don't have time for legislative process, make arrangements," Roth instructs Mercari.

"Consider it done," Mercari confirms.

Back on AzurNu, Chimera heads back to her dorm. As she reaches it, there is a figure waiting at her door.

"Anexichi!" Chimera exclaims. "What are you doing here?"

"Surprised to see me?" Anexichi questions.

"Of course, I thought you were staying at . . . in quarantine," Chimera remarks, catching herself.

"I decided to take your advice," Anexichi declares. "I'm gonna spend some time with Nya and take care of a couple other things."

"Awesome, that's good for you," Chimera says. "Well if there's anything you need, let me know."

"Actually there is, that's why I came here," Anexichi mentions.

"Definitely, just let me know what you need," Chimera states.

"I . . . was wondering if you could help me with something tonight," Anexichi inquires.

"Yea what did you need?" Chimera asks.

"Meet me tonight at the 23rd degree and I'll explain everything," Anexichi replies. "I really need your help. Can I count on you?"

"You have my word," Chimera responds.

"Thanks, this means the world to me," Anexichi proclaims. "I gotta get out of here but I'll see you tonight."

"See you tonight," Chimera confirms.

Anexichi heads out as Chimera opens the door to her dorm. Chimera freshens up and changes. Heading back to the room, Chimera retrieves her holpad and begins writing in it. She writes till the 18th degree when she hears the door open. Moments later, StarChild enters in. There is silence as the two stare at each other.

"Hey," StarChild says.

"Hey," Chimera replies.

"I . . . I just wanted to say I'm sorry for the way I acted," StarChild apologizes.

"It's ok," Chimera answers.

"I mean it," StarChild states.

"Me too," Chimera admits. "I know I haven't been around lately, but that doesn't mean I'm not here for you."

"I know," StarChild acknowledges. "Look, I'm going to the outer rim with Dug. We're going to visit his family for a few rotations. When I get back, let's spend some time . . . just me and you. Get things back to the way they used to be."

"That sounds good," Chimera agrees.

StarChild approaches and hugs Chimera.

"Be well," StarChild proclaims

"Be well," Chimera concurs.

Chimera returns to studying. A degree passes when her wristcom alerts again with an incoming call. She answers.

"Greetings Omega," Chimera answers, surprised.

"Greetings Chi," Omega begins. "I haven't spoken with you since . . . the project. I wanted to see if you had a few moments to briefly connect."

"Sure, when?" Chimera inquires.

"Tonight," Omega suggests. "I've received multiple reports of an impending attack from scouts. We may not have much time."

"An attack?" Chimera states, sounding alarmed. "I can meet now if you'd like. I'm supposed to help out Anexichi at the 23rd degree."

"Anexichi? Glad to see you two have come to terms. I was afraid you might kill one another at first," Omega jokes.

"Yea, it's a long story," Chimera says.

"Well I tell you what," Omega states. "I'd like to keep a low profile, so come to my compound. We can speak here and you can play me some more music on my pianotron."

Chimera laughs a bit. "Right, I'll see you in half a degree," Chimera confirms, before ending the call.

Chimera heads to Omega's chateau. Once she arrives, she and Omega greet one another and head to Omega's quarters. Chimera tells Omega about the mission experience with Corum.

"How did you meet Corum?" Chimera inquires. "I'm sure there are very few Reds that have a Grey in their contact list!"

"Well, we actually met through someone who was part of the reason I wanted to talk with you about," Omega reveals.

"Right, so what was it you wanted to talk to me about that was really important?" Chimera asks Omega.

"You see, Chimera, you are from a pretty complex past," Omega tells Chimera.

"How so?" Chimera questions.

"Most inhabitants here on AzurNu are born here," Omega

begins. "They grow up here, they die here; it's all they know. You've had the privilege of experiencing life outside of this city."

"I've never thought of it that way," Chimera admits

"Your past is richer than you know," Omega continues. "I know you are the one that has the ability to change the way things are here on Tychon. Spearhead a revolution, not just for Reds. That's why I choose you for the CorumGrey mission."

Chimera steps back. "Yes, and I hate to be the one to burst your bubble, but I'm not the hero that you keep pumping me up to be."

"Let me ask you, why did you come here?" Omega questions. "To AzurNu I mean."

Chimera pauses, glancing down before returning her gaze to Omega. "I came here to be a part of something. To be among what I thought was my kind, and to try and find out where I came from."

"Did it have anything to do with finding your father?" Omega inquires.

"Well, I can't write my story if I don't know my history," Chimera proclaims. "I feel like a piece of me is missing"

"And what if your history did the opposite of made you fit in?" Omega questions.

"Since my time here, you've always been a pillar for me. It's been anything but easy and you've always been honest with me. Tell me what you really want to say," Chimera suggests.

"ChimeraRed, sharp as always," Omega exclaims. He pauses,

looking at a holographic communicator on one of the tables in his room. "I received a call today . . . a call from an old friend," Omega begins. He becomes silent.

"Uh huh," Chimera confirms, trying to coax more information from Omega.

"Right before I spoke with you, we were mid projection when the call was cut off," Omega states. "I'm sending scouts from my Elite Guard to check on her and her child Tiadora's status."

"And who is this her?" Chimera questions.

"She is AuroraRed," Omega replies. "She is a distant relative of yours from the Bethelex region and she may have information on the true identity of your birth father."

"Why would she know about my father?" Chimera inquires.

"It's a bit complicated," Omega acknowledges. "But know that everything I haven't disclosed to you is for your own well-being."

"I keep hearing that!" Chimera replies. "Doesn't anyone think I deserve to know the truth, and that I can protect myself?"

"My young friend, there are elements of your past that if revealed, the Grey Army would search the ends of Tychon to destroy you," Omega admits.

Chimera is silent, as she stands up and walks around the room, pensive. She stares out the window watching the glistening lights of AzurNu. "Why are you telling me this now?" Chimera asks.

"Because as I said, there may not be much time," Omega

mentions. "Aurora and even your mother may be in great danger. War is at our doorstep and I want you to know your true history and how important you really are to the future of Tychon."

Chimera continues to stand pensive, listening to Omega's revelations.

"Scouts are leaving from the docks as we speak. Titan has issued a no fly protocol because of the threat of attack so they'll be flying a lightcraft to the location for what we covertly filed as a patrol mission. The scout team will report back to me immediately."

"I'm going!" Chimera exclaims.

"Out of the question!" Omega proclaims.

"You know I can't sit idle," Chimera responds. "Especially knowing that my family may be out there and in danger. I'm sorry, but I have to go with or without out your help."

"Chimera, I know you are a rock," Omega remarks. "As strong willed as a Mountain Gnarl, but this is a fight that you cannot win . . . alone."

"But that's what I mean. I am not alone. What I've been through the last few planetary rotations, and the beings I've met, showed me that," Chimera states proudly.

Omega rises from the table and moves to a corner of the room, placing his right hand under his chin with his left hand supporting it. He stares out the window, as if searching for something. "The scouts are leaving from dock 3. I'll make arrangements for you to join. You'll meet with a pilot by the name of IcanRed. Go now, before it's too late!"

Chimera leaves Omegas quarters and rushes to the exit docks. As she reaches the entrance, the guard stops her.

"Excuse me, this is a restricted area," the guard declares. "Do you have clearance to enter?"

"She's with me," a Red announce as he approaches behind Chimera. Chimera turns to see it is Liazo carrying a bright metallic case.

"Sorry sir, I didn't know she was with you," the guard says as he immediately opens the door.

Chimera follows Liazo into the docs. "Thank you, what are you doing here?"

"Omega thought you might need some help," Liazo explains.

"Yes, I need to find the scout pilot before they leave," Chimera states.

Liazo leads Chimera to the flight deck. There are several Reds in flight suits, sitting down playing a gambling game called Orbis.

"I'm looking for Ican," Chimera states.

One of the Reds points toward the other side of the docks, without taking his eye off the floating sphere of the game. Chimera and Liazo move to the other end of the docks, passing a collection of Red Defense Core ships with crews inspecting the ships.

"Looks like they're preparing for something" Chimera observes.

Liazo is silent.

Chimera and Liazo reach a light carrier ship with its preflight engines on. It is a small sized craft with a half circle-shaped cockpit and an enlarged under section. Its wings protrude from the cockpit in a diamond-shaped form.

"Excuse me, do you know where I can find Ican?" Chimera questions.

"Ican help you," the Red replies.

"Ok," Chimera confirms, waiting for the Red to assist her.

"You've found him, I'm Ican," the Red replies.

"Oh!" Chimera exclaims. "I see, you were being funny. I'm Chimera and this is Liazo. I'll be joining you on the patrol."

"Are you sure?" Ican questions. "This trip might get a little unsafe."

"I'll try to remember that when I pull you to safety," Chimera mutters.

"Alright, I see we have a hero joining us," Ican responds.

"Just load the ship, Icant," a Red retorts as he approaches.

"Very funny," Ican remarks.

"Hi, I'm HammerRED," the Red declares, stepping up to Chimera and Liazo. "And this is LazerRED," the Red adds, introducing a slender female Red with exotic features. Both Hammer and Lazer wear white and black space suits with white armor.

"Got it. I'm ChimeraRed and Liazo you probably already know," Chimera declares.

"Great," Hammer proclaims. "I'll be leading the patrol as captain and Lazer is our 2nd Lieutenant onboard. I see you've met 2nd officer Ican. First officer Jett is already onboard. We've got the Predator and two other ships running with us this evening so it's a full house. We're short on time so hop on board so we can finish up preflight."

"Ican, here's the updated flight briefing," Hammer states, handing a holographic pad to Ican. He moves over to the entrance of the ship and climbs in.

"Thank you again, I will see you shortly," Chimera remarks to Liazo.

Liazo bids Chimera farewell.

"I almost forgot, this is for you," Liazo states as he hands Chimera the metallic case.

"What is it?" Chimera questions.

"It's from few friends," Liazo replies. "The contents of this case are to remain unknown unless there is an emergency. And should there be, three is the key."

Chimera takes the case and boards the ship, trying to decipher the mysterious case and riddle presented by Liazo.

"Welcome to the Vega," the pilot on the left announces as Chimera steps on board. "I'm JettRED," he adds, slightly muffled by the profuse chewing of gum.

"I'm Chimera," Chimera confirms.

"Strap in," Jett instructs. "It's time to rock and roll."

"Got it," Chimera says, strapping herself in.

Jett and Ican complete the preflight check as Hammer and Lazer check their weapons and equipment.

"I guess you're some sort of VIP or something?" Ican asks Chimera.

"What makes you think that?" Chimera replies.

"They added three more ships to the escort when you joined the detail," Ican reveals.

"Omega," Chimera mutters, grinning.

"Vega 239 this is CD tower 3," the control tower begins. "We've received your request for takeoff. You've logged your patrol destination. Please advise, we need your waypoint and flight path before we can clear you for takeoff. Over."

Jett looks at Hammer. "Where we going cap?" he asks, between chews.

"Set a course for the grain farms on the west end of Tychon 1," Hammer replies. "We'll deviate from there."

"Copy that," Jett answers.

Jett logs the destination into the ship's navigation and prepares to turn power to full throttle.

"Power down and exit the craft," a loud voice commands on the dock's intercom system.

Chimera and the crew peer out the window to see Titan and six Defense Core soldiers standing to the left of the ship.

"What do we do now, sir?" Ican questions, turning to Hammer.

"Power down the ship!" Titan repeats, as he and the soldiers step in front of the Vega with weapons drawn. "I will not ask again!" Titan warns, his unusually large stature making him easily identifiable amidst the other soldiers. "Let's go!" Chimera exclaims

"Sir?" Jett questions, peering back at Hammer as Titan and the soldiers outside the cockpit remain with weapons drawn. Hammer looks over at Lazer who nods her head.

"You heard her boys, let's drop the Hammer!" Hammer exclaims.

"Copy," Jett confirms as he flips several overhead switches on the instrument panel and punches the power on button. The ship begins to rumble as it powers on but immediately decelerates. Jett checks several gauges on the ship.

"Uh, Vega 239, this is tower. It looks like you've been grounded. I repeat, you are not cleared for launch," the tower reports. "Power down and exit."

"Ican, are the rear thrusters vented?" Jett screams.

Ican looks down then shakes his head.

"Well open them up!" Jett exclaims.

"Do you know how to fly this thing?" Chimera questions, her voice slightly higher pitched than normal.

"Why do you think they call me I can?" Ican replies.

He flips a green switch on the instrumental panel and then pushes the throttle knob up. The ship powers on with a thunderous sound and vibrates the ground as it lifts up.

Titan and the soldiers began firing at the ship as it speeds off and heads down the exit tunnel toward the surface. The three other ships lift off behind the Vega, as one stays grounded, following Titans orders. The Vega and three other ships approach the exit tunnel when it begins to close.

"Why is it closing?" Lazer inquires.

"Must be Titan. He is really pissed off about something," Hammer acknowledges.

"I never liked him," Jett confirms, as he pushes the throttle and speeds through the closing door.

The Vega flies free of AzurNu, followed by the Predator. The remaining two ships are trapped as the exit door closes.

"What the hell were they shooting for?" Ican hollers once the Vega clears the exit door.

"That's Titan for you," Jett confirms, nonchalantly.

"Is everyone ok?" Hammer inquires

"Never better," Jett declares.

"Good to go," Lazer confirms

"I'm fine," Chimera confirms.

"Give me a systems check," Jett requests.

"I'm getting a little vibration in the controls and my power output seems a little off, but other than that everything looks good," Ican confirms.

"Alright, keep an eye on it," Jett instructs. "Looks like the Predator is the only other one that made it out so it's just us two on this one."

"Copy," Ican answers back. "Let's get to the destination quick. Dinner's getting cold and I have a nice piece of asparagus waiting for me back home." "Classy," Lazer responds.

Chimera shakes her head.

"What brings you on board?" Chimera asks Lazer.

"I owe Omega a few favors. Finally got the chance to pay him back."

"What about you?" Chimera asks Hammer.

"That's easy," Hammer begins. "Omega said there may be some Reds in need of rescue from a Grey attack. I jump at any chance to kill a Grey!" Hammer exclaims, wiping his weapon with a cloth. "What about you?" Hammer asks Chimera.

"Out to see the sights?" Ican asks.

"Not quite. Aurora is a relative of mine, and she might be the only one who can lead me to my birth father," Chimera discloses.

"Heavy," Ican declares

Hammer and Lazer are silent as they exchange glances.

"If she's there we'll find her," Jett reassures.

Chimera and the scout party fly east toward Aurora's location. Flying for about a degree, the team reaches their destination, the Bethelex region of East Tychon.

"Our destination should be a few clicks from here," Hammer confirms, checking the navigation on his wristcom.

"Let's set her down here," Jett suggests to Ican. "Radar looks clear but let's not take any chances."

Jett and Ican land in an area two clicks from Aurora's flat and the Predator lands nearby.

"We'll check it out and secure the area first," Hammer instructs, rising out of his flight seat.

"I'm coming too," Chimera confirms.

"We can't risk you getting hurt," Hammer warns.

"I can take care of myself," Chimera says as she grabs a laser rifle from the weapon rack and steps out of the craft.

"Warrior Princess," Ican jokes

"Can it, Ican?" Hammer states.

"She's got my vote," Lazer acknowledges as she exits the craft.

Chimera, Hammer and Lazer climb up an embankment and move cautiously. Stopping at the top of the hill, Hammer surveys the area for any movement or signs of life.

"Looks clear, let's go. Her flat should be right over there," Hammer declares, checking the coordinates on his wristcom.

Rising over the embankment, the three approach a flat cut into a rock with glasslike walls.

Chimera, Hammer and Lazer stop at what appears to be the entrance of the flat with weapons drawn. Hammer signals that he will enter first and check left, Lazer will check right and Chimera to secure the middle. Hammer knocks on the door, and on the first knock, the door creaks open. Alarmed, Chimera kicks the door opens and enters the flat.

"Chimera!" Hammer exclaims in a loud whisper as he enters in behind her.

"Here we go," Lazer remarks as she briefly checks the perimeter and then follows Chimera and Hammer inside.

Hammer checks the room to the left, which appears to be a nursery. There is no sign of anyone. He moves to the adjacent room. Moving to the right, he exits the room and enters the kitchen. Inside, Chimera is standing over a table with dishes scattered across the table and floor and two of the seats knocked over as well.

"They've been taken," Lazer suggests.

"We don't know that," Hammer states.

"Whoever was here left in a rush. They must have been kidnapped," Ican adds, entering the kitchen.

"We don't know that," Hammer repeats sternly.

Chimera remains silent, surveying the room for clues.

"Still fresh," Ican states, dipping his finger in a bit of the spilled soup on the table and tasting it.

"Why aren't you with the ship?" Lazer asks Ican.

"I figured you needed some help," Ican remarks. "Besides, there's not a ship in sight out here."

"They might still be here," Hammer warns.

"There's no one here!" Ican snaps.

"How would you know?" Lazer interjects.

"There's still other rooms to check. They may be hiding," Hammer suggests.

Chimera heads to one of the rooms to the right of the kitchen to check, as Hammer, Lazer and Ican continue to argue.

"Hello, is anyone in here?" Chimera calls. She checks around the room and is about to check it when a voice calls on the radio.

"Uh guys, you better get back to the ship," Jett declares. "I'm picking up activity on the scanners, looks like heavies."

Chimera is startled and knocks a holographic photo off the table behind her. It comes crashing to the floor as Hammer sprints into the room.

"We gotta go, now!" Hammer orders. "We got incoming!" he says hurriedly.

Chimera, Hammer, Lazer and Ican exit the flat and step outside. Ican is in front and continues toward the embankment.

"With caution, Ican!" Lazer suggests as she and Hammer survey the area before making a break for the Vega.

Ican looks up into the sky. "Looks clear to me."

Chimera takes a step outside when a laser strikes Ican, disintegrating him instantly.

"Incoming!" Hammer yells as he and Lazer shuffle back into the flat. A small Grey attack craft hovers by.

"We have a Red down, I repeat, we have a Red down!" Hammer screams through the radio.

"We gotta get to the ship before they level this place!" Lazer declares.

"I agree," Hammer confirms. "Jett, I hope those engines are fired up because we're gonna be coming in hot."

"Copy," Jett acknowledges.

"Can you give me eyes out there?" Hammer asks Lazer.

"Already done," she answers as she pulls a small hexad-shaped disc from a utility pouch. She expands it and it activates. She peers her head outside the house and then tosses the disc outside. It begins to float and rotate, scanning the surroundings as it rotates. Lazer activates her helmet closed and Hammer follows suite. A 360 scan of the outside appears on Hammer and Lazer's helmet visor.

"I need one of those," Chimera declares.

"On my count," Hammer instructs.

Chimera and Lazer both nod. Hammer counts down from three on his hand and when he reaches one, he motions to exit. Leading the way, Hammer rolls out of the flat and begins firing at the Grey craft. Chimera and Lazer join, shooting up at the craft that moves at supersonic speeds, dodging their shots.

"Go!" Hammer orders.

Chimera and Lazer jump down the embankment to the ship.

"C'mon!" Chimera calls to Hammer as she reaches the ship and then turns back to provide cover fire for him.

Hammers runs toward the ship and is almost onboard when he is struck in the side by a plasma beam.

"Just go!" he yells at Chimera and Lazer.

"Come on!" Chimera proclaims as she and Lazer rush back to assist hammer. They continue firing at the Grey craft and Chimera strikes it. The craft darts away, smoke emanating from it.

Chimera and Lazer hoist Hammer up and begin carrying him to the ship. Suddenly Chimera hears a soft hum behind her. She turns to see the Grey craft rising from behind the hill with its weapon turret spinning wildly. Chimera drops Hammer and tries to pull up her weapon as the turret stops jerking and locks onto them. There is a loud explosion as the Grey craft is struck and knocked out of the sky, exploding as it falls to earth.

Chimera turns to see Jett standing behind her and Lazer with an ion rocket launcher in hand, still chewing his gum profusely.

"I hate aliens," Jett remarks.

"Show off," Lazer mutters.

Jett helps Chimera and Lazer carry Hammer back onto the ship, laying him down on the Vega's floor.

"Well, this just puts a damper on my night's plans," Hammer retorts.

"Yea, I think that's gonna leave a mark too," Lazer remarks

sarcastically, catching a glimpse of Hammer's wound.

"Light scrape," Hammer declares, holding his side and trying to hide the pain in his voice.

"Where's Ican?" Jett inquires

Chimera looks up at Jett then shakes her head.

"Chimera help me strap Hammer into this floor gurney," Lazer remarks. "Jett, you get us home!" she adds, retrieving a med kit from the wall.

"Copy," Jett acknowledges as he throttles the ship to full power and the Vega rises gently.

"Predator this is Vega, mission is a scrub. We're 555 and heading back to base," Jett announces. Suddenly, something catches Jett's attention. "Oh shit!" Jett declares.

Before Chimera can ask what has happened, the ship banks hard to the right as several laser beams zip past the ship. Chimera is in her seat and Hammer is safely strapped to the floor of the ship but Lazer, who was tending to Hammer, is thrown toward the wall.

"We've got company," Jett announces.

"Thanks for the heads up," Lazer hollers angrily.

"More incoming?" Hammer asks.

"Four of them, Grey ramships," Jett replies.

"Can we outrun them?" Hammer questions.

"We would've been able to if Titan and his Defense Core didn't damage our injection core," Jett explains, still chewing away at his gum. "I noticed it when you guys were inside the house. If we try to jump to supersonic, we risk overheating and exploding," Jett explains.

"Can we take them out?" Lazer questions.

"Yeah, but I'm going to need somebody on the copilot turret," Jett states.

"I'll do it," Chimera offers.

"What?" Hammer asks.

"We don't have a choice," Lazer agrees. "I've got to take care of Hammer's wounds so he doesn't bleed out."

Chimera jumps into the copilot seat next to Jett.

"Uh, do you have any training," Jett asks.

"No, but I watched you and Ican fly for the last degree," Chimera admits.

"Here, put this bone dome on and strap in," Jett instructs as he hands Chimera a flight helmet. She puts the helmet on. "Alright, here are the basics," Jett begins as he gives Chimera a crash course in the weapon systems of the Vega.

As the Vega rises, suddenly an alarm sounds.

"We got a salvo of incoming plasma rockets," the pilot of the Predator screams over the radio.

"Copy that Ferrero," Jett replies. "There must be more ramships in the area."

"I see five missiles," Ferrero announces.

"And they've just locked on," Jett confirms.

The Vega and the Predator take immediate evasive action. The rockets approach at mach speed racing toward the Vega and the Predator.

The Predator darts right then left, dodging two of the missiles as they fly off into the distance. Three more missiles roar toward Chimera and the Vega. As the first missile approaches, Jett fires trace lasers, striking one of the missiles and destroying it.

"Nice shot!" Chimera exclaims.

As the second missile approaches, Jett turns the Vega hard left dodging the missile by only millimeters. The third missile strikes a rock pinnacle and explodes.

As the Vega and Predator fly west toward AzurNu, another proximity warning suddenly sounds.

"I'm picking up more contacts," Jett hollers.

"Missiles?" Chimera asks.

"ramships," Jett declares. "Four of them!"

"What's the plan?" Chimera asks, turning to Jett.

"Let's say hello," Jett instructs, as he switches the ship's thrust vectors and turns the Vega around.

"How's he doing back there?" Jett inquires turning to check on Hammer.

"Clean shot through the ribs, but I was able to stop the bleeding," Lazer announces. "We need to get him to a med bay asap."

"We're working on it," Jett declares, circling around to get a lock on the missiles.

"Watch my six," Jett proclaims to Ferrero.

"Copy," Ferrero replies.

The Vega rises to a higher altitude.

"Dammit!" Jett hollers.

"What?" Chimera asks.

"I can't lock onto them, some sort of field interference," Jett declares.

The Predator approaches, firing a warning missile at the Grey ships as they streak past.

"Hope you're ready for a little aerial combat," Jett warns. "Hit that button over there to your left," Jett instructs Chimera. "That'll arm your weapons. You got two choices: ion missiles or laser cannons. Two missiles in your payload so make 'em count."

Chimera nods.

Two of the ramships circle around and climb to engage the Vega, firing micro imploders. Jett navigates the Vega to fly downward toward ground, narrowly avoiding the employers as they explode.

"I think I know this area. We need get to Kybon Canyon," Chimera suggest. "We have a better chance there."

"Predator this is Vega," Jett calls. "We're gonna hit the deck and scramble to Kybon Canyon," Jett alerts as the Vega descends to a low flying position. The ground shakes and dirt is kicked up as the Vega and

Predator roar toward Kybon Canyon.

"Predator, you've got a Grey on your tail," Jett alerts looking out his cockpit window.

"Likewise comrade, you've got one above and one to your right," Ferrero responds.

"Here we go," Jett announces. He quickly pulls the Vega up and to the right. The Grey ramship above them comes into sight and Chimera fires an ion missile.

"Vexor 3," Jett calls, as the missile streaks toward the ramship. Just before contact the ion core of the missile shoots forward and strikes the Grey craft, exploding on impact.

"Target destroyed," Jett confirms. "Nice shot Chimera!"

Chimera tries to hide her grin, as she smiles.

"Tally one for the Vega," Ferrero announces. "Now it's my turn." The Predator rolls and turns to the left.

"Bait and switch?" Jett asks.

"Bait and switch," Ferrero confirms.

The Vega rolls left as well and the Grey ship follows. As the Vega straightens out, Jett glances out the window and waves at the Grey craft sarcastically. Suddenly, the Predator appears from above, and drops behind the Grey ramship and fires a missile destroying it.

"Two down!" Ferrero announces as the Vega and the Predator reach Kybon Canyon.

The Predator is ahead and the Vega is slightly behind. Suddenly, a ramship appears ahead.

"That's the Canyon over there," Chimera acknowledges, pointing to a giant tear in the landscape.

"Alright we're here," Jett reiterates, "but Ferrero you've got company!"

Without warning, the ramship fires its lasers at the two ships. The Vega descends quickly and avoids the lasers. The Predator tries to avoid the lasers but is struck on the right side.

"He's hit!" Chimera exclaims.

"Ferrero, what's your status?" Jett inquires. There is silence. "Ferrero, I say again status report?"

The click of the radio sounds for several moments, before a voice rings out.

"I can't believe I let these bastards scrape my paint!" Ferrero declares.

Jett laughs as Chimera and Lazer grin. Hammer shakes his head slightly, still strapped to the floor of the Vega and mildly sedated.

Without warning, the remaining two ramjets streak in from the right.

"Incoming right!" Chimera warns as one of the Grey crafts fires at the Predator. The Predator is struck again and the rear of the ship catches fire as it crashes to the ground in a large explosion.

"Ferrero!" Jett hollers. There is no response.

Chimera, Laser and Hammer are silent. After a few moments,

Jett springs back into action.

"Alright, Chimera, you say you know these canyons, it's your show now. It looks like we have two tailing us," Jett reveals, as the Vega twists and turns through the canyon. The Grey craft continues firing at the Vega, and the lasers strikes the canyon walls as the Vega avoids the shots.

"I've got an idea," Chimera suggests. "Can you transfer primary control over to me?"

Jett is reluctant, glancing at Chimera, but he does as she commands and transfers control to Chimera.

Chimera immediately pulls the ship all the way back and the Vega sores into the sky. The Vega continues climbing at a 90 degree angle as the Grey ships follow.

"What are you doing? We're gonna hit a stall if you don't level out," Jett warns, his head stuck to the back of the seat.

"Wait for it," Chimera remarks as the Vega climbs into the upper atmosphere and begins to lose momentum.

"Now!" Chimera hollers as she cuts the power to the Vega. As momentum stops and the Vega flips backward, the two ramjets behind come into sight. Chimera fires both ion missiles at the two ramships. The missiles soar toward their targets but both miss as the two ramships and the Vega hurdle down toward earth picking up speed.

"How many missiles left in your load?" Chimera asks Jett.

"I'm out!" Jett replies.

Chimera tracks the movements of the remaining ramjets behind and above her using the display on her flight helmet.

"There's a break in the Canyon in a few meters," Chimera states. "We can catch them off guard there."

Chimera rolls the Vega inverted and then pitches up, gaining a clear shot of one of the ramships. The other ramship approaches from behind as the Vega flies backward in a vertical position. The ramship begins to fire lasers at the Vega.

"You've got the shot!" Jett exclaims.

"Not yet," Chimera states.

The Grey ship above crosses the line of sight of the Vega and begins to descend.

"Now!" Chimera exclaims.

Chimera and Jett unleash a barrage of lasers striking the Grey ship above as Chimera pulls the throttle to max and the Vega shoots up out of the canyon right as the canyon comes to end. The Grey ramship doesn't see the upcoming canyon wall until the Vega rises up and it's too late. The Grey ship slams into the canyon and explodes.

"Genius!" Jett exclaims.

"Nice!" Lazer agrees.

"Let's set a course for AzurNu," Jett announces, flipping several switches to check the status of the Vega.

"Sounds good," Hammer moans.

Suddenly Chimera's wristcom rings and she peers down to check the source of the call.

"Shoot, I was supposed to meet Anexichi at the 23rd degree!" Chimera declares.

"You should tell her you might be a little late," Jett announces sarcastically, still chewing his gum as the ship bounces up and down periodically.

Chimera is about to answer the call when there is a large bang. Suddenly the Vega's engine's shut off. Jett checks the ships gauges.

"What's going on?" Chimera asks.

"Looks like we had a flameout!" Jett explains. "I'm gonna try to reprime the thrusters."

Jett tries to restart the ship's engine as the Vega continues to slowly glide downward.

"It looks like we're losing altitude," Lazer remarks.

Jett turns to Lazer and then to Chimera. "Brace for impact, we're going down. Chimera, you better get to the back. This might be a rough landing."

"I'm gonna stay up here and help you land this thing," Chimera insists.

"This one's not up for discussion," Jett remarks. "There's not much landing to be done. I need you in the rear so you don't take the brunt of the impact. You're of more use uninjured. Who do you think's gonna carry Hammers heavy ass?" he states winking at Chimera. Chimera hesitates for a few moments and then unstraps her seat harness and moves to the rear of the ship. Jett reactivates the comm frequency for AzurNu's tower control.

"Tower, this is Vega 239," Jett begins. "Multiple contacts; Greys. Predator is down, I repeat, Predator is down. We've lost all power and we're going down. Coordinates 31.7683° N, 35.2137° E . . . Vega Out."

The silence of the radio is interrupted by a loud crash followed by the crumpling of metal. The Vega hits the ground and rolls violently for several hundred meters before coming to a stop. The Tychonian night returns to silence as the Vega lays upside down.

After several moments, the door of the Vega suddenly flies open and out steps Chimera. She climbs out of the ship and staggers to her feet.

"Am I still alive?" she asks herself. She glances around and then looks down at the blood pouring from her arm. "I must be," she proclaims. She returns inside the mangled ship.

"Is everyone ok?" Chimera questions. There is no response. "Can you hear me?" Chimera asks, shaking Hammer.

"Yes, ouch!" Hammer exclaims, regaining consciousness. "As if getting shot and crash landing wasn't enough, now you want to shake me to death?"

"You're alive!" Chimera remarks.

A low voice to the right of Chimera begins to grunt. Chimera turns to see Lazer removing some debris from on top of herself.

"Lazer!" Chimera hollers. She rushes over and helps clear the debris pinning Lazer down. Chimera helps Lazer up, who is tattered and covered in dust.

"C'mon, we gotta carry Hammer out and then I'll grab Jett," Chimera instructs.

Chimera and Lazer unlatch the floor gurney and then carry Hammer off the ship. Activating the power on the gurney, it begins to hover.

"Is he gonna be ok?" Chimera asks Lazer.

"Yea, he'll be fine," Lazer confirms.

Chimera returns inside to help Jett. After a bit of time, Chimera emerges alone, standing at the damaged entrance bay of the ship.

"Where's Jett?" Hammer utters, tilting his head up slightly from the gurney.

"I'm gonna need a hand," Chimera announces to Lazer.

Lazer steps away from Hammer as she and Chimera return inside the ship. They return, carrying Jett shoulder to shoulder. They carefully lay him down and remove his helmet. He is bleeding from the nose and appears unconscious.

"Jett!" Lazer calls. "Wake up!" Jett does not answer. Lazer checks his neck for a pulse. Then she removes his flight gloves and checks his wrist. "He's . . . gone," Lazer utters sounding surprised.

"What do you mean gone?" Hammer questions.

"There's no pulse," Lazer responds.

Hammer unbuckles himself and tries to rise from the gurney but the pain is too great.

"Ahh!" he screams as the pain sharpens. He lays back down. "Get me out of this thing!" he screams.

"Hammer, you need to relax," Lazer urges. "You're gonna make things worse."

Hammer breaths heavily, his frustration intensifying with every breath.

"We're gonna get you home," Chimera reassures Hammer. Chimera turns to Lazer. "Have you radioed for help?" she asks.

"My wristcom is down," Lazer declares. "Totally dead."

Chimera checks her wristcom and tries to make a call. "Mine is down too," Chimera confirms.

Lazer checks Jett's wristcom. "Looks like his is broken and Hammer's is in the wreckage," Lazer remarks. "I'm gonna check the radio on the ship."

"Ok," Chimera responds.

After checking inside the Vega, Lazer returns. "Fried," she declares. "Looks like we're stuck out here with no radio."

"Must have been an EMP blast or something from one of the ramships," Hammer suggests.

"The Elite guard will send a search and rescue party right?" Chimera asks.

"There's no guarantee," Hammer responds. "We don't even know if Jett's mayday transmission went through. For all we know we might be out here on our own."

"If we don't check in after a few degrees, they'll send help," Lazer reassures.

"That is, if we were on a sanctioned op," Hammer remarks. "Have you guys forgotten we broke protocol? Cleared the flight deck after being grounded and ignored orders from TitanRED. They might think we've rogue. Trust me, help is the last thing they're sending."

"So what do you suggest?" Lazer inquires.

"We've gotta get our asses home," Hammer declares.

"We don't even know where we are," Lazer mentions. "Our wristcoms don't work and we have no navigation. We're practically naked out here."

"Well, we know we're somewhere west of Kybon Canyon," Chimera states.

"Somewhere doesn't really help," Lazer retorts.

"Well, my point is we're not completely lost," Chimera clarifies.

"No, just a little bit," Lazer replies.

"Lazer!" Hammer calls.

"No, I'm sorry," Lazer begins. "I'm just not good at pretending to be nice. The reality is we're stuck here in this infinity forsaken region with no gear and no help!"

"It's the 24th rotation," Hammer begins. "We're all exhausted and banged up. It's too dark so we're not gonna be able to see anything. I say we bunker down inside the Vega for the night. At first light, if help hasn't arrived we'll figure it out, but by infinity I promise we're getting home one way or another."

Chimera glances at Lazer.

"Optimist," Lazer mutters. "I don't agrees, but you're the captain." Lazer begins to steer Hammer's gurney back into the crashed ship.

"What should we do about Jett?" Chimera asks.

"We can bury him in one of the awning cloths from inside," Hammer states.

Lazer retrieves one of the cloths from the ship. Afterwards, she returns outside where she and Chimera wrap Jett inside of it. Using pieces of the debris, they create a mound around Jett, covering him in the loose dirt.

"Good-bye friend," Lazer states, kissing her fingers and then touching Jett's forehead with them.

"We will meet again," Hammer declares, still laying in the Gurney.

Chimera is silent. It is the 27th degree when the three return inside the Vega to rest for the night.

CHAPTER TEN

INDIGO

It is the 4th degree of early morning when Lazer awakes. Inside the Vega, she turns and finds Chimera awake writing on a holopad.

"What are you doing?" Lazer asks

"I couldn't sleep," Chimera admits. "Just writing some stuff down. I usually write in my wristcom but it's broken."

"So how is that holopad working?" Lazer inquires.

"Magnetic pulses shockwave, our holotech doesn't use magnetism," Chimera clarifies.

"You're pretty smart aren't you?" Lazer asks.

"I'm pretty ok," Chimera states.

"You said you couldn't sleep, worried about your family back at AzurNu?" Lazer asks.

"My family's not actually at AzurNu," Chimera begins. "My mother is in the Amran region. And my father . . . well, yea," Chimera remarks.

"I get it," Lazer declares.

"Is your family back at AzurNu?" Chimera inquires.

"It's just me," Lazer answers. "My parents are gone, both killed by Greys. And I'm an only child."

"I'm sorry," Chimera empathizes.

"I don't need any sympathy," Lazer proclaims. "My philosophy is when it's your time to go it's your time to go."

"I get it," Chimera replies.

Suddenly, Hammer mumbles something and repositions himself to lay the opposite direction, still asleep.

"What about the captain, what's his story?" Chimera asks Lazer.

"The Hammer, he's got fight in his blood," Lazer mentions. "Third generation Elite guard. His father was Elite guard and so was his father's father. His folks and younger brother are back at AzurNu, I think."

"You guys aren't, you know . . . ?" Chimera alludes

"What like together? Not at all, why would you think that?" Lazer questions, becoming defensive.

"Because, you guys argue like you are," Chimera jokes

Lazer laughs.

The two continue talking for a degree and a half. It is the 6th degree when Hammer awakes.

"What time is it?" Hammer asks, sitting up.

"The clock on my holopad says the 6th degree," Chimera

answers.

"Any sign of help?" Hammer remarks.

"Nothing yet," Lazer responds.

"Looks like we're short on options," Hammer declares. "We can try to find a beacon station, or we can try to find a pro AzurNu outpost."

"We have another option," Lazer announces. "Chimera has family in the Amran region."

"You have kin nearby?" Hammer asks.

"Yes," Chimera responds. "My mother's flat is in Khyber City south of the Mons."

"It's the closest location," Lazer begins. "There's no way we can make it back to AzurNu on foot. It's at least a planetary rotation away, maybe more."

"How long would the hike to your mother's flat be?" Hammer questions.

Chimera glances down at her holopad and begins to scribble something. After a few moments she responds, "Not for sure, but I say should be about 12 rotations."

"Hmm," Hammer states. "Not ideal, but it may be our most viable option. We can't wait around here for help. We'll be sitting coys."

"Let's gather what supplies we can from the ship and get ready for this quest," Lazer suggests.

"Ok," Chimera confirms.

Both Chimera and Lazer scour the ship, salvaging what supplies they can for the trip to the Amram region. After searching the ship, Chimera and Lazer exit carrying Hammer, two crates of supplies and backpacks.

"Inventory check, what do we have?" Hammer inquires, as they convene outside the Vega.

"We have food for about seven rotations, a tent for sleeping accommodations, a couple glow tubes for lighting and two flares," Lazer reports.

"Weapons?" Hammer asks.

"Nothing," Lazer responds. "Our blasters were all disabled by the EMP."

"Damn!" Hammer exclaims. "We'll have to try and improvise on the fly."

"Are we ready?" Lazer asks.

"Good to go," Chimera responds.

"Let's get Jett back inside," Hammer instructs.

Chimera and Lazer unbury Jett and carry him back inside the Vega. After placing him in the ship, Chimera and Lazer exit.

"What direction are we headed?" Lazer asks.

"We can use the mountains as a guide," Hammer states. "They should lead north, we'll move parallel to them and head east. Chimera, you say Iona is south of the Amram Mons?"

"Yea," Chimera replies.

"Sun is starting to rise, so let's get going," Lazer states.

As they prepare to move out, something on the ground catches Chimera's eye.

"What's that, over there?" Chimera mentions. "That metallic sheet in the ground.

Lazer peers over at what Chimera is viewing. "Looks like a piece of debris," Lazer remarks, as she starts to hover Hammer's gurney away.

"Looks like something else," Chimera declares, approaching the object. She kneels down and removes it from the ground. She retrieves a metallic case.

"What is it?" Lazer questions.

"It's the case, the case that Liazo gave me!" Chimera exclaims.

"Liazo gave you a case?" Lazer remarks. "What's in it?"

"I'm not sure," Chimera states.

"Can you open it?" Lazer suggests.

"I don't know how to," Chimera replies. "I don't see a button or anything, just this weird little square slot with three lines on the front." Chimera studies the case.

"The sun is rising and we have a long journey ahead of us," Hammer declares. "Let's get moving, we'll try and figure it out later."

As Chimera is about to put the case down, she suddenly remembers something. "Wait, the bracelet!" Chimera exclaims. "There's power in threes."

"Huh?" Lazer inquires.

Chimera slides her right sleeve up, flips the bracelet Omega gave her and inserts the square top of the bracelet into the metallic case.

The sound of an airlock unsealing is audible, and then the case pops open.

"You got it open!" Lazer declares. "What's inside?"

Chimera checks the contents of the case. "There's . . . some sort of super advanced rifle," Chimera begins, removing the weapon and tossing it to Lazer. "There's a weird handle thing with a Tychonian inscription on it," she continues, placing the handle inside a sheath on her back. "And, there's an orb," Chimera continues. "This must be for you, Hammer," Chimera retorts, tossing the sphere to Hammer.

"Very funny," Hammer states, catching the sphere from his gurney. "Wait," Hammer instructs, inspecting the orb. He unlatches himself from the gurney and sits up. He turns and examines the sphere. Hammer swipes his hand of the orb, causing blue shapes and numbers within the sphere to appear. Directional arrows, numbers and a needle appear shortly after.

"A compass!" Chimera hollers.

"That makes it easier," Lazer states.

"You're lifesaver, Chimera!" Hammer acknowledges.

"Thank Omega," Chimera replies.

Hammer checks their location on the compass. "Looks like we need to head that way," Hammer states pointing northeast. "Let's go."

Chimera, Lazer and Hammer, still gurney-bound, begin their odyssey to IonaRed. They trek through the Vulned region, a landscape made up of twisted rocks, springs of acid, sulfur hills and geysers filled with poisonous gas. The temperature in the region is extraordinarily hot, being a volcanic area.

After traveling through the Vulcned region for a day, the three setup their tent and rest for the night. The night is far from uneventful, as geysers spray gasses and volcanoes stream with lava. The next rotation, Chimera, Lazer and Hammer resume their journey, continuing in this fashion for three exhausting days.

On the fourth day, Chimera, Lazer and Hammer reach Mawton, the mountainous region east of Vulcned. Hundreds of large mountain peaks sprawl across the region. The three begin the voyage through the Mawton peaks using a nomadic trading trail to navigate the perilous mountains.

After three days of hiking through the treacherous lands of Mawton, Chimera, Lazer and Hammer arrive at a large drawbridge.

"Welcome to Prychon's Peak," Chimera announces, speaking above the unusually strong winds. "This bridge will take us through the peak and to the eastern part of the region. From here it should only be one or two days hike to Kori. After Kori, we'll be at Bethelex."

"Why's it called Prychon's Peak?" Lazer asks.

"Because it's deadly, just like Prychon," Chimera responds.

"Many Reds have perished here."

"You've been here before?" Lazer questions.

"No, but I've heard about it," Chimera explains. "I used to hear stories."

"Is that thing safe?" Lazer inquires, peering at the old bridge swaying from side to side.

"We don't have a choice," Chimera states. "This is the fastest way through the peak. If we try the other way, it'll add another three days to our hike."

"We're down to our last ration of food," Hammer announces. "We'll be hunting game to eat after today. We definitely can't afford to add any more days."

"I don't know, that's a pretty long way down," Lazer mentions, peering down over the mountain at the distance underneath the bridge. "That's gotta be half a kilometer at least," Lazer states.

"Hammer and I will go first," Chimera volunteers.

Lazer motions for her to lead the way.

"You ready?" Chimera asks Hammer.

"I really wish I wasn't stuck in this thing," Hammer responds.

"I'll take that as a yes," Chimera confirms.

Chimera pushes Hammer's gurney down the bridge as she follows behind. The bridge creeks with each step, as Chimera and Hammer inch across to the other side. The bridge sways from left to right, a result of the mountain winds moving it to and fro. The sound of creaking wood echoes off the mountain walls. After several more moments, Chimera and Hammer finally reach the other side.

"You see, it's safe," Chimera acknowledges.

"Easy for you to say," Lazer mutters.

"Ok, your turn," Chimera mentions.

Lazer slowly steps onto the bridge. She quickly grabs the guide ropes on both sides. The bridge creaks again as Lazer makes her way across.

"You're doing good, almost there!" Hammer coaxes.

"I guess this is the wrong time to mention I hate heights!" Lazer announces. Lazer is midway through, crossing steadily when the wind begins to kick up. The bridge increases its sway.

"The faster you cross, the faster you get it over with," Hammer suggests.

Suddenly, the sound of a crack rings out. One of the wooden steps Lazer is standing on gives way. Lazer's leg falls through the gap.

"Lazer!" Chimera exclaims as she darts back onto the bridge. "Hold on!" As Chimera reaches Lazer, two more pieces of the walkway give and Lazer falls.

Chimera grabs Lazer's right hand just as the planks crack.

"I got you!" Chimera assures, holding onto Lazer's hand. "Give me your other hand!" Chimera instructs.

"I'll have to drop the rifle if I do!" Lazer warns.

"You don't have a choice!" Chimera screams.

Lazer releases the rifle to the abyss beneath her and grabs Chimera's other hand. Chimera slowly pulls Lazer up to safety.

Hammer unstraps himself and sits up. He steps off the gurney to help but falls, overcome by pain. After helping Lazer onto the remaining part of the bridge, Chimera and Lazer crawl to the other side. The three of them lay crouched on the floor, all out of breath.

"That's Lazer, stubborn as ever," Hammer chuckles. "Second guesses the decision to save her blaster or save herself."

"And you said it was easy," Lazer states, breathing heavily.

Chimera begins to laugh.

"Well thanks, I owe you for that one," Lazer declares, still panting.

"It's no problem," Chimera answers. "The dangerous part is over now."

"Uh, unfortunately not quite," Hammer alerts.

"What do you mean?" Lazer questions.

Hammer points in the direction behind Lazer and Chimera. Chimera turns to see three a four-legged, slender creatures with course, reptile-like skin and four large canine teeth.

As an instinct, Lazer immediately reaches for her rifle and realizes she no longer has it.

"What the hell are those?" Lazer yells.

"Mountain Gnarls," Chimera states.

"Carnivores?" Lazer inquires.

"Definitely," Chimera replies.

Lazer grabs a stick from the ground. Hammer grabs two rocks. Chimera grabs the gurney, using it as a shield, and steps in front of Lazer and Hammer.

"Chimera, the blade handle!" Hammer exclaims.

Chimera grabs the saber handle from her back and holds it up. Nothing happens. As Chimera tries to figure out if the saber handle can help, two of the Gnarls attack. Chimera quickly blocks one of the attacking creatures with the gurney as it bites and tears at the stretcher. The impact knocks the saber out of Chimera's hands. The other Gnarl leaps onto Lazer. She raises her arm to shield herself and it bites her arm. She lets out shriek as she strikes the animal with the stick. Hammer throws two rocks at the animal, which seem to only aggravate it more.

Chimera tries to free the gurney from the Mountain Gnarl's mouth, who is still biting it. She shoves it forward and then jumps to assist Lazer. Hammer crawls over and grabs the tail of the Gnarl attacking Lazer while Chimera kicks its head. The third Gnarl jumps into action and pounces on Chimera from behind knocking her down. As it tries to bite Chimera, she searches around for a weapon. Lazer is pinned down by the second Gnarl and the third beast circles Hammer who is laying on the ground.

Chimera spots the saber lying next to her and reaches for it. She holds the Gnarl back with her right hand as she reaches for the saber with her left hand. The creature is about to bite Chimera's neck when she grabs the handle and strikes him with it. The creature jumps back for a moment. Chimera frantically searches for a way to activate the blade. She notices a small, clear surface on the handle of the blade. Again, remembering what Liazo stated, Chimera places three fingers on the surface.

Suddenly, a loud thunderous sound comes from the saber as it powers on. A blade doesn't emit from the saber, but a distortion of air is seen directly above the handle.

"What is it?" Hammer asks.

"I have no idea!" Chimera yells back. "I don't see a blade or anything, just this weird airstream of distortion."

The loud sound from the saber startles the Gnarls and they jump back.

"Get behind me," Chimera commands Hammer and Lazer as she rises to her feet. "Gnarls are notoriously stubborn."

The Gnarls regroup as the sound of the saber quiets to a pulsating hum. One of the Gnarls begins to creep back toward Chimera.

"I don't know what this thing does but if you want a taste come get it!" Chimera warns the beast.

The Gnarl accepts the challenge and jumps at Chimera. She swings the saber and the distortion field strikes the Gnarl, immediately disintegrating a large chunk of the animal. The upper and lower half of the Gnarl fall to the ground separately as blood from the beast spills out.

"This thing is wicked!" Chimera declares, glancing at the saber she holds.

Seeing Chimera slay the first Gnarl, the second beast charges at Chimera. With the swipe of her wrist she beheads it. The third Gnarl glances at its two dead pride members and then back at Chimera. It turns around and scurries off.

"Thank infinity," Hammer declares, letting out a huge sigh.

"Wow," a tattered Lazer remarks, limping over to Chimera. "What on Tychon is that?"

"I don't know," Chimera responds. "Seems like some sort of antimatter scepter."

"You've got the wrath of the infinity in that," Lazer states.

"Chimera storm," Hammer declares.

"It sounded like a terrestrial storm when it turned on," Lazer adds.

"I've never seen anything like it," Hammer admits.

"Neither have I," Chimera responds. She then peers up into the sky. "It's gonna get dark here quick here. We need to find shelter for the night. The temperature at night is deadly and the indigenous species as you can see aren't the friendliest."

"Sounds like a plan," Hammer agrees. "We're out of food so we'll have to tough it out for the night and see what we can find in the morning."

As the three continue on through Prychon's Peak, Chimera spots something.

"Look, up there," Chimera announces, pointing. "Looks like some sort of cave."

"Sounds like five star accommodations to me," Lazer remarks.

Chimera, Lazer and Hammer hike up to the opening.

"Lazer, can you toss me one of the glow sticks?" Chimera inquires.

Lazer retrieves one of the sticks from the container and hands it to Chimera. Chimera activates the glow stick and powers on her antimatter saber. She slowly enters the cave, the green hue from the glow stick shines on the cave walls like a green shadow. She moves through the cave cautiously, peering behind her periodically. Suddenly, there is movement in the darkness ahead of Chimera.

"Come out, or face death!" Chimera warns. The figure shuffles in the darkness. Chimera raises her saber as the figure emerges.

"There won't be a need for that!" the figure announces.

"You're a Red?" Chimera proclaims, as an elderly female Red shuffles over. She is hunchback and carries a long black staff to walk.

"I am NinaFortuna," the Red declares. "And this is my home."

"Oh, I apologize!" Chimera declares deactivating the saber. "I am ChimeraRed. I didn't think anyone was here. We were attacked and are trying to get back home. We needed accommodations for the night and stumbled across this cave. I didn't mean to intrude, we'll be on our way."

"You're more than welcome to stay here," Nina offers. "I haven't had company in quite a few rotations," Nina states, glancing at the blade in Chimera's hand.

"We really don't want to intrude," Chimera reiterates.

"Nonsense, you three will stay the night and I won't have it any other way. I'll light a fire and prepare cots for each of you."

"Thank you, how did you know I was with company?" Chimera questions.

"You said we," Nina replies.

"Right," Chimera confirms. "I'll call the others," Chimera states, as she returns to the entrance of the cave to retrieve Hammer and Lazer.

"Looks like we're welcomed for the night," Chimera announces. "Mind yourselves, she seems like she may be a little . . . sheltered."

"Spending the night in a dark cave with a crazy women, I couldn't think of anything more entertaining," Lazer remarks.

"We'll make the best of it," Hammer declares.

Chimera and Lazer unstrap Hammer and help him into the cave where they find the old women in the den, rotating a blue glowing sphere, speaking to herself.

"What is she saying?" Lazer whispers.

"I have no idea, I told you she was sheltered," Chimera whispers back. "Uh um," Chimera utters, clearing her throat to announce their presence.

"I see you have returned with your fellow journeymen," Nina

declares.

"Well this is Lazer . . . and this is Hammer," Chimera introduces, pointing to each of them. "We were together when our ship was attacked. We're lucky to be alive."

"Nice to meet you," Lazer proclaims, raising her palm.

"And thank you for allowing us as guests in your home for tonight," Hammer states.

"Oh, but you're so much more than that," Nina acknowledges. "Besides luck was not the determinant of your survival my kindred spirits. Come now, let me show you to your sleeping accommodations."

Nina leads them to a small adjoining room.

"You will be staying here in the guest suite," she announces to Hammer. Chimera and Lazer carry Hammer over to a cot in the corner of the room and he slides off the gurney and takes a seat.

"Suite?" Lazer mumbles to Hammer. Hammer glares at Lazer.

"Thank you," Hammer says to Nina.

Nina then hobbles over to Hammer and checks the bandages covering his wound.

"Ouch!" Hammer screams.

Nina analyzes the wound for several moments, poking and pressing the injury.

"I'm ok," Hammer clarifies.

"Lazer was it?" Nina begins. "You will be staying in the room over there to the left," Nina declares, pointing to another a wooden door.

"Chimera will be staying in the room on the other side of the den. Come now, Chimera, you can help me fetch stones for the fire and medicine for your companion."

"I'm ok," Hammer repeats, but Nina ignores him, limping out of the room. "Companion?" Hammer questions, looking at Chimera. Chimera shrugs, and exits the room to assist Nina.

Chimera finds Nina in the den, rummaging through a container searching for something.

"Thank you again, Miss Fortuna," Chimera mentions.

"You know when I was young, I was beautiful just like you," Nina declares proudly. "I had Reds fighting to be my suitor. Now look at me."

"Miss Fortuna . . ." Chimera begins.

"Nina, call me Nina," NinaFortuna insists.

"You're still beautiful," Chimera confirms.

"We both know that's not true!" Nina states.

Chimera is silent.

"Does your companion know who you are?" Nina asks.

"Who Hammer . . . no he's not my companion," Chimera clarifies, smirking.

"I see the way he looks at you," Nina whispers to Chimera.

"I assure you, there is nothing between us," Chimera reiterates.

Nina stops rummaging through the container. "Does he know

who you are?"

"What do you mean?" Chimera asks.

"Does he know . . . that you are the true heir to the throne?"

"Heir to the throne?" Chimera retorts. "I'm sorry, I'm not sure know who you think I am . . . but I am ChimeraRed, daughter of IonaRed."

"You are the illegitimate miracle of Tychon. You are not your mother's daughter," Nina proclaims.

"How dare you insult me you!" Chimera snaps. "What would you know? You're a recluse."

"I know . . . that everything in your world will cease to exist . . . very soon." Nina warns. "Your friends will become enemies; your enemies will become allies. Beware of the third harvest moon, as your father predicted."

"My father?" Chimera exclaims. "Is this some kind of joke?"

"The real question is, do you know who your mother is?" Nina inquires, grinning.

"I've told you, I am the daughter of IonaRed!" Chimera announces, louder this time.

NinaFortuna remains silent for several moments. "The Phoenix leads the way. Follow the Phoenix," she suggests.

"Is everything ok?" Lazer asks, entering. "I heard yelling."

"Yeah, I was just going to my room," Chimera replies as she heads to the room to the left the den. Nina grins as Chimera exits, her chin resting on her oversized staff.

"Like I said, entertaining," Lazer remarks as she returns to her room as well.

Chimera retires for the night, removing her armor and placing it neatly on the ground. She places her saber next to it. She sits down on her cot and begins writing notes in her holopad. Before long, she falls asleep, holopad in hand.

It is the 30th degree when Chimera is suddenly awoken by the presence of something. Sitting up, she finds the NinaFortuna in her room kneeling down as she examines Chimera's saber.

"No, don't touch that!" Chimera exclaims. "It's very dangerous," she adds as she rises out of her cot.

"The blade of Kybon," Nina announces. "I have not seen this in ages."

Chimera retrieves the device from Nina. "What are you doing sneaking in here like that, and how do you know what this thing is?" Chimera asks, holding the saber.

"It's a very unique saber," Nina states, smiling. "I have seen all three."

"You still haven't answered my question. What are you doing here?" Chimera inquires.

"Well, I came in here to bring you some food. You stormed off before I had a chance to offer you any," Nina explains, as she picks up a tray of food next to Chimera's belongings and brings it to her. "You will need to be well nourished if you are to complete your journey through Kori."

"Thank you," Chimera states, as Nina shuffles off, humming to herself. Once she leaves, Chimera smells the food and then examines it. She glances around and then begins to devour the meal.

Lazer is beginning to fall asleep when Chimera enters.

"Lazer," Chimera whispers.

"What?" Lazer responds startled. "And what's that in your hand?" she asks pointing.

"It's a piece of bread!" Chimera replies.

"Why?" Lazer questions.

"I haven't eaten all day, I'm hungry!" Chimera declares. "Will you forget about the bread! Meeting in Hammer's room, right now!" she states, still whispering.

Chimera and Lazer head to Hammer's room, where he is fast asleep.

"Wake up," Chimera says, shaking Hammer. He brushes Chimera away and turns the other way. Chimera grabs his nose and squeezes it closed. As an instant reaction, Hammer grabs Chimera's hand and brings her into a headlock. He wakes up and turns to see he's holding Chimera, who quickly drops her bread and reverses the move and exits the headlock, bending Hammer's arm in a painful position.

"Are we gonna have a meeting or wrestling with each other?" Lazer declares, as she picks up the piece of bread, dusts it off and begins eating it. "Let him go, Chimera."

Chimera glances at Hammer and then releases him.

"Did you just eat my bread?" Chimera whispers angrily.

"Why are you guys in my room? It's the middle of the night," Hammer asks, confused.

"Chimera Storm called an emergency meeting," Lazer states, popping the last piece of bread into her mouth.

"Maybe I should just let the crazy old lady kill you both," Chimera warns.

"What are you talking about?" Hammer asks.

"I came in here to tell you guys that we need to get out of here," Chimera begins. "Like immediately, I have a bad feeling plus the old lady is crazy!"

"What happened?" Hammer inquires.

"First she started telling me all this crazy stuff about being an heir and my mother not being my mother," Chimera explains. "Then, while I was asleep, I had this weird dream something happened at AzurNu. I wake up and find the old woman trying to steal my saber. She gives me the creeps."

Lazer and Hammer look at each other.

"What?" Chimera questions.

Lazer and Hammer do not speak.

"There's something you guys are not telling!" Chimera barks. "Spit it out."

"We didn't want to say anything . . . but Lazer found a skull in the closet of her room," Hammer admits.

"A skull!" Chimera blurts. "We have to get out of here, tonight!"

"We can't," Lazer begins. "Hammer is in no condition to make the journey across Kori. His wound is getting worse and his gurney has about half a rotations power left. If the infection doesn't kill him, frostbite will."

"So what do you suggest?" Chimera asks.

"You make the journey, Chimera," Hammer answers. "Cross Kori and get to Iona. You can send for help once you arrive."

"No way!" Chimera argues. "I'm not leaving you guys here in this cave with this crazy lady."

"There's no other way and you know it," Lazer proclaims. "I would go in your place, but you're the only one that knows the way."

"There has to be another way," Chimera suggests.

"We'll be fine," Lazer urges. "If we can fight off three Mountain Gnarls, I think we can handle a little old lady."

"Yeah, but I won't be there to protect you this time," Chimera retorts.

"Very funny," Hammer responds.

"If I go I'll have to gather all that I can carry and sneak out before sunrise. I'd cross Kori in two days and send help as soon as I arrive," Chimera confirms.

"Is everything ok?" a voice rings out startling Chimera and the others. They turn to find Nina standing in the doorway.

"Yea . . . uh everything's fine," Chimera acknowledges. "We were just . . . checking on Hammer. We thought we heard him call for help." Chimera turns and makes a face at Hammer.

"Ahhhh, uhhhhh, I'm really in a lot of pain!" Hammer cries out.

"Oh my dear, I'll get you some more medicine," Nina states as she turns to leave the room.

"Lazer's gonna stay here with Hammer tonight and keep an eye on him," Chimera tells Nina as she gives Hammer a thumbs up.

Nina abruptly stops and turns around toward Chimera.

"You should know . . . the place you seek to go cannot be reached by craft of the sky, nor by land on foot," Nina remarks.

"Huh?" Chimera inquires.

"Before I retire for the night, I wanted to give you this," Nina declares. "I present all my guests with gifts."

"That's what we're afraid of," Lazer mumbles.

Nina hobbles over to Chimera and produces a small marble-like ball from one of her pockets.

"What is it?" Chimera asks.

"It is Tychon," Nina remarks. "With this, you have the world in your hands. Keep it with you and you will never be lost."

"Thank you," Chimera remarks.

Nina turns and exits the room.

The next rotation before sunrise, Chimera awakes, gathers her belongings, grabs food rations from the den and stops by Hammer's room.

"And so the Indigo rises," Lazer declares as Chimera enters.

"What?" Chimera inquires.

"Nothing, it's a saying from a datasphere I used to read a lot," Lazer clarifies.

"Well, when we get back to AzurNu, maybe I can read it," Chimera states. "Be well, both of you. I'll see you shortly."

"Goodbye, Chimera," Lazer responds.

"Wait," Hammer declares. He stands up and limps over to Chimera. "You're gonna need this," Hammer states as he hands Chimera the compass sphere.

"Thank you," Chimera responds, as Hammer embraces her and hugs her tight.

"Be well, Chimera," Hammer declares.

Chimera turns and exits.

Chimera begins the journey across the final region, Kori. The temperature is freezing and the cold winds are blistering, as Chimera fights through the thick snow. She travels for a full rotation before stopping around the 27th degree to rest. She consumes a ration of food smuggled from NinaFortuna and then builds a makeshift shelter by hollowing out a mound from the snow. Once the shelter is complete, she hunkers down for the night.

Early morning around the 7th degree, Chimera awakes to another icy Korian blizzard. Adding an extra layer of garments, she continues on her way, trekking through the snow for 13 degrees. About 5 degrees away from her destination, Chimera suddenly collapses. She lays on the frozen tundra, suffering from hypothermia and exhaustion. Her eyes begin to close and she slowly slips unconscious.

Chimera awakes in a dark room, lying on a bed. As she comes to and regains her sight, she sees an unfamiliar Red feeling her forehead. Startled, Chimera jumps up, frantically searching around for her saber.

"Who are you?" Chimera screams, covering herself with a cloth from the bed. "And what have you done with my saber?"

"You're awake!" a voice suddenly rings out.

Chimera turns as another Red enters, arms spread in a wide embrace.

"Iona?" Chimera declares, confused.

"Chimera! Of course it's me!" the woman responds as she darts over and hugs Chimera.

"How did . . . how'd you find me?" Chimera asks.

"He did," Iona replies, pointing to the other Red in the room.

"I'm sorry, I didn't mean to startle you," the Red responds. "I'm CortusRed. Riktor and I went out into the snow storm and found you out there freezing. It's a miracle you survived."

"Thanks for saving me and all, but what are you doing here?" Chimera asks.

"He's been helping me with things around the flat since you've been gone," Iona explains.

"I could've gotten you a bot for that," Chimera responds.

"If he and Riktor hadn't found you when they did, you would've frozen to death," Iona acknowledges.

"Great, I'm forever indebted to him," Chimera retorts.

"Chimera!" Iona snaps. "How dare you speak like that!"

"I'm not the half-grown Red that left here," Chimera responds.

"It's fine," Cortus remarks to Iona.

"Cortus and Riktor went out searching for you. They found you after 5 or 6 degreess, unconscious in the snow," Iona explains. "The least you can do is show some gratitude."

"It's been a long journey," Cortus states. "She needs her rest."

"I've had enough rest," Chimera assures, stepping back from Iona.

"What happened to you Chi?" Iona questions. "You used to be such a sweet girl. And now you show up out of nowhere, half dead in Kori? Omega told me you disobeyed his advice and went out with the scout crew."

"Yea?" Chimera replies starkly. "Did he also mention that he told me all about how Aurora knew where my father was? I still don't understand why you lied to me!"

"And so you risked your life to prove a point?" Iona remarks. "My Chimera, why ever did you move to AzurNu. It's changed you."

"That was the point," Chimera declares. "But right now it's not about me. Aurora is in trouble. Seven Reds are already dead! Two more are stuck in a cave on Mawton! If I don't get help and find Aurora, all of it will be in vain!" Chimera pleads. "I need to contact Omega immediately."

"Seven Reds killed, how?" Iona proclaims. "And who's stuck in Mawton?"

"When we reached Bethelex, Aurora was missing," Chimera begins. "When we left, our escort ship was destroyed and two Reds from my crew were killed during the mission. We were shot down and now two more are stranded in some crazy lady named NinaFortuna's cave. They're gonna die there unless I get to them!"

Iona is silent for several moments. "I can't believe this is really happening," Iona says to Cortus, turning away from Chimera.

"Did you hear me?" Chimera exclaims. "Right now, there are Reds that need our help!"

Iona sighs. "We've been trying to contact Omega for three rotations. We lost communication a few rotations after you went missing," Iona admits. "I haven't been able to get through to him . . . or any other Reds since."

"Isn't there another way to contact them?" Chimera inquires.

"Wristcom and Holo-com are the only two means of reaching them," Cortus answers, comforting Iona.

Chimera glares at Cortus. "Do you mind giving us some privacy, so I can speak alone with my mother?"

"Sure, sure," Cortus agrees as he releases Iona and begins to step away.

"I'm sorry. Will you give us a moment?" Iona asks Cortus.

"Of course," Cortus responds, as he excuses himself and exits the room.

Iona moves closer to Chimera. "Why didn't you call for help my love?"

"My wristcom is down," Chimera states. "All of our wristcoms were disabled in the crash."

"I'll have Cortus take a look at it," Iona offers. "He might be able to fix it."

Chimera turns and begins searching for her wristcom.

"All your things are over there in that corner?" Iona asks, pointing to the corner.

Chimera retrieves her wristcom from atop her bag and hands it to Cortus. "And where is my saber?" Chimera asks.

"That weird handle thing? It's right over there underneath your bag," Iona directs.

Chimera walks back to her gear and lifts her bag, uncovering the blade of Kybon.

"I have to get back to Hammer and Lazer, and I need to get more help to find Aurora," Chimera announces, holding the saber.

"You're in no condition to go back out into the wilderness and risk being killed," Iona states.

"I'm not gonna leave them stranded!" Chimera declares.

Just then, Cortus pokes his head into the room.

"I'm gonna grab Keniah, we'll be right back for supper," Cortus states.

"As should you," Iona proclaims to Chimera. "You haven't eaten a full meal in three rotations."

Chimera is silent.

"Ok," Iona states, folding her arms. "Cortus and Rictor will ride their terrain hunters out to NinaFortuna's tomorrow. Once you get some supper, you can try contacting your friends from AzurNu through our Holo-com. That's my offer and it's not up for negotiation."

Chimera glances over at Cortus who turns his palms inside out, as a confused look slides across his face.

"Supper will be ready shortly, go ahead and wash up," Iona instructs as she exits the room.

"Wait, hold on . . . how did I get volunteered for this mission?" Cortus asks following Iona out of the room.

"And she wonders why I left," Chimera states.

At supper, Chimera and Iona are joined by Cortus and his daughter.

"Chimera, this is my younger daughter, KeniahRed," Cortus introduces.

"Hey," Chimera greets.

During supper, Chimera is relatively silent.

"So, I heard you survived a crash, walked across half the planet and killed like ten Greys!" Keniah exclaims.

"Keniah, not at supper," Cortus urges.

"When I get older, I wanna be just like you," Keniah whispers to Chimera.

Chimera smiles.

Throughout the remainder of supper, there is an awkward silence as Chimera, Iona, Cortus and Keniah quietly eat.

After supper, Chimera heads to the den to try to contact Omega using Iona's Holo-com. Chimera checks her holopad for the coordinates and then dials Omega's coordinates. There is no answer.

Chimera then tries to contact Anexichi, who also does not answer.

"Why isn't anyone answering?" Chimera questions aloud.

Iona enters the den shortly after. "I made you some tea honey," Iona offers, handing Chimera a thermos.

"Thanks," Chimera acknowledges, as she takes the thermos.

"Well, all done?" Iona inquires, as she begins out the room.

"Yeah," Chimera confirms. She rises and is about to exit. "Wait, I'm gonna try one more," Chimera declares. She checks her holopad and then dials one last set of coordinates.

After several rings, a voice answers on the other line.

"StarChild, can you hear me!" Chimera exclaims.

"Chimera, Chimera is that you?" StarChild responds.

"Yes," Chimera replies.

"My infinity, I thought you were . . ." StarChild begins.

"Dead?" Chimera answers back.

"You left and . . . you said you would be back," StarChild explains. "But you never did. I checked everywhere and tried calling but got no answer, what happened?"

"It's a long story, and I'll tell you all about it but right now I need your help," Chimera responds. "I need you to get a hold of OmegaRed and have him contact me here. I need him to send more scouts. Aurora's been taken and we need to find her!"

"Chimera, I'm so sorry, but I don't think that's possible," StarChild answers.

"You can do it," Chimera urges. "I know it seems near impossible to get through the Elite Guards security at his chateau but if you say you have a message from me they'll take you to him," Chimera suggests.

"No, Chimera, it's not that," StarChild responds.

"Then what is it?" Chimera questions.

"You really haven't heard have you?" StarChild asks.

"Heard what?" Chimera inquires, as a confused look permeates her face.

"There was an attack here at AzurNu," StarChild declares. "We don't know how, but they found us."

"Who found you?" Chimera inquires, the urgency evident in her voice.

"The Greys," StarChild admits. "They struck the night you left with ramships and all types of craft. I was getting ready for my trip with Dug when they broke through our defenses and got inside. So much was destroyed and . . . a lot of Reds were killed."

"No!" Chimera screams, dropping the thermos in her hands onto the floor. "How?"

"Everything. It happened so quick," StarChild remarks. "It was like . . . they were looking for something. Anyone they didn't kill, they took!"

"You have to find Omega for me, he's the only one that can help!" Chimera pleads.

"Don't you get it, like I told you it's not possible!" StarChild proclaims.

"Why?" Chimera snaps.

"Because he's dead!" StarChild reveals. "Omega was killed in the attack. They froze his body for cryo a few rotations ago."

Chimera is silent, as tears begin slowly rolling down her face

"Chimera, are you still there?" StarChild inquires. "Hello?"

After several moments of silence, a distraught Chimera speaks again. "What about enforcement, didn't they do anything?" Chimera asks fighting back tears.

"Enforcement?" StarChild asks. "I don't know, but that's not the worst part."

"Omega is dead, how could it get any worse?" Chimera asks.

"After the attack, two soldiers from the Red Defense Core came to the dorm," StarChild reveals, "asking questions and looking for you. They said you fled AzurNu just before the attack and that you might have had something to do with it. Titan placed a bounty on you, and said if you return to AzurNu, you'll be detained immediately. Tell me it's not true, Chimera! Tell me you're not the traitor Titan said you were?"

"Star, you know me!" Chimera replies. "You know I would never do anything like that. Omega was like a father to me, and you're like a sister to me. I would never do anything to risk something happening to either of you. I left to find my father. I had nothing to do with the attack."

"I believe you," StarChild admits. "What are you gonna do?"

"I'm gonna do whatever I can to make everything right," Chimera vows. "I won't let this attack go unanswered, but I have to get a hold of Liazo."

"That might be bit difficult too," StarChild mentions.

"Was he killed in the attack?" Chimera questions.

"No, Titan had him detained after Omega was killed," StarChild states.

"That coward!" Chimera snaps. "What about Nya? She's second in command after Omega. She can free Liazo and send for help."

"With Titan spreading the rumor of you being a traitor it'll be a stretch to gain her support," StarChild warns. "Besides, Titan's been granted executive powers given the circumstances."

"I can't catch a break here," Chimera retorts. "What about Anexichi? She can convince her mom to help!"

"That option is less likely than the first two," StarChild remarks. "She's in the infirmary, recovering from injuries she got during the attack."

"Injuries, no wonder she didn't answer," Chimera replies. "Can you get a message to her?"

"I don't think she'll want to hear it," StarChild continues. "When I was there visiting a friend of mine at the infirmary, she was there upset about something. Something having to do with you not meeting her the night you disappeared. That, and . . . the rumors of you being a traitor."

"I have to fix this!" Chimera declares. "I need to free Liazo and get to Anexichi, but first I have to find Aurora. I know she's the key to everything."

"Maybe Iona can help?" StarChild mentions. "Does she already know about Omega?"

"Not yet," Chimera responds. "And it's better that way. Besides, she's always keeping secrets from me. It's my turn now."

"If you say so," StarChild remarks. "Is there anything I can help with?"

"Yes, I need you to find Athos," Chimera requests. "Have him reach me at the holo-com coordinates I contacted you on. His dorm his 425, but I'm not sure if he's still at AzurNu. I don't have his coordinates in my holopad."

"Ok," StarChild agrees. "Anything else?"

"That's it for now," Chimera declares. "Is Dug ok?"

"Yea, thankfully his kin and my kin are all safe," StarChild confirms.

"At least that's some good news," Chimera states. "Well, get that message to Athos if you can and I'll be in touch with you."

"I will," StarChild responds. "Be well Chi."

"Be well," Chimera answers back.

"And Chimera," StarChild begins.

"Yes?" Chimera replies.

"Whatever you do, be careful," StarChild proclaims.

"You too," Chimera responds as she ends the call.

On Tychon 2, a medium-sized Grey transport known as an Arcship lands. Touching down on the outskirts of Helum, a wealthy residential region for Greys, four Greys emerge and gather at the foot of the ship.

"Remember your tasks," a Grey in metallic armor announces to the other three Greys in white flight suits. "Prychon and his entourage will be emerging from their meeting with MakuGrey at the 21st degree. The compound has security fields and watch stations at the north and south end. Azzo, you are lead. You move the target into position and deliver the gifts. Atmos and Ruko, you take point. If Lord Prychon moves outside the security shield, either of you will end it."

"Understood, Tyranus," Azzo confirms.

Azzo motions for Ruko and Atmos to move out as he exits. Azzo uses a changing device to change his attire into a metallic dark gold armor. Azzo, Ruku and Atmos retrieve small speeder crafts from the Arcship and head out, speeding toward MakuGrey's compound.

Atmos heads to the north end of the compound as Ruko moves to south side. Atmos and Ruko disable the security fields at the north and south end. Shortly after, Prychon, Nintius, Seyfert and the remainder of Prychon's entourage conclude their secret meeting with MakuGrey and make their way from Maku's compound. Atmos launches a large, egg-shaped drone into the sky and directs it toward Prychon's entourage.

"Distraction airborne," Atmos confirms. The drone hovers toward the compound.

"What's that?" one of the guards from Prychon's entourage proclaims, pointing at Atmos's drone.

"It must be an attack," Seyfert warns.

"It's unlikely," Tachyon responds. "No one knows of this meeting."

"Remove the threat!" Prychon declares.

One of the guard raises his weapon and fires at the drone. It launches a burning sphere-like device that seeks the drone and destroys it.

While the entourage is distracted, Azzo enters the compound from the south end and heads toward the entourage. Ruko launches a small round bot into the sky.

"Trace destroyer airborne," Ruko declares.

Azzo approaches the entourage dressed as a compound guard in purple metallic armor, as the entourage makes their way up toward the ship.

"Sire, we've got incoming, we're not sure but it may be an attack. It may be some sort of assassination attempt. Have you swept your transport before reboarding?" the undercover Azzo asks.

"Send sweeper drones aboard immediately!" Seyfert orders.

Azzo drops a small square cube onto the ground near the entourage as guards send a drone to sweep Prychon's ship.

"Gifts delivered," Azzo whispers through his headset, as he turns preparing to slip away.

From the south end of the compound, Ruko activates the Trace destroyer bot, which fires four small missiles into the sky.

"Trace destroyer airborne"

Azzo begins to retreat, back toward the other end of the compound when Seyfert notices Azzo leaving and the security shield suddenly deactivating.

"It's a trap!" Seyfert hollers as he activates a second security field. A few moments later, three explosive devices rain down exploding on the platform. Several of Prychon's guards are killed, however Prychon, Tachyon and Seyfert are protected by the secondary shield.

"Get Prychon onto the ship!" Tachyon demands.

Another explosion from the ground erupts, throwing Tachyon and several guards to the ground.

Azzo darts to the exit.

"Stop him!" Seyfert exclaims, pointing and the fleeing Azzo. Four guards retrieve land speeders from Prychon's cruiser.

"Order 77, return to ship," Azzo declares as he continues back toward his Arcship.

Seyfert quickly retrieves his weapon and repositions himself. Seyfert fires at the fleeing Azzo, striking him in the back. Azzo falls to the ground.

"Azzo!" Ruku calls.

"Seyfert, we need any possible conspirators alive!" Tachyon demands.

Seyfert grunts as he turns away from Tachyon.

"He is correct," Prychon confirms as he is rushed to safety inside his ship by his guards.

"Check the perimeters, he's not alone," Seyfert instructs. Two guards rush toward the north end of the compound and Atmos's location.

Seeing Azzo struck down, Ruko immediately summons his trace destroyer. "Atmos, return to the ship at once!" Ruko orders.

"Already on my way" Atmos confirms, as he gathers his equipment and mounts his awaiting land speeder. Just then, four royal guards approach on speeders. Atmos accelerates away toward the city, evading the pursuing guards. He twists and turns through the upscale streets and alleys of Helum.

Ruku returns to Tyranus, who waits in the Arcship. Atmos races toward downtown Helum, leading the pursuing guards away from the Arcship. Shimmering blue lights accent grey megastructures as Atmos speeds toward the financial district of Tychon 4. The symmetrical streets and flyways come into view as Atmos approaches the hustle and bustle of ships and Greys seeding the bureaucratic underbelly of Grey Society.

Back at Maku's compound, Tachyon and Seyfert continue to argue.

"Seyfert, you are a maniac!" Tachyon declares. "Why shoot that Grey? If he is part of an assassination plot, we need to interrogate him! That is the only means of finding the source."

"Anyone who threatens Lord Prychon's reign must be slain with no hesitation," Seyfert snarls.

"I'm going to retrieve the fleeing conspirator," Tachyon remarks as he boards one of the other ships in Prychon's convoy. See to it that Prychon makes back to the Palace safely," Tachyon instructs Seyfert.

East of their location, Atmos reaches an entryway into the finance district. He accelerates and is about to enter the city when a laser strikes Atmos's speeder. Atmos is sent flying to the ground as his damaged speeder deactivates. A ship quickly descends from above, and Atmos looks up to see one of Prychon's convoy ships. The injured Atmos is beamed up into the ship and taken.

Back at Iona's home, Chimera searches through her old room, viewing projections and memories from her childhood. Iona comes and joins her.

"Can I ask you something?" Chimera inquires.

"Sure," Iona responds.

"I noticed . . . there aren't any holographs of me earlier than three lunar cycles, why is that?" Chimera questions.

"Well . . ." Iona begins.

Suddenly, the Holocom beeps as an incoming call initiates.

Iona walks over and checks the Holocom.

"Are you expecting a comm from an Athos?" Iona questions.

"Athos, yes!" Chimera exclaims as she darts over to the Holocom. "Hey Athos," Chimera begins.

"Hey Chimera," Athos responds.

"Where are you?" Chimera asks.

"I've been traveling. I'm returning from the Sirez region. I stopped at AzurNu and now I'm headed to Broadcast Central," Athos explains.

"Well, I need your help," Chimera blurts out.

"Sure, is everything ok?" Athos questions.

"AzurNu was attacked," Chimera begins.

"Yea, I heard," Athos explains. "I was in Sirez, otherwise I would've been there when the attack happened. I stopped by to check on a few friends and pick up the last of my stuff. I ran into StarChild who said you were looking for me?"

"I'm so glad you're ok," Chimera declares. "Yea, I needed your help. Omega was killed . . . and Titan, he thinks I had something to do with the attack. I've been blacklisted from AzurNu."

"Serious, that's absurd" Athos states.

"Exactly," Chimera declares. "I have to get help. I need to put together a team to find Aurora. She is the key to rallying support . . . and to finding my father."

"Phoenix, he'll be able to help!" Athos exclaims. "He's connected with the rebels in the Anti region. Tell you what, I'll divert to your location and link with you. We can head to Broadcast Central together. We'll link with Phoenix and rally support."

"That sounds like a plan but I've got a problem," Chimera remarks. "Two crew members of mine, Hammer and Lazer, are stuck in Mawton. An acquaintance of my mother will be hiking out to rescue them. It'll be at least three rotations before they return. I don't want to leave them."

"They can meet us at Broadcast Central," Athos announces. "Send me the coordinates and I'll send another transport for them.

"Are you sure?" Chimera questions.

"Yea, it'll be best that way," Athos confirms. "You'll get a head start on mobilizing support. Plus it'll be safer. Broadcast Central is protected by the rebels. Titan and his defense core are a joke."

"I know what you mean," Chimera confers.

"The best part is you can meet some creators from the Tychon Broadcast Group," Athos declares.

"I'm in," Chimera agrees.

"Awesome, I'm on the way," Athos remarks. "You focus on your recovery in the meantime."

After two rotations, Athos arrives in his transport. Chimera gathers her belongings and bids farewell to Iona and Keniah.

Iona approaches Chimera as she prepares to leave.

"I really wish you wouldn't leave again," Iona urges. "You should stay here with me, it would be best."

"I can't," Chimera replies. "There are a lot of Reds that need me right now."

Iona is silent. She turns and reaches for something. Retrieving it, she hands Chimera her wristcom. "Cortus fixed it, so you should be able to contact me now."

Chimera takes the wristcom, as Cortus emerges from one of the rooms. "Thank you," Chimera motions to Cortus, who nods.

Outside, the transport door of the ship opens as Athos awaits at the top of the gangway. Chimera exits the flat and boards the transport.

"Good evening," Athos greets.

"So good to see you," Chimera confirms.

"Likewise!" Athos replies. "Shall we, it's half a rotation to Broadcast Central and we need to make one stop along the way."

"Let's go!" Chimera agrees.

Chimera and Athos head to the Techno region. Along the way, Chimera updates Athos on everything that has occured since her departure from AzurNu, from the disappearance of Aurora to NinaFortuna's bizarre prophecy. After 11 degrees, Chimera and Athos arrive at Broadcast Central.

The transport descends on the landing pad of the heavily fortified compound. As the transport door opens, Chimera and Athos are greeted by a group of Reds led by PhoenixRED. Suddenly, from the crowd Hammer and Lazer emerge.

"Lazer, Hammer!" Chimera exclaims, as she exits the transport.

"Welcome to Broadcast Central, home of the creators," Phoenix declares.

TO BE CONTINUED

LIVE RED

For More information on Music from the
ChimeraRED universe and all other things Red
visit **WWW.CHIMERARED.COM**

TBG Publishing

This book was art directed by Phoenix Red. The font used for the cover and chapter titles are Cinzel and Anamatic SC. The text for the contents of the book were set in 13 point Times New Roman.